THE GOOD COP

THE GOOD COP

A Dick Hardesty

mystery novel by

Dorien Grey

GLB PUBLISHERS ®   **San Francisco**

FIRST EDITION
Copyright © 2002 by Dorien Grey
All rights reserved. Printed in the U.S.A.

No part of this publication may be reproduced or transmitted in any form or by any means, electronic or mechanical, including photocopy, recording or any information storage and retrieval system now known or to be invented, without permission in writing from the publisher, except by a reviewer who wishes to quote brief passages in connection with a review written for inclusion in a magazine, newspaper or broadcast.

Published in the United States by
GLB Publishers
P.O. Box 78212, San Francisco, CA 94107 USA

Cover by GLB Publishers

This is a work of fiction. Names, characters, places, and incidents are either the products of the author's imagination or are used fictitiously, and any resemblance to actual persons, living or dead, events, or locales is entirely coincidental.

Library of Congress Cataloging-in-Publication Data

Grey, Dorien.
   The good cop : a Dick Hardesty mystery / by Dorien Grey.-- 1st ed.
      p. cm.
ISBN 1-879194-75-9 (alk. paper)
1. Hardesty, Dick (Fictitious character)--Fiction. 2. Private investigators--Fiction. 3. Gay police officers--Fiction. 4. Police murders--Fiction. 5. Gay men--Fiction. I. Title.
PS3557.R48165 G66 2002
813'.6--dc21

2002011236

Published 2002
10 9 8 7 6 5 4 3 2 1

CHAPTER 1

Everything has a beginning. Very rarely, it's something spectacular, like an undersea volcano suddenly breaking the surface and spewing ash to color sunsets around the world as it forms a new island: something everyone is instantly aware of and always remembers. But most beginnings are small, and quiet, like an individual drop of water joining another drop, and then another to form a rivulet which joins other rivulets to become a stream, which eventually becomes a river. And people who sail up and down the river or sit on its banks hardly ever give a moment's thought to how the river got there—of what went into creating it. And that's a shame, because every one of those drops of water has a history, and today is built on all the yesterdays of the world.

I was thinking about that the other day when I came across a picture of my friend Tom. Tom was a cop....

* * *

I probably should tell you right now that this might not be the story you're expecting. I know I certainly wasn't prepared for it. There's something to be said for a certain degree of basic predictability in life, but…

Well, hey, nothing's perfect. Things were going okay… maybe even just this side of okay…and I was keeping fairly busy. My car was beginning to nickle-and-dime me to death and I was doing my best to set a little bit aside for the all-too-soon time when scotch tape and baling wire wouldn't keep it running anymore. But since I insisted on throwing my money away on such frivolous things as food and rent and insurance and electric bills, it was a long, slow process. That condo in Key West was just going to have to wait awhile.

I hadn't had a really interesting case in some time. Just routine, by-the-numbers stuff, and most of my assignments were still referrals from members of the gay Bar Guild. I'd been doing some investigating work, too, for a couple local attorneys, which helped. But as for job-related excitement, there wasn't much going on.

Luckily, my social life kept me from getting too bored. The local gay community was blossoming, with new bars and restaurants opening (and closing) left and right. The gay business area of town now known even by straights as "The Central" was spreading out, and it was becoming possible, if one were so inclined (and I generally was), to shop, eat, and be entertained without leaving The Central.

Oh, and we had another new Chief of Police. Chief Robertson, who had replaced the rabidly homophobic and good-riddance'd Chief Rourke, had done his best to drag the police department kicking and screaming into the present; Robertson was a definite step in the right direction as far as the gay community was concerned. Things were beginning to change, slowly, and the department was developing a core of good people like Lieutenant Mark Richman, with whom I'd developed a nice working relationship over the course of a couple cases involving both me and the police.

But while the community was warily optimistic about the changes in the department, one of Chief Robertson's proposals to update the department involved building a number of police substations, to make them more directly responsive to potential problems in various parts of the city. The first two to be built were in the Marshfield district, a largely black area which had been demanding better police protection for years, and in The Central. While Robertson meant it as a positive outreach to the gay community, most gays, accustomed to the department's long history of homophobia and former chief Rourke's storm-trooper tactics in particular, took it as a new form of harassment. But despite much muttering and suspicion, ground had been broken and construction started when Robertson dropped dead of a heart attack in his office.

Deputy chief Michael Cochran, next in command, took over as interim chief. Since Cochran had been a crony of Chief Rourke and a was a charter member of the department's hard-core old-schoolers, many of the advances made by Chief Robertson began to backslide while an inner-department battle raged between the hard-liners and the more moderates as to who would be appointed as new full-time chief. And construction of the Beech Division Substation, in the heart of The Central, was slowed by minor but consistent acts of vandalism.

As if the squabbling within the department weren't bad enough, there was the city's growing problem of gangs, which had in recent years become so severe that Chief Robertson had set up a Gang Control Unit to deal with them. But the gangs took full advantage of the bickering within the department to expand their respective turfs—which included Arnwood Street, where many gay bars were located. The incidents of gay bashing and robberies along Arnwood increased dramatically, and the department was too caught up in its own inner turmoil to do much about it. It definitely was not a priority for acting chief Cochran, who was having enough trouble just trying to hold on to whatever control he had over the department.

So you see, I wasn't totally cut off from the World of the Breeders. And a lot of the work I did for Glen O'Banyon, one of the city's most prominent attorneys even though he made no secret of being gay, involved at least some peripheral contact with his straight clients.

* * *

But I was going to tell you about Tom. Tom Brady. I'd known Tom since college. He was a year or two behind me, but everybody knew Tom. Tom was a Golden Child if ever there was one. He looked like the 40's movie star Tyrone Power and was probably—and justifiably—one of the most popular guys on campus. He came from an incredibly wealthy family—his father owned a national chain of high-class hotels, though Tom never mentioned it. The fact that he chose to attend a small liberal arts college over any one of the ivy league schools that would have been glad to have him was a good indication that Tom had his feet firmly on the ground. He drove a six-year-old, beat-up car—it was a convertible, though, I remember, although something was broken in the lowering/raising mechanism so that top would never come down.

Of course I had a huge crush on him, as did every girl on campus, and a lot more guys than let on. Tom had a girlfriend, Lisa, whom he'd been dating since grade school.

I saw a tee-shirt once that said: "How dare you assume I'm heterosexual!" A lot of truth in there, and it worked perfectly for Tom. No one ever questioned his sexual orientation; it was simply assumed—by the straights, at least—that Tom was straight. Isn't everyone?

Tom and I were on the college boxing team and one night after we'd both stayed in the gym until it closed, he asked me back to his off-campus room and erased all doubts about where his sexual priorities lay. We became pretty good friends, and it was then that I found out that Lisa was lesbian. "Protective coloration," he used to joke. The three of us used to hang around together, and often we'd go to campus social events with Lisa's "close friend" Carol. After the event, Tom and I would go to his place, and Lisa and Carol would go to Carol's. I found it interesting even then that though the four of us were always together and everyone "knew" Tom and Lisa were a couple, no one really thought Carol and I were, to my vast relief.

Ah, the stupid games we play. But there was (and regrettably often still is) something to be said for "protective coloration," and I never faulted Tom—or Lisa—for taking advantage of it.

After I graduated, we sort of lost touch, but I heard that Tom had moved to Reno to start learning the family business at one of his dad's hotels. I could imagine he was not too thrilled about it, because while we'd never talked about it directly, I got the idea Tom had other plans for himself. But then I lost track of him completely, though I never forgot him.

* * *

I was sitting in my favorite bar, Ramón's, one Saturday evening having an Old Fashioned and a sporadic chat with the owner, Bob Allen. It was still relatively early, and Jimmy, the regular bartender, was also there, so Bob and I had some between-waiting-on-customers time to fill each other in on what had been happening in our lives since our last get-together. Bob had just moved off to the aid of a parched customer when I felt a hand on my shoulder and a warm voice I recognized immediately: "Now, as I was saying…" I turned around to see…Tom Brady! I practically jumped off my stool and grabbed him in a bear hug, which he returned, with hearty back-slapping.

"Tom!" I said when we finally broke our hug and withdrew to arms' length but without letting go completely. "When did you get into town? And how long are you staying?"

Tom grinned that glacier-melting grin of his that I'd only seen in an occasional erotic fantasy since our college days, and carefully looked me over from head to foot. "You're even better looking than you were in school," he said. "I didn't think that was possible."

I grinned. "And you," I said, "are still so full of bullshit your eyes are brown."

We released our mutual elbow-hold, and he pulled up the stool beside me. We both sat down, facing one another. I had a chance to take stock of him, and there was a lot to take stock of. He still looked exactly the same as he had in college, as though the intervening years hadn't passed. And he was still drop-dead beautiful.

Before my crotch had a chance to put its two-cents worth in, I thought I'd get back to the subject at hand. "So what *are* you doing in town? And how long *will* you be here?" I repeated.

"A long story," he said. "We moved here two weeks ago, and with luck it will be permanent."

The "we" wasn't lost on me, you can be sure.

"We?" I asked.

Bob came over to take Tom's drink order, and I introduced

them. They shook hands, exchanged a few words, and then Bob gave me a quick raised eyebrow and a smile, and went to get Tom's drink.

"Lisa and I," Tom said, picking up where we'd left off. "We got married about two years ago." He foresaw my next question and raised his hand quickly to head it off. "I know, I know…you always did have more guts than I did when it came to telling the world to go fuck itself. But it just seemed the easiest course for both Lisa and me. Her family expected it; my family expected it; we're best friends, and this way everybody is happy. Our lives are our own. We just live in the same place and get a break on our income taxes. Of course now the folks are starting to bug us about having kids, like *that*'ll ever happen—at least not the 'old fashioned' way. We've been talking about adopting, maybe, sometime down the road."

Rather than letting my mouth get the better of my mind, I decided to drop that whole can of worms before it was even fully opened.

"As long as you're happy," I said, a little lamely, I'm afraid, then made a valiant effort to save the situation by jumping back into neutral territory. "So what the hell are you doing in Ramón's—not that I'm not delighted that you are, and not that it isn't a great place, but it's a little off the beaten path."

He nodded. "Kismet!" he said. "We rented an apartment over on Spring and Warner."

"No shit?" I said, grinning. "That's only two blocks from my place. We're practically neighbors!"

And any time you want to come by to borrow a cup of sugar…my crotch volunteered happily….

Luckily, he couldn't hear it. "As I say: Kismet," he said. "I was going to look you up the minute we got settled in…which we're still not, completely. Anyway, as to what I'm doing here, we decided we deserved a night away from unpacking. Lisa and Carol went to a movie; I decided to check out the local action. Sure am glad I did."

"That makes two of us," I said, deciding not to pursue the

'Lisa and Carol' reference at the moment. There would be plenty of time for that later, I hoped. "Now tell me everything that's happened to you since we last saw each other...."

* * *

I was struck, as we talked, at how two people with such totally different lifestyles can still be good friends—and Tom and I had never stopped being friends, even though we'd not seen each other in a long time. Our lives had taken two very different paths, but the foundations of our friendship remained solid. I've always believed that the mark of a true friend is one with whom you can pick up a conversation in mid sentence after 20 or 30 years, and while it hadn't been anywhere near that long for the two of us, the rule certainly seemed to apply.

Tom, I learned, still worked for his father's hotel chain, which had just purchased the Montero here in town. The Montero was a city landmark, a recently restored grande dame of a hotel that the elder Brady considered to be the crown jewel in his empire. He intended for Tom, who had quickly worked his way up from the smallest hotel in the chain to the biggest, to start out as assistant manager and eventually become manager, but Tom had other ideas which he didn't go into at the moment and I did not interrupt him to ask. One thing that struck me, though, was that a potential assistant manager of the Montero could certainly afford to live in a better location than Spring and Warner, which was a nice enough neighborhood but hardly what one could even charitably call upscale. My mind was piling up questions, but I just shoved them into a mental closet for now, and let him talk.

When he'd arrived back at the point of his moving here, it was my turn, and I filled him in on the intervening years which, in retrospect, seemed like yesterday afternoon.

Tom seemed impressed, but then that was one of the secrets of his charm: He always made whomever he was with feel important.

"The Montero's looking for a new chief of security," he said. "If you're interested…"

"I really appreciate that, Tom," I said, "but I like what I'm doing now, even if it drives me nuts sometimes."

"You'd have a pass key to all the rooms…" Tom added his face breaking into a very sexy grin. He paused and I waited for the hoped-for punch line, which he delivered: "…which, since I'll be keeping a room there, would include mine."

My crotch put on a full-volume recording of "Stars and Stripes Forever" and it was only with effort that I got it to tone it down.

I mirrored his grin and he laid his hand on my leg.

"You care to go do a little reliving of old times?" he said.

I reached for my glass and drained it.

"Guess," I said as we both got up, waved to Bob and Jimmy, and headed for the door.

* * *

Odd but interesting going to bed with someone again after many years. Even before we got to my place, I was remembering everything about Tom: what he liked, how he liked it, the incredible things he could do with his tongue. So by the time we walked into my apartment and shut the door there was so much electricity between us it reminded me of those electrode machines in the Frankenstein movies. One thing I definitely remember is that Tom always liked to take the lead, to set the pace. So while I was ready to rip his clothes off and get down to business on the living room floor the second the door closed, Tom had other ideas. After about a three minute rib-cracking, face-melding clench into which we crammed nearly eight years of missed encounters and didn't come up for air, I was *definitely* in a clothes-ripping mood.

But Tom broke it off and stepped back. He didn't say a word, just raised one finger in a cautionary, *ah-ah-ah* gesture. I recognized it immediately.

Okay, Tom, I thought. *You lead, I'll follow.*

The very first time Tom and I ever got together, that night after boxing practice, he'd done the same thing, and I wondered if he was doing it deliberately now, remembering it as I did. It was one of his favorite games, and I came to think of it as "The Tease." We seemed to play it every time my testosterone level was about to blow the top of my head off. It was excruciating but in the long run...infinitely worth it.

He stepped back, holding me by the shoulders at arms length, looking at me with that slightly knit-eyebrow, slightly cocked-head expression that I seem to recall seeing on lion tamers' faces when they want their charges to pay close attention. Slowly, still holding my right shoulder with one hand, he inched his other hand down the front of my shirt and, in slow motion, unbuttoned each button. Then he returned his hand to my shoulder and pulled me slowly toward him. When our faces were about three inches apart, he slowly opened his mouth and in what seemed like super-slow motion, closed the gap between us.

When he sensed I was getting a little too eager, he broke the kiss and backed away. Now it was my turn, and I echoed his unbuttoning routine. It took every ounce of self control I could muster, but I knew it was part of the game, so I did it. My turn to repeat the slow motion kiss. When he broke it off—*he* had to, because *I* certainly wasn't about to—I took a step forward and he took a step back. It was all part of a symbolic dance which guided us slowly toward the bedroom: one action (shirt-tails pulled out of pants; shirts slid off shoulders and dropped on floor; belt buckles undone, etc.), one step at a time. After eight years, we still timed it perfectly.

And by the time we reached the bed, we were in our shorts and I was about to explode. Neither one of us had said a single word, but we didn't have to. Tom moved in front of me and pushed me gently back onto the bed, then slid my shorts off, then his, and slowly—really slowly, lowered himself on top of me.

He rubbed the side of my face with his chin and I felt the tip of his tongue tracing the outline of my ear. Eight years, and I knew exactly what came next.

"Foreplay over," he whispered, and the lions came out to play.

* * *

I'd been invited to Tom and Lisa's for dinner the following Friday, and the intervening week literally flew by. I was working for Glen O'Banyon gathering information on a patent infringement case with possible implications of fraud, which involved tracing down the paper trail of exactly which of the parties had gotten the basic product idea to whom and when. Hardly the kind of stuff that makes the hair on the back of your neck stand up, but I never minded working for O'Banyon because it paid pretty damned well.

Tom had started his job at the Montero, but he called me at least three times during the week, which produced a strong teenage-testosterone response every time. I mean, it wasn't as though I'd been exactly celibate for the past eight years—or even the past eight days, for that matter—but maybe there was a large element of reliving a very nice part of the past that made it special. I realized, too, that Tom had probably been the first guy I'd really thought I was in love with. I had no illusions about Tom being Mr. Right—I was afraid our lifestyles were just too different for that—but it was certainly a pleasant interlude.

* * *

Friday evening finally rolled around, and I left the office a little early so I could stop at the liquor store near home and pick up a really nice bottle of wine as a housewarming gift. A quick shower and change of clothes and I was ready. I was for some strange reason mildly nervous of seeing Lisa (and, I was pretty certain, Carol) again, but....

It being a nice evening, I decided to walk to their apartment, rather than fight trying to find a parking place, and besides, I could use the exercise.

When Tom had said "Spring and Warner" he *meant* Spring and Warner—the building was a relatively new high-rise on the southwest corner. I rang the buzzer, and after a wait of no more than three seconds, was buzzed through to the small lobby. I took the elevator to the sixth floor and found my way to Apartment 6-G. I had my fingertip about half an inch from the buzzer when the door opened to reveal an incredibly handsome, grinning Tom. We shook hands and, as soon as the door had closed behind me, exchanged a bear hug. Over Tom's shoulder, I could see Lisa and Carol coming out of the kitchen, smiling.

If I didn't know better, I would have sworn I'd wandered into a typical heterosexual family scene. Both Lisa and Carol looked great, and both were what my lesbian friend Mollie Marino calls "lipstick lesbians"—very feminine. I doubt very much, had I not known them all before, that if I met them at a straight cocktail party, I'd have any idea they were gay.

I exchanged hugs and cheek-kisses with the women and we all went through the usual mildly awkward confusion that ensues when old friends first see one another again after a long absence. I handed Lisa the wine which she acknowledged with profuse thanks and then insisted that Tom and I sit while she and Carol went into the kitchen.

The apartment, I noticed as Tom and I sat side by side on one of the two love seats facing one another across a glass-topped coffee table, was very comfortable and, again, gave not the slightest hint that the occupants were anything than an average heterosexual couple.

Carol came back into the room carrying a tray of hors d'oeuvres, followed by Lisa with another tray with wine glasses and a bottle of wine, which they set on the coffee table.

"We'll have your wine with dinner," Lisa said. "This here's chattin' wine," she added with a smile. Tom poured the wine as the women sat on the opposite love seat, and we all leaned forward to click our glasses together in a toast.

"To old friends," Tom said.

"And to new beginnings," Carol added, looking at Tom.

???? I thought.

* * *

It was a great evening. We talked about our college days and exchanged favorite memories, and caught up on news of classmates and mutual friends, and laughed a lot, and the years melted away and it was another place and another time.

Dinner was excellent—pork roast with garlic roasted potatoes and some kind of succotash that Lisa's grandmother had taught her to make, and a Bavarian torte for desert. The wine was pretty good, too, I was delighted to discover: I'd just asked the owner of the liquor store what he'd recommend—my knowledge of wine isn't much above the level of Mogen David Port.

Tom and I sat on one side of the table with Lisa and Carol on the other. It was obvious that the two women were lovers, and had been ever since college. We talked a bit about it, and about the inconveniences of Tom and Lisa's arrangement, which meant Carol and Lisa couldn't live together. But they'd apparently worked it out to their mutual satisfaction, and while I couldn't imagine such a situation for myself, it wasn't my place to pass any sort of judgment on it.

"We're *so* glad we found you again, Dick," Lisa said. "We don't have many gay friends here," Lisa said, "and it's going to be even harder now."

I'm afraid on this yet-another-reference-to-something-apparently-important I couldn't keep my face from reflecting the question I hesitated to ask.

All three apparently noticed my confusion and exchanged smiles. "Tell him, Tom," Lisa said, reaching across the table to tap his hand.

Tom turned toward me. "I'm joining the police force," he

said. "I'm going to be a cop."

"*Whoa!*" I heard myself say, then just sat there like someone had just beaned me with a frying pan. The three of them sat quietly, looking at me with identical smiles.

"Are you sure?" I asked, feeling immediately stupid for having done so. "I mean, do you have any idea of what you'd be getting yourself into?"

He nodded. "I know," he said. "But it's really what I've wanted all my life."

"But..." I started, then couldn't remember what I'd intended to come after it.

Fortunately, Lisa stepped in. "My dad was a policeman. You knew that, didn't you, Dick?"

I shook my head. "No, I don't think I ever did," I said.

She nodded and smiled. "Yes, he was," she said. "Right up until the time I started college, when he took early retirement. That was back in Hartford. But the interesting thing is that his partner for eighteen years was a man named Kensington Black."

That was news! "*Our* Kensington Black?" I asked, as though there were thousands of men named Kensington Black...

She smiled again. "*Our* Kensington Black," she said. "He's my godfather. And when he came out here to be chief, and then Tom's dad wanted to send him here to help with the Montero, things just sort of clicked."

I should have mentioned, when I was talking about the hassles in the police department, that finally, at the urging of the mayor, the Police Commission chose to eliminate the intramural hassling by going outside the department—and outside the state—for the new chief. They finally picked one Kensington Black, who had done wonders reducing the crime rate of one of the East Coast's older, deteriorating cities. Chief Black was rumored by his many detractors in and out of the department to be to be a closet liberal. Everyone in the gay community hoped they were right.

"Kismet yet again," Tom said. "I decided it was time to make the change. And while Chief Black of course can't guarantee that I'll be accepted, having him as a family friend sure can't hurt, and I'm sure he'll be glad to put in a good word with the applications committee if one were needed. I submitted my application the first week we got here. There's a lot of paperwork involved: background check, even a lie detector exam. Fortunately, if I was gay or not wasn't one of the questions."

"But..." I started again, and forgot again.

"And, no," Tom said, apparently having a better idea of what I was trying to get out than I did, "he doesn't know I'm gay."

I took a deep breath. "I'm really glad for you if this is what you really want," I said, "but you must know how homophobic this police force has always been. I don't want to be the voice of doom, here, but I'm not being melodramatic when I say you could very well be putting your life in danger."

Tom shrugged. "I know," he said, "but this force isn't all that much different from any force anywhere, and things won't change until somebody *makes* them change: There's got to be somebody willing to take the first step toward integrating the force: especially this one. I know it won't be easy, but I know Chief Black, and I know he's a good, decent man who's determined to make changes that need being made. He won't let anyone get out of hand."

He grinned at me and moved his hand down to lay it on top of my leg. "Besides," he said, "it's not like I'm going to go around waving the rainbow flag or hang around the locker room groping my crotch and drooling. But I know there are already other gay cops on the force—there *have* to be. Maybe, when there are enough of us...I just want to make a difference; to show the straights that we've got the ability—and the right—to be as good a cop as any heterosexual."

I shook my head slowly. I was impressed by his altruism, but was really concerned about his walking into the lion's cage without a whip and chair. Still, it was his life. "Well," I said finally, "if that's what you really want, and you realize what you're getting into, go for it. I wish you the best."

He grinned. "Thanks, Dick," he said. "I knew you'd understand."

I wasn't sure I did, but.... And I really wondered what Tom's dad had to say about all this, or even if he knew yet. But it wasn't my place to ask—at least not now. Knowing me, I knew I'd manage to bring it up at some point.

The grandmother clock on the credenza struck 11, and I automatically looked at my watch for verification.

"Wow," I said, "it's getting late. I guess I'd better be going."

Tom, whose hand still rested on my knee, squeezed it slightly. "You don't have to go, do you?" he said with a grin that made Western Union obsolete.

I felt a wave of…what?…awkwardness. I mean, here we were, sitting across from his wife (yeah, yeah, wife in name only, but still…) and his wife's lover and I was suddenly feeling very midwest/middle class…well, stodgy. I hated that.

Carol deliberately reached over and took Lisa's hand. "We're going to go spend the night at my apartment," she said as they exchanged smiles. "We thought maybe the two of you would like to have the place to yourselves."

Oh, my, yes! my crotch—which was never much one for social conventions—said eagerly. I looked at Tom, who just grinned at me.

"Gosh," I said. "If I'd have known, I'd have brought my jammies."

"I don't think you'll need them," Tom said.

And I didn't.

* * *

Time has an annoying habit of sneaking by when you're not paying attention, and that's what happened to the next several weeks. The patent case I was working on dragged on and on and involved far more detail than I'd have any interest in relating here. In the end, however, I was able to determine that the defendant had indeed engaged in a little skulduggery. Unfortunately, it was the defendant whom Glen O'Banyon was representing. Oh, well, you can't win them all, and even a lawyer as good as O'Banyon can't always be on the right side. (In fact, it's precisely because he was as good as he was that clients who knew they were in the wrong sought him out.)

Tom's application to the Police Academy was accepted with what must have been unprecedented speed, and he was told there'd been a "last minute" opening in the very next class when one of the scheduled recruits had had to withdraw for personal reasons. The speed of the process surprised even him, and turned out to be a little more life-disruptive than he'd anticipated. He'd notified his father before putting in his application, and while the older man was understandably less than overjoyed by Tom's decision to leave the family business, he knew his son had a mind of his own, and didn't try to stop him. Tom had assumed he'd have at least a month or so before his acceptance came through, and even considered postponing entering the Academy for a class or two to give his dad time to make other arrangements for an assistant manager. But he realized that part of the speed of his approval was undoubtedly due to his association with Chief Black—though Tom had of course never even mentioned it in his application or in the pre-admission interviews. Postponing his entry was, he decided, out of the question. He entered the Academy exactly two weeks after our reunion dinner.

He did love the Academy, though, and he was like a little kid when he described everything he was learning. Apparently he was doing very well and was at or near the top of his class, which came as no surprise. While I still had my doubts about what he might be facing in the future, I was glad for him.

* * *

As for me, though most of my cases during those weeks were considerably less interesting than watching paint dry, my social life provided enough stimulation to keep me from getting totally bored. My friend Jared Martinson, who had been driving a beer truck for well over a year while he worked on his doctoral dissertation in Russian Literature (a long story), finally finished it and, after making his oral presentations, hoped to have everything tied up so that he could receive his official diploma at the next graduation ceremony. Though we were jumping the gun a bit, I and some of our mutual friends held a little surprise party at my place to celebrate. I'd not been used to throwing parties since when Chris and I were together, what seems like a couple hundred years ago, now. It took up a lot of time, pulling everything together, but it was worth it and everybody seemed to enjoy themselves.

Basically the same group of friends as were at Jared's party had gradually established an informal weekly Wednesday night get-together at Bob's bar, Ramón's. I got a kick out of thinking of the group—for no other reason than that I'd heard the name as a kid and loved it—as "The Elves, Gnomes, and Wee-People's Marching and Chowder Society." But I kept the name to myself, lest one of the other "members"—not one of whom could be considered an elf, gnome, or wee-person…or a fairy, for that matter—not appreciate my humor and be tempted to punch me out.

I'd arrived early—surprise—for one of our get-togethers to find only Bob and his lover Mario there before me. Bob was behind the bar as a backup for Jimmy should one be needed, though Wednesday wasn't the busiest night of the week and we met and disbanded fairly early due to its being a weeknight.

"Any news on the house?" I asked Bob as soon as I'd pulled up a stool and sat down. He and Mario had made an offer on a great old Victorian house in one of the areas being saved from the urban sprawl by gentrification. It needed a lot of work, of course, but it was basically solid with, they'd told me, beautiful woodwork and even a small coach house in back.

Bob grinned. "We should be closing any time now," he said.

"That's fantastic!" I said, and meant it. "I'll volunteer for the moving crew whenever you're ready."

"Glad to hear it," Bob said. "If you hadn't volunteered, I'd have drafted you."

Jimmy was at the front of the bar talking with a couple customers, and while I couldn't hear the conversation, I did catch the name "Nightingale" several times. The Nightingale was a small bar on one of the side-streets just off Arnwood.

"Something happen at the Nightingale?" I asked Bob when he brought my Manhattan over to me.

He nodded. "It got held up last night," he said as he put two maraschino cherries on a plastic pick and dropped them into my drink.

"No shit?" I said, only mildly surprised. "There seems to be a lot of that going on these days."

"Yeah," Bob nodded. "Way too much. Three guys just walked right in and robbed the place. Luckily, it was near closing and there weren't more than three or four guys in the place, but still…. That takes a lot of balls."

"Gang members?" I asked.

Bob shrugged. "Probably, I'd imagine."

"Well," I said, "hopefully things will get better once Chief Black gets settled in."

"I sure don't envy him," volunteered Jimmy, who had come to our end of the bar for another bottle of gin and who never seemed to miss out on much.

"I do know that business at Venture has sure picked up," Mario observed. Mario was a bartender at Venture, which was closer to The Central and therefore considered relatively safe. "Kind of a double-edged sword, though…we're glad for the extra business, but sorry it has to be at the expense of the Arnwood bars."

At that point, Tim and Phil walked in and joined us. Tim hadn't made it to the past few gatherings, the increase in business at the coroner's office, where he was a junior medical examiner, having picked up considerably in wake of the police being distracted by the upheavals at headquarters.

Greetings exchanged and drinks ordered, Bob grinned at Phil and said: "You look a mite tuckered, Phil...Tim not letting you get enough sleep?"

Phil grinned. "Sleep? What's that? It's the trying to juggle a new job, go to night classes, and move all my junk *and* Tim's to the new place all at once that's wearing me out."

"Hey, I help when I can," Tim said, defensively.

"Uh huh," Phil said, unconvinced.

"That's what happens when you get married and settle down," Mario said.

"Watch it, Mario," I said. "Don't use the 'M'-word or you'll have Tim bolting for the hills."

Tim grinned. "That's right. Tell the press we're 'just good friends.'"

The back door opened and Jared came in, spectacular as always. Another round of greetings and handshakes, and Jared took the stool beside me, his knee automatically finding my thigh.

"What'll it be, Jared?" Bob asked as Jared exchanged a wave with Jimmy at he far end of the bar. "Or should we start calling you 'Dr. Martinson'?"

Jared shook his head. "Not quite yet. Now that my dissertation defense is out of the way and everything's been submitted, it'll still probably take a while."

Bob put Jared's drink in front of him, then moved around from behind the bar to pick up his own glass, and raised it: "To Dr. Jared Martinson," he said, adding "...whenever."

We all joined in the toast, with glass-clicks all around.

"Well," Tim said, "I'll bet you'll really be sorry to have to give up your beer delivery route. Maybe they'll let you keep it on weekends."

Jared grinned at him. "Uh, tempting as that sounds, I don't think I'd want it even if they offered," he said. "There's talk that our union dues are going to at least double after the contract negotiations are over."

Jimmy, who had once again wandered to our end of the bar

for something, and again without breaking stride or even looking at us, said: "Jeez, the whole town's goin' to hell in a handbasket. Gangs, unions, organized crime. A girl just isn't safe on the streets anymore." And, having gotten what he came for, he went back to the front of the bar, leaving me still amazed at how he was able to keep track of our conversation even from that distance.

"Well, not to worry," I said. "I think that once Chief Black gets it all pulled together, it'll be okay. They do have some good people on the force."

"Yeah," Bob said. "And in the meantime we can all just put a deadbolt on our closet door and wait for it to pass over."

Ah, if only we'd known….

CHAPTER 2

Tom graduated #1 in his class, and had his picture on the front page of two of the local papers. He did look like a poster boy for police recruitment, and a particularly large amount of attention was given to the graduation of Tom's class by way of assuring the citizens that the department was still functioning.

I took Tom, Lisa, and Carol out to dinner as soon after Tom's graduation as we could arrange it, and Tom and I were able to reestablish at least semi-regular phone calls with promises to get together privately the first chance we had.

* * *

Never turn your back on time, not even for a minute, because when you do, it disappears. Monday becomes Friday and June becomes January. I kept busy, though don't ask me to give a detailed account of any case I worked on—none of them was sufficiently interesting for me to really remember. The social side of my life kept me from getting too bored, and there were the usual number of tricks coming and going: Nice guys, most of them, of course, or I wouldn't have gone home with them, but no one I was particularly distressed not to see again.

Tom, of course, was on cloud nine. I always looked forward to talking with him on the phone because his enthusiasm and pure joy at doing what he loved always gave me a boost. He was particularly excited when his request to be assigned to the Gang Control Unit was approved. He was the only rookie in the unit, which was obviously an acknowledgment by his superiors of his potential. He always had stories to tell and I enjoyed hearing them.

He was, from everything I could gather, extremely popular with his fellow officers, not one of whom suspected he was gay.

He did admit, somewhat embarrassed by what even he referred to as "selling out," to keeping a photo of Lisa taped to the inside of his locker. At the same time, he kept his eye out for other officers he felt might also be gay. He was willing to bide his time to be sure he was firmly entrenched and accepted by everyone as a "good cop" before he took whatever next step he was considering in reaching out to the other maybe-gays.

So, things were starting to settle down and I plodded along from ho-hum case to ho-hum case. I tried very hard, with marginal success, not to think about it, for whenever I did, my mind whispered *Do the words 'dead-end job' ring a bell, Dickie-Boy?* Of course that wasn't really fair or accurate. I'd had several really interesting cases and knew perfectly well I'd have more. But an occasional bout of self-pity is good for the soul.

Part of my problem was that while I considered myself to be adrift in a Sargasso Sea of non-progress, luckily my friends were doing quite well for themselves.

Phil had signed a contract to be the official underwear model for Spartan Briefs, thus providing teenage and adult gay (and closeted) males across the nation with an endless supply of fantasy fodder.

Jared had applied for a teaching position at, and been accepted by, Mountjoy College, a small but prestigious liberal arts college noted for the large number of its graduates who went on to government foreign service. I, like his other friends, was relieved that Mountjoy's campus is only about an hour north of the city, so we'd still be able to see him regularly.

And Tom had earned a citation for rescuing a fellow officer involved in a serious traffic accident in which the officer's squad car had caught fire, trapping him inside. Tom had risked his life to pull the other cop to safety. He'd been on the force less than a year, and was rapidly becoming, as he had been in all other aspects of his life, their golden child.

So it was with considerable pleasure that I picked up the ringing phone in my office to hear Tom's voice.

"Hi, stranger," I said. "How's our resident hero doing?"

"*Please* don't do that 'hero' routine," he said, not angrily but in a tone that said he meant it. "...like anybody else would just have stood there and watched Jake die."

"Sorry," I said, mildly embarrassed. "You're right, of course. But how *are* you doing?"

The good humor had returned to his voice when he said: "I've got the weekend off! The whole weekend! Well, I'm on call, of course, but...and Lisa and Carol are going out of town—some mutual friend's wedding—and the apartment's just sitting here empty, and I was wondering if you'd like to come over and spend the weekend with me."

Gee, let me think that one over, I thought.

"Sure!" I said. "That sound's great! You want to go to dinner Friday night as a weekend kickoff?"

"Yeah, I'd like that." There was a slight pause, and then: "It's not like I don't love my job, but I really do need to kick back for awhile and just be me."

"We'll work on it," I said. "What time Friday, then?"

He was quiet again for a second, apparently thinking, then said: "I get off at 3; why don't you come by around 6 or so? Will that give you time to swing by your place and pick up your toothbrush? But you probably won't need to bring much in the line of clothes," he added.

I got the message, and was sure he was right.

* * *

I left work around 4:30 Friday, went home, showered, changed clothes, and tossed a few things in an overnight bag. It wasn't like I was going to Tibet, and I could always just walk home and get anything I needed. But I liked the whole idea of a "get-away weekend," even though it was only a couple blocks.

At two minutes to six, I was ringing the buzzer to apartment 6-G, overnight bag in hand. I rather hoped I wouldn't run into any of Tom's neighbors in the hallway. While the real reason why some guy was walking into Tom's place with an overnight bag probably never would have occurred to them, it might have seemed a bit odd.

Well, why didn't you just pack everything in a pizza box and pretend you're making a delivery?, my mind said sarcastically. *What the hell are you worried about, anyway?*

Well, it had a point, and I guess I was just a tad…conflicted?… about this whole Tom and Lisa situation. It really bothers me when people don't feel, for whatever reason, that they can just be who they are. Every now and then, when self-realization rears its ugly head, it dawns on me what a heterophobe I really am. I'm certainly not proud of it, but it's a part of me and so I live with it.

Tom had the door open even before I reached it. We did our shake-hands-at-the-open-door-and-bear-hug-when-the-door-is-closed routine. Apparently his training at the academy had included a lot of physical workouts, because his hug was just this side of rib-cracking. Tom motioned me to a seat, then said: "Too early for a drink?"

I shook my head vigorously. "Perfect time," I said.

"I've got something to show you, first," Tom said, and went to open a drawer at one end of the credenza. He reached in pulled out a small wooden case, which he opened with a key from his key ring. When he brought the case over and opened it, I saw that it was lined with cotton batting, in the center of which was…a gun in a small leather holster.

"It was Lisa's dad's off-duty weapon," Tom said, obviously delighted. "…from when he was on the force. He sent it to me for my graduation from the academy. What a great thing for him to do."

I recognized it as a short-barrel .357 magnum—much easier to conceal than the regulation model. It looked brand new—though, if Lisa's dad had had it, it had to be at least 15 years old, if not older.

"Uh, doesn't the Police Department furnish you with a gun?" I asked, hoping he knew I was kidding.

Tom grinned. "Sure. But we're allowed to carry a weapon off duty, and everybody has their own. The rules vary from department to department: Some won't allow anything but your service revolver, which can get a bit cumbersome when you're not in uniform. I was planning on buying one, but then this came. It really means a lot to me. Our service issue is a .38, and I had to qualify on the police firing range to carry this one before I could carry it officially. I always keep it locked up when I'm home, though."

I noticed, as I was slipping the gun back into the holster, that the small strap that attached the holster to the wearer's belt was broken. Tom saw me looking at it.

"I know," he said. "I can't figure out how in hell that could have happened. Leather's not supposed to do that. But it is pretty old, so I suppose….I had to order a new one; it should have been here by now."

I put the gun and holster back in the case, which he took, carefully locked, then went to replace it in the drawer.

"So," he said, turning back to me with a smile, "how about that drink? A Manhattan, I assume?"

"Great, thanks," I said. I got up from the settee and followed him into the kitchen while he went to the cupboard for the liquor.

"Grab the ice cubes out of the freezer, would you?" he asked as he reached for glasses. "And there's some salsa in the fridge—chips should be in that cupboard right by your head."

Between the two of us, we got everything organized. I carried our drinks back into the living room while he followed with the chips and salsa. I set the drinks on the coffee table, then sat back down on the love seat. After tearing open the bag of chips and putting the bowl of salsa beside it on the coffee table, he plunked down beside me, his hand immediately laying itself casually on my knee.

He turned to me with a smile. "Nice to see you."

I put my hand over his. "You, too," I said.

He leaned forward and kissed me—not a "wow, let's get it

on right now" kiss, but a kiss that conveyed a lot more: the kind of kiss straight guys might give their best buddies if they dared. I recognized it for what it was, even though I had to send a mental shorthand message to my crotch to cool it for the moment. The good stuff would be coming along later.

We picked up our drinks and sat back, hands still joined.

"So how come you're not married?" Tom asked, then broke into a broad grin. "No, not Lisa-and-Tom married—you know, Dick-and-Joe married."

I shrugged. "Good question. Wish I had an answer."

We were quiet for another minute or so, sipping our drinks, and then I couldn't resist asking: "What about you? Don't you want a lover?"

Tom stared pensively into his glass, lips pursed. Then he brought his eyes back up to mine. "Sure," he said. "Some day. Maybe I'll be lucky enough to find somebody in the same boat as Lisa and I—though I realize that's not exactly a very deep pool for fishing. I'm really glad Lisa has Carol, and I do admit it would be nice to have someone just for me. But I realize that not many guys would be able to adjust to this kind of a relationship. I don't imagine you would."

I didn't know if he was being rhetorical or specific, but I think I could figure it out, and I was both embarrassed and a little ashamed of myself because he was right…I couldn't.

Tom took a quick, quiet intake of breath and gave my hand a quick squeeze. "So," he said, "for the foreseeable future…."

"Well," I said, trying to lighten the air a bit, "it's surely not as though you were doomed to a life of celibacy." I gave him a wicked smile. "Not as long as I'm around, anyway."

He pulled back his head and opened his eyes wide as if he were totally surprised. "Well, thank you sir," he said, then let his expression segue into a softer smile. "I just might take you up on your kind offer."

"Any time," I said with a smile.

Now! Now! my crotch yelled, and I quickly squeezed my legs together to shut it up.

* * *

We took our time finishing our drinks, talking about everything and nothing, laughing and reminiscing. When our glasses were empty, Tom said: "Like another? Or are you in a hurry to go out? I was thinking maybe we might just order in a pizza or something."

"Fine with me," I said. "I'm plenty comfortable just staying in."

"Good," Tom said, getting up from the love seat, picking up the glasses and heading for the kitchen. "Where's a good place to get delivery pizza around here?"

"Momma Rosa's about as good as they make 'em," I said. "And it's pretty close-by."

"Great," Tom said from the kitchen, where I could hear the clink of ice cubes being dropped into our glasses. "You want to call them? The phone's just around the corner in the hall, and the book's in the little drawer in the phone stand."

"I think I remember the number," I said, getting up and moving to find the phone. "Large sausage, pepperoni, green olives, onion and…half mushroom for you, half anchovy for me. Right?"

"You *are* good!" Tom said from the kitchen. "How in hell can you remember that after all these years."

I dialed Momma Rosa's and listened as the phone rang several times. "It hasn't been all *that* long," I said, hand over the mouthpiece. And at that moment, it really didn't seem so. "And if you'll recall, we practically lived on the st…"

"Momma Rosa's" a voice said.

I placed the order.

* * *

About 25 minutes later, Tom had just excused himself to go to the bathroom when the buzzer rang. "I'll get it," I called to Tom, getting up to go to the door.

When I heard the knock, I opened it to find Jeff Barber,

whose parents owned the laundromat I'd gone to for the past several years—in no small part because Jeff, now about 18, was a singularly tasty piece of eye candy who had been rather blatantly coming on to me since he was around 16. I never took him up on his offer, to the ill-concealed disappointment of my crotch, but….

Jeff was carrying a large Momma Rosa's pizza box, and seemed as surprised to see me as I was to see him.

"Dick!" he said with a very large and very sexy grin. "I didn't know you lived here!"

"I don't," I said, reaching into my back pocket for my billfold. "Just visiting a friend. And what are you doing delivering pizzas?"

"I'm starting college pretty soon, and need the extra money," he said, the grin never fading. The very tip of his tongue appeared at one corner of his mouth and slowly traced the inside of his lower lip.

Gee, I sure wish I'd brought my Dictionary of Sexual Signals, I thought.

I took out a bill considerably larger than the cost of the pizza, and we did a hand-off exchange. He reached into his pocket for change, but I told him to keep it. "For your college fund," I said.

At that moment, Tom came back into the room and Jeff gave him a long, hard, and very appreciative look.

"You've got nice…friends," Jeff said in a lowered voice that left no doubt whatsoever what he meant.

"Thanks," I said.

"I'm still holding you to your promise," Jeff said as he gave Tom a big smile and small wave, which Tom returned.

"You've got it," I said, as he turned and went out the door.

As soon as the door had closed, I walked the pizza over and handed it to Tom, who was grinning at me. "Hitting on pizza delivery boys now?" he asked. "Have you no shame?"

I returned the grin and explained the situation, and that I'd once told Jeff that he was way too young for me, but that if he was still interested when he turned 21….

"Why wait?" Tom asked. "He seems pretty eager right now, and he's old enough to know what he wants."

"Yeah," I said. "I know. Hard to explain—maybe the old midwest, middle class ethic, but I just wouldn't feel right about it. No accounting for how the mind works."

"Ah, Hardesty the Heartbreaker," Tom said as he set the pizza on the coffee table and opened the lid.

* * *

A nice night, in every way. No sense of hurry, none of the "Hi, my name's Dick…ya wanna go home and fuck?" urgency of picking up a trick a few minutes before Last Call. Lots of time to explore, and experiment, and enjoy. That Tom hadn't had a chance to be with anyone for quite a while certainly showed, but in a nice way.

We got to sleep around 2 or so, woke up for a spontaneous somewhat-delayed replay at about 4, then went back to sleep, totally relaxed and comfortable.

* * *

An equally nice day Saturday. Not having to be concerned with laundry and dry cleaning and vacuuming and grocery shopping made it seem like a real vacation. Tom woke me around 7:30 in a most enjoyable way, and it occurred to me that if someone could just invent an alarm clock to do that, nobody in the world could object to waking up.

Tom loaned me a spare robe, and we sat barefoot in the kitchen having coffee and talking. The subject got around to Tom's relationship with his dad. His mom had died when he was 11, and it wasn't easy for his dad taking over the family as well as trying to run his growing business. Luckily, Tom had always been independent, and his dad tended to give him free reign, which Tom recognized and appreciated. In exchange, Tom more or less took care of his younger sister, Maureen. He had a brother, Art, five years older than Tom and their dad's favorite, though he never gave any overt recognition of it, and Tom understood. I gathered from what Tom said that the two brothers were a lot alike in many ways, but unlike Tom, Art had been fascinated by the family business, and their dad obviously had intended to turn the business over to him at some point.

I more or less just sat and listened as Tom talked. I'd known he'd had a brother, but this was the first time Tom ever talked about him at any length. Art had been killed in a head-on collision with a semi after the semi driver claimed to have fallen asleep and swerved into Art's lane.

Tom was a junior in high school at the time, and was of course devastated by his brother's death. But his father was, if possible, even more so. Tom didn't fully understand it at the time, but his father was convinced that Art's death was not an accident. It happened at the height of a set of bitter union contract negotiations, and the semi that hit Art was driven by a member of one of the unions involved—the Amalgamated Hotel Workers of America headed by one Joe Giacomino. Nothing could be proven of course, but the elder Brady, and later Tom, were absolutely certain that Giacomino was behind it. Giacomino was currently serving a non-related 20 year prison sentence for racketeering.

While Tom did his best to fill Art's shoes when it came to the business, both he and his dad knew Tom's heart wasn't really in it. So when Tom decided, shortly after moving here, to join the force, his father reluctantly understood. Tom's sister, Maureen, had recently graduated from college and had started to work at their father's corporate headquarters. Maybe, Tom hoped, she could take his place, eventually.

One of the reasons Tom had been sent out to the Montero was because of the forthcoming labor negotiations; his dad wanted him to get experience in dealing directly with labor contracts, and all evidence was that the upcoming local contract talks were going to be rough in the extreme. The contracts of several unions were all coming up for renewal at the same time, and those unions with reputed ties to organized crime—notably the A.H.W.A.— apparently were planning to take advantage of the current upheaval within the police department to try to expand their influence. So Tom felt doubly guilty for letting his father down by not being there for him. His father was, in fact, coming out from the east coast the following week to begin preparations for the talks.

Coincidentally, the newly elected head of the Amalgamated Hotel Workers of America local was one Joe ("Joey") Giacomino, Jr., *not* coincidentally the eldest son of Joe Giacomino, Sr.. This was to be little Joey's first major contract negotiation, and he was understandably going to be taking a lot of heat not only from union headquarters, but from dear old dad.

* * *

It's kind of surprising how fast time can go by even when you're not doing anything special, if you're spending it with someone you enjoy. Tom had some home movies from college, and we watched them, laughing at triggered memories and wondering about now-lost friends who were once so close to us. We didn't even get out of our robes all day. (Well, I take that back—we did, a couple of times, but we always put them back on afterwards.)

We were, in fact, lying in bed when I heard the grandmother clock in the living room strike 5. "Well, do you think we should try for dinner out tonight? I have to admit I'm plumb tuckered from all this exercise."

Tom reached over and rolled me over to him, chest to chest. "Sure," he said, the tips of our noses about two inches apart. "Where should we go?" I was lying on his left arm, but his free right hand, fingers splayed wide, was making large circles across my shoulders, then slowly spiraling downward. I reached down with my own left hand and grabbed his wrist, keeping him from moving further south.

"Now look, buddy," I said, moving my nose forward until it

was pressed against his, hard; "I'm the Scorpio here. Nobody's allowed to be hornier than me, and even I admit I could use a little break."

Tom grinned, moving his head back just far enough to be able to look into my eyes. "Hey, I've been out there in the desert a long time," he said. "You can't blame a guy for trying."

"Who's blaming?" I asked. "Give me a couple hours to recharge my batteries and we can start all over again. Fair?"

He gave the facial-expression equivalent of a shrug. "Fair," he said, and I rolled back off his arm and onto the pillow.

"So where for dinner?"

I thought a moment."Well, let's see; there's Calypso's, or Napoleon, or…"

"You pick," he said. "The place you took us to the other night was nice."

"Rasputin's," I said. "Sure, we could go back there if you'd like. But I think you might like Napoleon. There are a lot of nice places around; you might as well sample them all."

"You lead, I'll follow," he said.

"Can I have that in writing?" I asked.

* * *

We got up, took a communal shower, jostled around each other for use of the mirror while shaving, causing Tom to nick himself to the point of drawing blood. At that point, after tearing a small piece of toilet paper off the roll and sticking it to the cut, he put his razor down and said "Okay, I'll go and make us a drink while you finish up here. Let me know when it's safe to come back in." And with that he wrapped a towel around himself and padded off toward the kitchen.

Of course I felt guilty, but not very, so took my time getting my hair into some semblance of order, stealing some of Tom's after-shave and, though I normally never use the stuff, applied some underarm deodorant from a stick I'd had lying, unopened, in my dopp kit for a couple years or more. As I was leaving the bathroom, I met Tom coming in, a drink in each hand. I took one, nodded a thanks, and we did a classic shoulder-turn pass as I left and he entered through the door at the same time. I stopped just long enough to make a quick turn and yank his towel off. Teenage stuff, but fun.

* * *

We took our time finishing our drinks and getting dressed, talking all the while. I think we were probably both rather surprised that we never seemed to run out of things to talk about, but we didn't. We shared a lot of the same interests. Tom had an endless string of stories to tell about his adventures working at his dad's various hotels, and while his chances for any long term relationships were limited by circumstances, he never wanted for willing bed partners. Hey, when you look like Tom…! He'd get hit on constantly by women, too, of course, but all he had to do was mention Lisa and they'd usually get the picture.

I gathered the Lisa-and-Tom thing just sort of evolved. Straights seem to find it almost impossible to imagine that a boy and a girl can really be best friends, without sex having to enter into it. And of course, both Tom and Lisa had always known the other was gay. So rather than try to go it on their own in the "Oh, Tom, you've got to meet my niece; you'd love her," or "When are you going to find the right man and settle down, Lisa?" world, since it was always assumed that they were a "couple," they just went along. The vast majority of straights, Tom and I agreed, tend to be dumbfoundingly, infuriatingly smug when it comes to assuming that their way of life is the only way of life.

I called Napoleon and got reservations for 7:30. As we were getting ready to leave the apartment, Tom seemed mildly distracted.

"Problem?" I asked.

"Sort of," he said, going over to the credenza to take out his gun case. "What am I going to do about my gun? There's no place to put it dressed like this, and I'd stand out like a sore thumb if I tried to wear my shoulder holster under a jacket."

"Do you have to have it on you?" I asked. "Maybe if you put it under the front seat of the car…we'll park as close to the restaurant as we can."

Tom shrugged. "Sure; that'll be okay," he said.

Since Lisa and Carol had taken Tom's car to drive to the wedding, Tom and I walked back to my place to pick up mine. As we were walking over, Tom was apparently more than a little self-conscious about carrying the small case.

"This is damned awkward," he said. "Maybe I should have ordered two new holsters. But who'd ever expect a leather strap to break?"

Despite having to walk to my place for the car, we arrived at Napoleon…thanks largely to my magic ability for always being early…at 7:15. Tom didn't seem to mind, and we'd pretty much managed to ignore the clock all day anyway. I'd been telling Tom—at his insistence—about some of the more interesting cases I'd worked on, and about my friends and how some of them got to be my friends. I kind of avoided getting back to Tom's earlier question of why, if I thought I'd like to have a lover, I didn't have one. Actually, I knew, the answer was simple: It's a lot easier to want something than to get it.

And I realized again, as I talked, that whatever professional doldrums I might be in at the moment, they wouldn't last forever.

Dinner was nice, and relaxing, and comfortable—much like the past 24 hours-plus had been. As we were leaving Napoleon, Tom suggested we stop at a couple bars before heading back to his place. I realized he was really enjoying what was probably his first completely free weekend since he'd arrived in town, but I was mildly concerned about going to the bars—for his sake, certainly not for mine.

"Sure, if you want to," I said, "but what about…uh…." I didn't know exactly how to say it.

Tom looked at me and grinned. "You mean what if somebody from the department sees me?"

I gave a cursory shrug.

"Well," he said as we reached my car and I unlocked the passenger's side door for him, "if I run into a fellow cop in the bars, chances are he's there for the same reason I am, so I don't think he's going to be telling anyone who can cause any trouble, do you? And as far as anything else is concerned…I told you, I'm not going to lock myself in a closet and turn my life off. If something happens, I'll deal with it then, not before."

He was right, of course, and I admired his attitude. I was still a little concerned. He'd just started a career he really loved; I didn't want to see him jeopardize it, but I realized it was his life and his choice as to what he wanted to do with it.

"So," I said, "where would you like to go?"

Tom got in the car and I moved around to the driver's side, which he leaned across the seat to unlock. I got in, hoisted my rear off the seat to reach into my pocket for the keys, and turned on the ignition.

"I dunno," Tom said, picking up the conversation where we'd left it. "You know the bars here a lot better than I do. Where would you suggest?"

"Well," I said, checking for traffic and then pulling out into the street, "depends on the mood you're in. There's Glitter, if you don't mind 10,000 guys on the dance floor at once, or risking having your ears bleed from the sound system—but it can be fun if you're up to it. Or the Male Call, if you want to go back home and change into your leather, or…"

Tom reached over and laid his hand on my leg. "How about just someplace kind of laid back? I'm not out for cruising—I just feel like being around some of my own people for a change."

"I think I know just the place," I said, and took a right on Parker, headed for Griff's. I remembered that Tom had one characteristic that was a dead giveaway that he was gay: he loved Broadway musicals, and Griff's was a really nice, comfortable piano bar.

We found a place to park just across the street from Ruthie's, a quiet lesbian bar my friend Mollie Marino and her lover Barb had taken me to once. Ruthie's and Griff's were only about five doors apart on the same side of the street, separated by an alley that sided Ruthie's.

For whatever reason, lesbian bars were seldom hassled, either by the police or by gay bashers, but about a month before, two women had been attacked, dragged into the alley, and raped after coming out of Ruthie's, apparently by gang members. There had understandably been quite a furor at the time, but since the area wasn't noted for gang activity and there had been no incidents before or since, things had sort of gotten back to normal.

* * *

As I'd hoped, Guy Prentice was holding sway at the piano, belting out "The Boston Beguine" from New Faces of 1952 (Guy knew every song from every musical that had run on or off Broadway from 1922 to the present, and I'd never seen him fail to remember one.)

Griff's never had to worry about exceeding occupancy limits, but it always had a nice crowd, both in number and in disposition. After getting a heads-up greeting from Guy, who didn't miss a beat in his playing, Tom and I went to one of the small tables on a step-up platform that lined the front end of the bar. It was just high enough to allow an unobstructed view over the heads of those sitting at other tables between the platform and the piano. The waiter came over and took our order and went off to give it to the bartender.

"I like it," Tom said, approvingly.

"Thought you would," I said, grinning.

I exchanged wave-and-nod greetings with Jim Marsh and Cory Lockhart, sitting at the stools around the piano. Jim and Cory used to hang around with Chris and me before Chris went off to New York.

Our drinks arrived, and we settled back to enjoy the music.

During his break, Guy got up from the piano and moved around the room, exchanging greetings with the regulars and accepting compliments on his talent, which was considerably larger than the venue in which he was playing. I'd often wondered why he seemed happy to stay at one place so long, but was very glad he did.

He worked his way to the platform, and to our table.

"Good to see you, Dick," he said, putting a hand on my shoulder. "It's been a while."

"Unfortunately," I said, then introduced Tom. Guy gave him an appreciative once-over, then turned to me and said: "I'm glad you're getting on with your life, Dick. Still in touch with Chris?"

"Sure," I said. "We write a couple times a month and talk on the phone regularly. He's got a new lover, as I think I told you last time I was in. He's doing well, and I'm glad for him."

Guy nodded. "Well, give him my regards when you talk with him next." Then, turning to Tom, he said: "Got any requests for the next set?"

"Do you know anything from 'Boy Meets Boy'?" Tom asked.

Guy grinned and gave him a wide-eyed, raised-eyebrow look. "Do I know anything from 'Boy Meets Boy'?" he asked incredulously. "Honey, I know *everything* from 'Boy Meets Boy'! What would you like to hear?"

"'Tell Me, Please'?" Tom said, then gave me a quick look and if I didn't know better, I'd swear he blushed.

"You got it," he said. "Well, time to get back. Good to see you, Dick; nice to meet you, Tom. Come back."

"We will," we echoed in unison.

Was that a blush? I wondered. *And if so, why?* Of course, I knew the lyrics by heart, and realized that maybe Tom might be afraid I'd think he meant them to apply to me. But that was hardly likely...even though the die-hard romantic in me gave it a wistful thought.

About ten minutes into his second set, Guy segued into almost the entire score from 'Boy Meets Boy', moving from the rousing 'It's a Boy's Life!' into the far more...*out with it, Hardesty!*...okay, romantic...'Tell Me, Please.'

You're a marshmallow, Hardesty, my mind said, derisively and I immediately got a mental picture of my guardian angel, wings and halo highlighted, responding sweetly: *Fuck thee!*

I forced myself not to look at Tom, and to zero in on Guy and the words to the song:

Tell me, please, does anybody love you?
Do you have a special love affair?
Someone who worries about you,
who's always true and tender too
and waits for you somewhere?

You're hopeless, Hardesty, my mind sighed.

* * *

Guy finished his second set and remained at the piano, engrossed in conversation with a couple of the patrons sitting closest to him. Jim and Cory finished their drinks and got up to leave. We exchanged another wave and smile as they went out the door.

"I'm really glad we came here," Tom said. "Just what I needed—like this whole weekend has been."

I thought again of how tough it must be for Tom, really, being in a demanding, dangerous job surrounded by too many homophobes, being in a relationship which, no matter how close friends he and Lisa were, did not and could not supply him with the kind of emotional support he wanted and needed.

"Well, we've still got one more day to go," I said.

Suddenly the front door burst open and Cory ran into the bar, shirt torn and face bloody.

"Call the police!" he yelled at the bartender. "Jim's hurt!"

Everything started happening at once: the bartender reached for the phone; two guys closest to the door grabbed hold of Cory and led him to a stool. The rest of the bar got to its feet, including Tom and me, and moved toward the door, but Tom pulled out his wallet and flashed his badge. "Stay here!" he said in a voice which commanded attention. He turned to me. "Give me your keys!"

I fumbled for them and handed them to him as he went out into the street, with me at his heels. Ignoring me, Tom raced across the street to my car, and to the car's passenger side door. I meanwhile ran instinctively toward the alley between Griff's and Ruthie's, where probably ten people were roiling around, fighting. I could see someone on the ground—Jim, I guessed—while several guys stood or bent over him, kicking and punching him. One had a pipe or club of some sort in his hand, using the end of it as a battering ram to punch Jim in the side. Jim had managed to curl himself into a fetal position to try to protect himself. I managed to grab one of two guys who had a woman forced against the wall, punching her, while out of the corner of my eye I saw another woman kneeing a guy in the groin. Several other women were coming out of Ruthie's, attracted by the noise, not knowing what was going on. A couple started toward the scuffle, but at that point, I heard Tom yelling: "Police! Knock it off! Now!" and saw him running toward the group, his wallet and badge in one hand, a gun in his other.

The women coming out of Ruthie's backed off immediately, but not the attackers, including the guy I'd pulled off the woman. He punched me, hard, in the stomach, and I came up with an uppercut that snapped his head back sharply and sent him crashing backwards into the wall.

I saw one of the group kicking Jim step back, reach one hand behind his back, and bring out a gun he'd apparently had in his waistband, just as the guy with the pipe standing over Jim raised it over his head with both hands.

I heard Tom yell "Freeze!" and saw the start of the downward swing of the pipe, toward Jim's head. Then there were three quick shots, a couple screams, and the sound of running as four or five of the attackers headed down the alley. The guy I'd been fighting with tried to follow, but I grabbed him and slammed him into the wall again. A couple guys from Griff's and some of the women from Ruthie's appeared and held him to keep him from getting away as the sound of approaching sirens grew closer. I saw Cory running to kneel down beside Jim, trying to turn him over.

When I looked around, there were four people on the ground: Jim, the guy with the pipe, the guy with the gun…and Tom.

CHAPTER 3

The rest was a blur. I immediately ran over to Tom and was relieved to see him struggling to sit up. He had his right hand against his left shoulder, and blood seeped between his fingers. While I'm sure it hurt like hell, it appeared that it wasn't life-threatening. He managed a weak grin and tried to get to his feet, but I told him to stay where he was. I stayed with him until the squad cars started pulling up, and I was pushed back with the crowd. A moment or two later, the ambulances arrived and took Jim and Tom away: Cory and the two women were battered, but did not require an ambulance; the two attackers were beyond needing one, and were covered over with yellow tarps.

Cory had wanted to go immediately to the hospital to be with Jim, but the cops asked him to stay to give his statement. Other cops on the scene started taking the names and addresses of everyone who had seen anything at all, and a couple plainclothes detectives showed up and took Cory and the two women aside to question them. I recognized both the detectives and hoped to hell they wouldn't see me.

I just wanted to get the hell away from there, but a squad car was blocking my car and I couldn't. I wanted to stay as far out of it as I could, for obvious reasons. I knew they'd ask me about Tom, and what we were doing there. I just tried to slowly back myself away, but then Cory looked around and pointed at me and I knew I'd had it.

Shit!

One of the plainclothesmen—Detective Crouch…no, Couch—looked at me, nudged the other—Detective…Carpenter—and they waved me over to them.

"Detectives," I said by way of acknowledgment. I'd had a minor run in with the two partners on an earlier case, and I'd managed to piss Detective Couch off royally. From the way he looked at me, I could see he hadn't forgotten.

"You know Officer Brady?" Carpenter asked.

"Yes," I said, "I went to college with him and his wife." *Sliiide that one right in there, Hardesty*, I thought.

"And what was Officer Brady doing in a gay bar?" Couch asked, scowling at me, then added: "Oh, yes, that's right. You're...*gay*...aren't you?'

One of Chief Black's innovations had been to require every officer in the department to attend classes in dealing with minorities—including gays—which was widely applauded by the citizenry, but generally regarded as a waste of time by some of the department's old guard.

While I was glad to see Chief Black's sensitivity training program was having some effect, in that Couch didn't use one of the other words he undoubtedly would have preferred, the way this guy said "gay" made it sound like an infectious disease.

"Yes," I said. "Your point being...?"

"So what was Officer Brady doing in a gay bar?" Couch repeated.

"Because I invited him to come," I said. "His wife is out of town for the weekend, so we decided to spend some time together. Officer Brady puts friendship above passing judgment. And I think we should all be pretty damned glad he *was* in that bar, or it could have been a lot worse for the people whose lives he probably saved."

"Yeah," Couch muttered, "two lesbos and a..."

Carpenter shot him a withering look, and Couch abruptly shut up. "I apologize for my partner," Carpenter said. "He..."

I turned to Couch and stared at him until he looked at me, defiantly. "Detective Couch," I said, being very careful not to let my anger show, "I'm sure you're a good detective and a good man, but you have one *hell* of a lot to learn. I might suggest *you* consider spending some time in a gay bar. It might do you good." Realizing he would undoubtedly take that the wrong way, I looked at his partner, who had always struck me as being a little more open minded. "You can interpret that for him sometime,"

I said.

Carpenter gave me an almost imperceptible nod, then immediately said: "So exactly what happened here?"

And I told him what I knew.

* * *

While I was really concerned about Tom, I didn't try to go to the hospital. I knew he'd be in deep enough shit without having a known faggot hovering over him. I was pretty sure they would keep him overnight and probably release him in the morning. I'd call him at home then.

* * *

The shooting was the lead story on the morning news, and made the front page of the Sunday paper. While the newspaper article had obviously been hastily patched together, owing to the relatively short time between the incident and press time: "2 Dead in Gang Attack", the TV reports did go into a bit more detail, including giving Tom's name. It was interesting for what all the reports didn't say as well as for what they did: Two women had been attacked outside "a bar" on Parker Boulevard, and two men coming to their aid were severely beaten, one of them reported to be in critical condition in City General hospital. When an off-duty policeman arrived on the scene a gunfight ensued in which two of the attackers, believed to be members of the Turf Lords gang, were shot and killed by the officer, who himself sustained a gunshot wound to the shoulder.

One of the TV stations (I flipped back and forth between them) even somehow had managed to show Tom's photo, apparently from the award ceremony after he'd saved the officer trapped in the burning squad car. I had a sneaking suspicion that the fact that not one of the reports mentioned the gay aspect of the story just might have been in response to a request from the department. I somehow found that fact more than a little disturbing.

I also felt guilty about not going to the hospital to see Tom, or to make sure he got home okay if, as I suspected and hoped, they had released him. But I knew it would not be a good idea. I waited until about 10:00 Sunday morning, then called his apartment. There was no answer, and I began to get worried.

I'd just determined to take a walk over to his place and check when the phone rang.

"Dick Hardesty," I said, wondering as usual why I always insisted on using my last name when I answered the phone, even at home.

"Dick, hi. It's Tom."

Well of course it is, I thought, relieved to hear his voice.

"Tom!" I said, mildly surprised by the sound of relief in my own voice. "Where are you? *How* are you?"

His voice sounded tired when he said: "I'm home, and I'm fine. Sore, but fine. I've been here about an hour, but I haven't been answering the phone. Did you try to call?"

"Yeah," I said. "I've been worried about you, and I wanted to apologize for bailing out on you last night. But when I realized you were probably going to live, I just felt that discretion was the better part of valor."

Tom managed a small laugh. "Probably just as well," he said. "I had department people all over me most of the night, wanting every detail of the shooting. Luckily they spent more time on the shooting itself than on what I was doing in a gay bar; I gather they'd talked to you at the scene from what one of the detectives said. But I suspect the gay issue will resurface soon. If I hadn't been shot and effectively taken off the duty roster, I'd probably have been suspended as a matter of course while they investigated. There'll be a hearing, of course, which is standard procedure when a police officer is involved in a fatal shooting." He paused, then said "You want to come on over? We could talk easier in person, I think."

"Sure," I said. "Did you have breakfast? I could stop at the deli and get something."

"No, thanks," he said. "I had breakfast—at least that's what they called it—at the hospital while I was waiting for them to release me."

Again I felt guilty for not having been there to bring him home, but forced myself to put it aside. "Okay," I said. "I'll come right over."

When we hung up, I grabbed a quick piece of toast and a glass of orange juice, then put on my shoes and left for Tom's. About halfway there, I remembered his gun case, which was still lying open on the floor of the passenger's side of my car, and I returned to get it.

* * *

Tom opened the door looking pale and tired, but otherwise none the worse for wear. He was shirtless, and had a large bandage from the base of his neck to his left shoulder. His left arm was in a sling. We shook hands, then he closed the door and, seeing that I'd brought his gun case, he reached out with his free arm and gave me a sort of sideways hug, careful not to involve his left side. I returned the hug gingerly.

He grinned as we released the hug. "I'm not made of glass, you know," he said.

"I can see that," I said, giving his bare torso an appreciative once-over.

"Want some coffee?" he asked as I followed him toward the love seats, pausing to lay the gun case on the coffee table.

"Sure, if you've got some made—or I could make some, if you'd like." I said.

"Thanks, mom," he said, "but you don't have to fuss over me. I managed to make a pot when I got home."

I aborted my rear-end's descent onto the love seat and followed him into the kitchen.

"Have you called Lisa?" I asked.

Tom reached into one of the cabinets for a coffee mug. "Nah," he said. "They'll be back tonight. No point in spoiling their day."

He poured my coffee, then refilled his own cup which sat beside the coffee maker, and we went back to the living room and sat down side by side on one of the love seats.

"Did you hear how Jim's doing?" I asked, putting my hand on his leg.

Tom took a swig of coffee before nodding and saying: "Yeah, I stopped by to look in on him just before I left. He's out of intensive care, but still in pretty bad shape. Several broken ribs, a ruptured spleen, and some internal bleeding, from what I understand. His partner…Cory?…was with him. He was lucky he ran for help, or they both could have ended up dead—the women, too."

"They seemed to have come through it pretty well, all things considered," I observed. I'd only caught a couple glimpses of them after the incident. They both looked like they'd been in a fight, but I guess it wasn't bad enough for them to have to go to the hospital. But Tom was right, they were pretty lucky.

"What about the gay thing?" I asked.

Tom put his cup down on the coffee table, made a slight grimace when he apparently moved his left shoulder too fast, then leaned slowly back upright and looked at me with another grin, as if apologizing for the grimace. "The two detectives who interviewed me first were the ones who talked to you: Couch and Carpenter. They wanted to know exactly what my relationship with you was. I skipped over the part about us spending a lot of time in bed together. But I did tell them we had been friends since college: you, me and Lisa," he added, then scowled and shook his head. "Damn it! I hate having to run and hide behind Lisa! I hate not being able to just say 'Yeah, I'm gay; so what?' But I just haven't been around the department long enough to do that yet. Maybe, in a couple of years…."

Dream on, kid, I thought.

He carefully leaned forward to pick up his cup and take another mouthful, draining it. "The taller one…Carpenter…did most of the talking," he continued. "Couch didn't say much but he glowered a lot. I got the feeling you aren't one of his favorite people. It was pretty obvious that as far as he's concerned, no real man could ever be friends with a fucking faggot. But they really didn't push too hard. Later, two guys from Internal Affairs came in and I guess they had talked to the first two, because they didn't ask any direct questions about it, either. But I'm not foolish enough to think I'm off the hook just yet."

I finished my coffee and offered to go get Tom some more, but he shook his head, then gave me a big grin.

"You know one thing I found out about being shot?" he said.

Puzzled, I shook my head. "No," I said. "What's that?"

"It makes me horny as all hell!"

I looked at him, wide-eyed. "Are you serious?" I asked, incredulous.

"Oh, yeah," he said.

"And how in the hell are we supposed to manage that without sending you back to the hospital?"

Tom reached over with his good hand and slid it behind my neck, pulling me toward him.

"Improvise," he said.

* * *

I stayed with Tom until Lisa and Carol got home around 8. They were both shocked to find out what had happened, and Lisa was angry and a little hurt that Tom hadn't called her immediately.

The phone had rung almost constantly all the time I was there, but Tom had been advised not to talk to anyone —especially the press. I thought of volunteering to field calls, but immediately realized that would not be the smartest thing in the world to do, given the circumstances. A police officer involved in a shooting outside a gay bar having his phone answered by a man other than the officer himself…uh, no….

I went home about nine o'clock, to find several messages on my answering machine: Jared, Bob Allen, Glen O'Banyon— now that was a surprise—Tim and Phil; all of them had heard I'd been at the scene of the shooting. How in hell they'd found that out, I have no idea, since while Tom's name had been mentioned, mine certainly hadn't. But I should have realized that a story like this would sweep through the entire gay community in a heartbeat. And the fact that Tom was gay was part of the beat.

Since Glen O'Banyon had left his home phone number—the first time I'd ever had it—I returned his call first. The phone rang several times and I was just about to hang up when I heard the receiver being lifted and O'Banyon's voice: "Glen O'Banyon."

"Glen, hi. Dick Hardesty. Sorry I missed your call; I just got home."

"No problem," O'Banyon said. "I heard about the shooting—as a matter of fact, that's about all I've been hearing about all day. How do you manage to do it?"

I was puzzled. "Do what?" I asked. "I didn't do anything; I was just there."

There was a note of mild amusement in his voice when he said: "My point exactly. You have a magic knack for being 'just there.'" Then his voice took on a more serious note. "Your friend Tom Brady is turning into something of an instant hero in the gay community. I've never met him, but would like you to pass along word to him that if he needs legal representation, have him give me a call."

I was more than a little impressed. While O'Banyon's being gay was an open secret, he had always been careful never to flaunt it. His power and success gave him access to the upper strata of straight society, and his financial support and leadership qualities had earned him a seat on the boards of several influential charities. He had also been very shrewd in avoiding making enemies in the department, partly by having established, and largely supported, a scholarship fund for the children of police officers killed in the line of duty. Not even the most homophobic members of the force would dare openly attack him. So given all these factors, his offer meant a hell of a lot.

"Tom will be very grateful to hear that, Glen." I said. "Thank you. I certainly hope it never comes to that, but if it did...well, Tom wouldn't want you to put yourself on the line for him."

"Nonsense," O'Banyon said. "That's what lawyers do, and if anybody in the department gets his nose out of joint, tough. If Chief Black were totally in charge now, your friend very well may not need one at all. But given the power struggles going on in the department, I'm pretty sure Chief Black's enemies will jump on this as a way to undermine him. The very idea that there may be a gay officer in a department with as strong a tradition of rampant homophobia as ours is, I'm afraid, just too explosive an issue for Black's foes to ignore. I suspect this whole thing has the potential to get very messy."

"Yeah," I said. "Plus, were you aware that Tom's wife is Chief Black's goddaughter?"

"Ah, so it's true. I'd heard something about their being related; but I don't think a goddaughter/godfather relationship exactly qualifies as nepotism. Still, it's interesting to note, and I'm sure it will add fuel to the fire." He was quiet a moment, then said: "Just let Officer Brady know I'm here if he needs me."

"I'll do that, Glen," I said, sincerely impressed. "Thank you again."

"Keep me posted," he said.

We hung up shortly thereafter and I called Jared, Bob, and Phil and Tim in order. Each of them expressed their admiration for what Tom had done, and any support they may be able to provide if the issue of Tom's being gay became a major problem. And each commented on the sense of...pride probably describes it best...sweeping through the community at the thought that one of their own might actually be on the front lines of integrating the police force. Everyone knew, of course, that there were other gays on the force, but this was the first time a specific name had emerged, and in circumstances so directly involving the community.

If all the gay cops on the force served openly, Toms actions would still have been considered heroic, but that he was the first of our own on the force to whom the community could point with pride...well, it elicited a rather unrealistic degree of hope that other gay officers would somehow begin opening their closet doors. Still, it was hope, and the community clutched at it.

While this was all, indeed, kind of euphoric, it was also a bit more than altruistic. The hard fact of the matter was that Tom was *not* openly gay to the department and while the department's reaction was yet to be seen, it was almost inevitably going to be negative, and harsh.

* * *

I arrived at the office Monday morning to find a message from Lieutenant Mark Richman, asking me to call him. The message didn't say "immediately" but it didn't have to. I didn't get calls from Lieutenant Richman unless it was important.

I put the plastic lid back on the styrofoam cup of coffee I'd picked up at the diner downstairs, dialed the City Building Annex's number, and asked for Richman's extension.

"Lieutenant Richman," the familiar voice said. I'd not talked to him in some time but had no trouble in recognizing him.

"Lieutenant. This is Dick Hardesty returning your call."

As usual, on the phone, he was all Police Lieutenant efficiency. "Thanks for calling, Dick," he said. "I was wondering if you might be free for lunch today. There's something I'd like to talk over with you."

Now, I wonder what that might be? my mind asked.

"Sure, Lieutenant," I said. "The park or Sandler's?" We'd established a sort of pattern, in the several cases I'd worked on in loose conjunction with Richman, of meeting either at the fountain in Warman Park, or at Sandler's Café, both of which were about two blocks from the City Building Annex where the police department headquarters were located.

"How about Sandler's? Noon?" he said.

"I'll see you there," I replied, and we hung up.

I knew full well Richman knew I'd been with Tom at the shooting, and I also knew full well that it wasn't the shooting he wanted to talk about. Richman was officially in Departmental Administration, but he apparently wore a lot of hats. He worked closely with the head of the Homicide Division, Captain Offermann, and it was as Offermann's leg man that we had had most of our previous contacts. But in this instance I was pretty sure this call was more related to his administrative duties than to Homicide.

* * *

I didn't even try to call Tom. I knew he still wouldn't be answering his phone, but I was curious if he'd had any contact from his department superiors. I decided to either wait until I heard from him, or I'd drop by on my way home.

I got to Sandler's early, of course, and was on my second cup of coffee when I saw Richman come in. The more I saw of that guy, the more attractive he became. I knew part of my attraction was something of a matter of "forbidden fruit" (no pun intended) in that Richman was unrelentingly straight. But that didn't make him one bit less sexy. He was in full uniform, which was just a little unusual since he was normally in civies when we met outside of his office.

He came directly over, shook hands, and sat down opposite me. The waiter had followed him to the table, so he didn't say anything until his coffee was poured and the waiter moved away.

"We've got a problem," he said, not looking directly at me as he placed his napkin on his lap.

"I know," I said.

He reached for the sugar and poured about a quarter-cupful into his coffee, then picked up the spoon and began stirring, slowly. His eyes moved up to mine and locked on them, as was another part of the ritual of our meetings.

"*If* Officer Brady is gay…" I knew and appreciated the fact that he would not ask me directly, "…the repercussions can be gravely serious for the department, especially now. Chief Black is a good man, and I think he's exactly what the department has needed for some time. But he has powerful enemies, and he hasn't been here long enough to fully establish his control. There are still too many…" The waiter returned, order pad and pencil in hand.

Without looking at the menu, Richman ordered his usual meatloaf platter and I ordered the turkey club I'd seen written on the chalkboard in the window as I'd come in.

Richman watched as the waiter headed off for the kitchen, then picked up in mid sentence: "…of Chief Rourke's cronies around who were perfectly satisfied with the way the department was run in 1933 and see no reason for it to change. They resent Chief Black's vision of what the department should be, and will do anything in their considerable power to undermine him. Most of them will be retiring within a couple years, but until then, Chief Black is going to have to keep a very tight rein. The question is, frankly, if he'd be able to handle such an explosive issue right now, given his short time on the job."

As usual, once eye contact had been established between us, it was broken only to blink. I didn't get the impression that I needed to do anything other than listen at the moment, so that's what I did.

Richman took another sip of his coffee and set the cup down. "The issue of gays on the force is serious enough without its being compounded by the fact that the officer in question is married to Chief Black's goddaughter. The fact that Brady *is* married is a strong factor in his favor: Most of these old-timers simply can't comprehend that somebody can be both married and gay at the same time. The old 'he's married so he can't be gay' mind set. That he was at a gay bar with an openly gay man can be explained by the fact that you are an old friend of both him and his wife. But the 'guilt by association' factor is always there. Now, if he were to come out publicly and deny being gay...." He looked at me, studying my face, and gave the barest hint of a smile.

"He wouldn't do that," I said. "Tom's a man of honor and strong principle. Why should he have to deny something that has nothing whatever to do with his qualifications as a police officer? It's like asking someone to deny being a Democrat, or a Republican: It's totally irrelevant and nobody's damned business."

Richman nodded. "In a perfect world...." he said. "But how we're able to handle this entire situation depends to a large extent on the reaction of the gay community."

The waiter arrived with our lunch, and we ate in silence for a moment, dropping our mutual eye-lock with the conversation.

When I felt the pause had gone on long enough, I said: "So what, if anything, would you like from me?"

Don't say it! I cautioned my crotch.

The eye-lock resumed, Richman waited until he'd dipped a forkful of meatloaf into the gravy around his mashed potatoes, conveyed it to his mouth, chewed a bit, and swallowed, before gesturing toward me with his fork and saying: "I've already heard the rumors—Brady's being looked on as a community hero: and *if* he is gay, that's completely understandable. To have the department looked on favorably for a change by the gay community would normally be a real plus. But the hardliners definitely won't see it that way.

"We've done everything we can to encourage the mainstream media to act responsibly and not make an issue of the rumors. Luckily, most of them are on Chief Black's side and so far they've done a good job of just sticking to the pertinent facts of the incident. Of course there are no guarantees that someone won't see the opportunity to boost sales or ratings too tempting to resist. We'll just have to wait and see.

"But while we have very little control over how the general public views this incident, we have absolutely none over the gay community, and it's the gay community that holds the fuse and the match."

I'd hardly touched my sandwich, but took a few bites while Richman took a momentary pause to scoop a forkful of succotash through the mashed potatoes and into his mouth. Having done so, he shook his head slowly, swallowed, and resumed talking.

"We have a slight advantage, too, in the fact that very few if any of the old schoolers have a clue as to what's going on within the community. But you can be sure they're going to suddenly be very alert to every ripple this causes. As long as the story stays within the community, the chances of the hardliners being able to grab something and run with it is limited. But the minute articles start cropping up in Rainbow Flag or 'Go, Brady!' banners show up on the front of gay bars, or the activists decide to hold a rally or march on city hall to demand 'more' gay cops, we're all in deep shit."

He finished his coffee, laid his knife and fork on his now empty plate, and edged it slightly forward toward the center of the table to indicate that he was done. Then he again resumed our eye lock.

"So," he said, "the bottom line is this: Chief Black's enemies are looking for any reason to discredit and even get rid of him. They would love nothing better than to use this incident as a chance to get at Chief Black by demanding that he fire Brady. That would be an unmitigated disaster, for the department and for any hope it may ever have had to improve relations with the gay community. To fire a cop for saving the lives of three members of that community would send a horrific message and do incalculable and possibly irreparable harm.

"We don't want the gay community to give them a reason. At this point *no one*..." and both his facial expression and the tone of his voice got his message across clearly "...knows for sure that Tom Brady is gay. And we're going to do our level best to make sure that no one on the force officially asks. From everything I've heard, Tom Brady is a damned good cop, and like it or not, *if* he is gay and wants to keep his career, the gay community has to cooperate."

I knew without question that he was right, but wasn't quite sure just what he wanted me to do about it. "I'll do whatever I can," I said, "but I'm hardly what anyone would consider a 'community leader'—they're the ones you should be talking with."

The waiter came to take our plates and ask if we wanted dessert. Richman asked for some peach cobbler—*That man is a bottomless pit!* I thought, inexplicably flashing on a split second of erotic fantasy—and I passed. The waiter poured us more coffee, and turned to get the cobbler, which was in a cooler just a few feet from our table.

"We would if we could," Richman said when he'd left, reaching again for the sugar and again picking up the conversation where it had left off, "but we're skating on very thin ice, here, and no one from the department can approach these people directly without giving the hard liners even more ammunition. The official stand of the department regarding this shooting is that it involved an off duty officer who arrived on the scene—the circumstances of how he happened to be there are totally irrelevant. We don't want sexual orientation to enter the equation. We have, as I said earlier, the advantage that most of the hardliners can't accept or even comprehend the idea that a man can be married to a woman and have sex with another man. Totally beyond their ken, and we want to keep it that way.

"So while you may not consider yourself a community leader, you've got contacts with the people who are. Glen O'Banyon, for one; and you've got close links with the Bar Guild. Try and get them together with the gay papers and the Gay Business League and anyone else who will listen. Just ask them to please, please keep a low profile on this thing. You've got a right to be proud of Officer Brady whether he's gay or not, but don't give the hardliners any more reason than they already have to use Brady to destroy the Chief."

He was silent again, and we finished our coffee as the waiter brought the check.

"On me," Richman said, reaching for it.

* * *

I found a message from Tom when I returned to the office, asking me to call, but called Glen O'Banyon's office first. His secretary, Donna, told me he was in court, but that she would have him call me as soon as he possibly could. I then dialed Tom's number.

Lisa answered the phone. "Brady residence." Obviously, she'd taken the day off work to be with Tom.

"Lisa, hi, it's Dick. Is Tom around?"

"Sure, Dick," she said. "Hold a second." I heard the receiver being set down, and a moment later picked up, and then Tom's voice.

"Hi, Dick. Thanks for calling back."

I told him where I'd been and gave him a rundown on my conversation with Richman. "So you've got some pretty heavy support in the department," I said.

"I think I'm going to need it," he said. "And I think Richman is right in asking the community to keep it cool."

"Have you had any word from the department?" I asked.

"Not a word. Jake called to see how I was doing but...."

Somehow, I read a lot into that last word, and I got a small knot in my gut. I'd have expected he would have been swamped with calls from his fellow officers. That the only guy who'd called was the one whose life he probably saved...*shit!*

But there was only a moment's pause before he continued: "The reason I tried to reach you is that my dad's coming into town tomorrow to get ready for the union contract talks. I was wondering if you'd like to have dinner with us at the Montero?"

"Sure," I said. "I'm looking forward to meeting your dad."

"You'll like him," Tom said.

"Hey," I said, "he's your dad. How could I not like him?" I knew that one of the major reasons I was being invited was to provide Carol with a "date". God, what stupid, stupid games! But I didn't resent them for playing it: I just wished it wasn't necessary.

"Seven thirty?" he asked.

"Great," I said. "You want me to drive?"

"It might be a little easier, if you don't mind."

"And we'll meet Carol and Lisa at the hotel?" I asked, teasing.

"You're a riot, Hardesty!" he said.

* * *

I had a lot of people I wanted to call, but decided it best to wait until I heard from O'Banyon first. He was, after all, the key to organizing the people in a position to do something—or, in this case, to *not* do something.

Luckily, O'Banyon returned my call within the hour, and I quickly outlined my meeting and conversation with Richman.

"He's right, of course," O'Banyon said, "and whatever we do should be done quickly. And we need a place to meet...." There was a brief pause while we both thought.

"How about the M.C.C.?" I said. "It's centrally located, and I know Reverend Mason would be glad to cooperate. I'm sure we could use one of their meeting rooms."

"Good idea," he said. "Why don't you give him a call and see if we can get one for...what...tomorrow night around 5:30? I'll call Lee Taylor at the Gay Business League right away, but then I have to get back to court. Could you do me a favor and call the editors of Rainbow Flag and...what are those two bar papers? We might as well make sure we don't leave anybody out."

"Bottoms Up and Tattler," I said. "Sure, I can call them all. Can I say I'm calling for you when I talk to them? I don't think 'Dick Hardesty' by itself would be much of an incentive for anyone to come to a meeting."

"Of course," he said. "And you know the president of the Bar Guild, don't you?"

"Mark Graser," I replied. "Yeah. I can call him, too."

"I'd appreciate it," he said. "And if you can think of anyone else who should be there.... And we should probably just try to get the word around generally. The more people who know what's going on, the better."

"I'll get right on it," I said. "Give me a call at home tonight, if you can, and we can bring each other up to date."

"I'll do that," he said. "And now I've got to call Lee Taylor and get to court. Later."

* * *

As soon as we hung up, I got out the phone book to look up the number of the M.C.C. and called. I was in luck when I heard Tony Mason's voice saying "Metropolitan Community Church: Reverend Mason speaking."

I got right to the point and invited him to be part of the meeting, since he had a strong voice in the community. He was glad to cooperate, and offered us the large basement room normally used for the church's Sunday School. He quickly added that he'd be sure there were enough adult chairs to seat everyone. I thanked him and made a mental note to stop by the store on my way home to pick up a couple pounds of coffee, sugar, powdered creamer, and some styrofoam cups. I knew Tony would be sure there was coffee available, but since the church was run on a tight budget, it was sort of a tradition for those who used the church for social events to restock whatever supplies were used.

I had to rummage through my desk drawer to find copies of Rainbow Flag and Tattler…I didn't have a copy of Bottoms Up and would have to make a quick run the two blocks to Hughie's—the closest gay bar to my office—to pick one up. I looked for the editors' names and their phone numbers, then called.

Charles Conrad had just taken over as editor of Rainbow Flag and was doing a really great job with it. I'd never met him, but knew his predecessor. So I was a bit surprised, when I introduced myself and told him I was calling for Glen O'Banyon, to have him say: "Oh, yes! Dick Hardesty: You were with

Officer Brady at the shooting!"

Now how in the hell did he know that? I wondered.

Probably because he's a newspaper editor, Dumbo, my mind answered. *They get paid to know things.*

"Uh, yes…" I said.

"I'm glad you called," he said. "I was going to try to get in touch with you. We'd like to interview you and Officer Brady for the cover story we're doing for next week's issue on the shooting."

Uh, not if I can help it, I thought.

"That's just the reason I'm calling, Mr. Conrad," I said. "We're having a meeting of community leaders tomorrow evening at 5:30 at the M.C.C.. Mr. O'Banyon specifically asked that you be there, and I strongly recommend it."

"Is it in regard to Officer Brady and the shooting?" he asked.

"While I can't go into specifics right now, yes."

"Then I'll be there," he said. "I'm sure you can appreciate what a story like this means to the community. A hero cop! A gay hero cop! What a story!"

If only you knew, I thought, but said: "I agree. So we'll see you tomorrow?"

"Count on it," he said. But before I could say goodbye, he said: "We've been trying to reach Officer Brady ever since the shooting, but he's not taking our calls. Could you put in a good word for us? And will he be there tomorrow?"

"He's not taking anyone's calls," I said, "and with good reason. We'll fill you in on all the details tomorrow. 'Bye." And with that I hung up. If he wanted to assume that Tom would be part of the 'We'll', let him.

I next looked up the number for Hype II, Mark Graser's bar. The original Hype was the first gay bar to have been torched in a string of disastrous bar fires some time before, and Mark was president of the Bar Guild. The bartender, or whoever it was who answered, said Mark hadn't come in yet. I had his home number, so called it without even putting the phone back on the cradle. I caught him just as he was getting ready to leave the house, told him of the meeting, and got his promise to attend.

Tattler's number was an answering machine. I left a brief message mentioning Glen O'Banyon's name, the time and the place of the meeting, and saying we sincerely needed them to be there. I figured a mention of someone as powerful and well known as O'Banyon would, for the editor of a small paper distributed mainly as a give-away in bars and filled mostly with ads for other bars and little local bar-gossip columns, be sufficiently flattering to warrant their attending.

I glanced at my watch and seeing it was three thirty, figured I'd just have time to run down to Hughie's, have a quick beer (oh, I know, it was still pretty early in the day, but a beer's just a beer, and I'd feel funny just walking in, grabbing a paper, and walking back out—even bars have a code of etiquette) and make it back to call the Bottoms Up editor before it was time to go home.

CHAPTER 4

Hughie's was, is, and probably always will be Hughie's. Most people walking in for the first time would—as soon as their eyes became accustomed to the fact that no lightbulb in the place was over 25-watts—consider it really tacky. I liked to think of it as "lived in" which, for some of the hustlers who frequented the place, it almost was.

There was the usual number of hustlers, a few fewer johns than usual—business would pick up as soon as the office workers and young-executive crowd got off work. And, as usual, there was Bud holding sway behind the bar. I didn't think he'd even seen me come in, until I noticed him grabbing a frosted mug out of the cooler and pouring a dark draft. He had it on the bar by the time I walked over to it.

"How's it goin', Bud?" I asked, as I asked every single time I'd ever been in the place.

"Pretty good, Dick. You?" he asked, face expressionless as he took the bill I handed him and turned to the cash register. I was thinking, as I raised the icy mug to my lips, feeling a couple drops of condensation drip onto my shirt, that maybe I should buy Bud and myself little matching tape recorders, so that when we saw each other all we'd have to do is press the little button. "How's it goin', Bud?" mine would say. "Pretty good, Dick. You?" his would respond. Save us quite a few breaths over the years.

Bud headed back from the cash register with my change, but I just waved it off. He nodded and dropped it into the jar alongside the cash register.

When my eyes were able to discern more than just vague figures, I noticed a really cute, kind of skinny kid about two stools down from me, looking at me and grinning from ear to ear. I wondered at first if he knew me, then decided maybe he mistook me for somebody else. I nodded to him in a casual greeting which he apparently took as an invitation. He scooted over to the stool beside me. "How's it goin'?" he asked, using words I'd heard somewhere just recently.

"Pretty good," I replied, playing a little Hardesty game with myself. "You?"

"Okay," he said brightly. "I'm horny, though. Are you horny?"

One of the things I truly do enjoy about hustlers is their subtlety. If you want beating around the bush, go somewhere else. But rather than respond as I automatically wanted to ("Hey, kid, I'm a Scorpio. Scorpios are *always* horny!"), I didn't want to lead him on, so I opted for: "I just came in for a beer and a paper," I said.

But then, not wanting the kid to think I was brushing him off—he *was* really cute, and hustlers *do* have feelings—I said: "How's business?"

He'd lost his grin only momentarily, then immediately got it back as he showed me his right forearm which, aside from a small, apparently self-applied tattoo, sported an obviously new if not very expensive watch. "I got this the other day," he said like a proud little kid who'd been given an unexpected present. "A john gave me a fifty dollar tip!"

I smiled. "You must be pretty good," I said.

"Oh, I am!" he said. "You really should check it out yourself." I'd noticed that instead of the ubiquitous beer bottle, he had what looked like a mixed drink—coke and something, I guessed. It was nearly empty, and he raised his glass, tipped it all the way up to drain it, then set it slowly on the bar.

"What are you drinking?" I asked, then immediately realized he'd probably take it as an invitation.

"Just coke," he said. "I don't drink."

Well, that was certainly different, I thought.

"Want another?" I asked, rather surprising myself, since I have a long standing rule to never let myself get suckered into buying drinks for hustlers. But it was just a coke, after all, and this kid got to me, in some odd way.

"Sure," he said, still grinning. "Thanks."

I motioned to Bud, who nodded, reached into the cooler, scooped some ice into a glass, then filled it from the mixes tap. He brought it over and put it in front of the kid. I handed him another bill and indicated he should keep the change.

"My name's Jonathan," the kid said as he gestured his glass at me in a 'thanks' gesture. "I just got here a couple weeks ago, and I sure like this town. Lots of rich guys here. Are you rich?"

I smiled again, looking at the kid in front of me and thinking for some reason of a puppy.

"No," I said. "I'm not rich." I took another drink of my beer. "I gather you haven't been hustling all that long?" I asked.

He took a small sip from his coke—I got the impression he wanted to make it last—and shook his head. "No, not really. Just since I got here. I'm 19 but I tell everybody I'm 21. I've been trying to find a regular job, but they're really hard to find unless you've got a car, and hustling pays *really* well. Maybe I'll just do this for a while. I had the same guy pick me up twice now, and he gave me a fifty dollar tip *both times!*"

I strongly suspected that Jonathan was assuming fifty dollar tips were going to be common, and that he hadn't been selling himself long enough to find out what the life really was like for most hustlers. I didn't envy him the learning process.

He might have been conning me, but I think I've been around long enough to know when someone is and when they're not. And I didn't really think Jonathan was. He didn't have the usual tough-guy bravado hustlers adopt as a survival mechanism. *Give him time,* my mind sighed.

"You're serious about getting a real job?" I asked.

"Sure," he said. "But like I say, I can make a *lot* of money hustling. I've been working since I was 12. Not hustling, of course, but working. Maybe now I can take it easy for a while."

Hardesty! Stay out of it! my mind commanded.

But Jeezus, he's just a kid! I thought.

And you can't save the world, my mind responded, gently.

"Well, I tell you what," I said. "There's a diner on the ground floor of the building I work in, and I see they've got a sign in the window for a busboy. If you'd be interested, you could check it out."

He grinned yet again. "Sure! I been a busboy a couple times. Maybe I will. Where's this at?"

I gave him the address, then finished my beer.

"Well, good luck, Jonathan," I said, extending my hand. I wasn't really surprised to know that I sincerely meant it.

"You aren't horny?" he asked, looking disappointed.

"Not right now," I said, lying through my teeth, of course.

I got up to leave, and Jonathan quickly chug-a-lugged his coke and got up, too. "Maybe you can show me where this place is?" he asked.

Hardesty! Don't be an idiot!

"Sure," I said. I stopped by the door long enough to pick up a copy of Bottoms Up, then stepped out into the sunlight, an eager Jonathan at my heels.

* * *

All the way to my building, Jonathan talked. Talked and talked and talked. About having hitchhiked here from Cranston, Wisconsin, about his brother Samuel and his brand new nephew, Joshua; about how excited he was to be out into the big world all by himself for the first time, about…well, you get the idea. And though he had no idea he was doing it, his words painted an impressionists' self portrait: A picture of naivety, innocence, sweetness, and…okay, I'll use the reference again…puppy-dog…charm. I didn't know the kid from Adam, but my gut ached to think what he had in front of him. It wasn't my place to warn him, and what could/would I have said that would have registered with him, anyway?

We reached my building and went into the lobby—for some unknown reason the "Help Wanted" sign was in the small window looking out onto the lobby rather than in the larger windows facing the street.

Jonathan noted the glass-cased Building Registry. "Which one's you?" he asked, and I... reluctantly...though I've always deeply resented the fact that in this world you have to be guarded with people you don't know...pointed to "Hardesty Investigations, Suite 633." It was far from being a "suite" but I guess they figured "room" would make it sound too much like a hotel.

"Wow!" Jonathan said, obviously impressed.

I offered him my hand again. "Well, I've got to get back to work," I said. "Good luck with the job."

"Thanks a lot," Jonathan said with a big smile. "And thanks for the coke."

I turned and headed for the elevator, leaving Jonathan staring at the "Help Wanted" sign.

* * *

I'd managed to reach Cathy Brower, editor of Bottoms Up, the only bar paper to give equal time and space to the city's lesbian bars. She, too, was planning what would be something of a first for the bar give-away—a front-page editorial—on the incident and the fact that a gay cop had come to the rescue of his own people.

Non-minority straights could not possibly begin—or be expected—to understand how deeply this incident was resonating in the gay community. What Joe Straight just naturally assumes—that the cop who protects him and his wife and kids goes home to his own wife and kids every night just like he does—was something the gay community had never experienced. This was only one incident, and one cop, but it was a true milestone for us.

Again, I didn't mention the true purpose of the meeting, but Cathy said she would attend. I just hoped we would be able to convince her to go along.

I stopped by Ramón's on the way home to talk to Bob Allen

and let him know what was going on. Jimmy, the bartender, who never misses anything, joined Bob in saying that rumors were beginning to circulate in the community that Tom was going to be fired because he was gay. Even though Bob, at least, knew for sure that Tom *was* gay, once again the fact was that Tom had not been openly "accused"—a fascinating word, when you think of it—of being gay and that nobody in the department either knew it for sure or could prove it. Tempers were beginning to heat up, and some of the anger, amazingly, was directed at Tom. Why didn't he just come right out and say he was gay? Was he ashamed of it? Did he get married to try to hide it?

It's almost impossible to deal rationally with questions like that, and fortunately they were in the minority—again, no pun intended. Obviously those who asked them had no idea of who Tom was or what he was trying to do, or what was really at stake.

Bob's lover, Mario, came in and joined the conversation. He said much the same thing was happening at Venture, where he bartended, and undoubtedly at every other gay and lesbian bar in the city.

The thing that nagged at me was that I knew in my heart of hearts that if Tom were ever, as Richman had hinted at, asked directly if he was gay, yes or no, he would never deny it.

I told them about the upcoming meeting, and that I'd invited Mark Graser of the Bar Guild. Bob wondered if he and a couple of the other Guild members might be able to come, too, but said he'd call Mark to see what he thought. I encouraged them all to do their best to explain the reality of the situation to whomever would listen—that what could and should be done in a perfect world simply could not be done in this one; not at this time and in this place: That in order for the community to move forward, it had to stand still for the moment.

* * *

I was a little later getting home than I'd intended, and I had a couple messages from Jared and Phil and Tim, which I returned. Jared, who was in his final weeks of driving his beer delivery route, said basically the same thing as Bob, Jimmy, and Mario; that there was a split within the community between those who thought the fact of Tom's being gay should be shouted from the rooftops, those who were afraid Tom would be fired and were becoming preemptively angry at the department, and those relative few who criticized Tom for not striding out of the closet in a suit of white armor, waving the gay flag.

Tim had been hearing rumors, in his job as junior medical examiner at the City Building, of an openly gay cop on the force, and that he had to be fired in order to keep the department morally pure—which, considering the number of hypocrites and bigots still in positions of authority within the department, would have been laughable if the issue weren't so serious.

When Tim turned the phone over to Phil, I told him about meeting Jonathan at Hughie's, and how bad I felt for what I'm sure he'd be facing if he didn't get out of hustling.

"You do have a thing about hustlers and Hughie's, don't you?" he teased. I'd met Phil there, as a matter of fact, before he turned his life around and got out of the business. But then his voice turned a little more serious, and he said: "It's all up to him what happens," he said. "Some of the guys who were hustling when I was are still out there on the streets; some managed to get out; a few are dead. It isn't the life of glamour this kid apparently thinks it is now, and he'll find that out pretty fast. Are you going to see him again?"

"Not on purpose," I said. "I guess I just saw something in him...."

"Yeah, I know," Phil said. "But it's up to him. If he's smart, and lucky, he'll do okay."

Phil was right, of course.

We talked for a bit about the upcoming meeting, and the need for everyone to be aware of all aspects of the situation and cool it.

Tim came back on to remind me that they were having a housewarming party the following Saturday, and for me to be sure to bring somebody if I wanted. "How about your friend Tom Brady?" he said. "He could probably use some relaxation. There'll be some straights here, if he thinks he needs some 'protective coloration.' As a matter of fact, you can bring him and his wife and her girlfriend if you'd like. It's already an established fact that he has fag friends, so being here shouldn't cause too much more hassle."

Probably not a very good idea, I thought, but: "Yeah, I'll ask," I said. "Thanks; I'll let you know as soon as I can."

We hung up and once again, phone cradled between shoulder and ear, I immediately dialed Tom to tell him of the meeting and that I might, as a result, be a little late getting to the Montero for dinner. He said that he, Lisa, and Carol would go on ahead and meet me at the hotel.

* * *

I'd barely put the phone back on the cradle before it rang. I picked it up immediately.

"Dick Hardesty," I said.

"Dick. Glen here. I've been trying to call, but your line's been busy."

"Yeah," I said, "sorry about that."

"No problem. Did we get the room at M.C.C.? I talked with Lee Taylor, and he'll be there. He wants to ask several of the other League members. I hope the room's big enough."

"It should be," I said, then told him that everyone I'd contacted would undoubtedly be there.

"Good," he said. "I've got to be in court all day tomorrow, and I may be late getting there. If I am, start without me—it's pretty much your show anyway."

My show? How in hell did that happen?

"Uh..." I said

"Well," O'Banyon said, "you're the one Richman came to.

You know more about exactly what was said than I do. You'll do fine. I'll see you there."

* * *

I won't go into all the details of the meeting. Between Glen O'Banyon and me, we'd contacted fewer than a dozen people: 42 people showed up, and the room was just barely big enough to hold everyone. The largest contingents, of course, were from the Bar Guild and the Gay Business League. Things got a little rough in spots, particularly when the editor of Rainbow Flag made the strong case that the story was real news for the gay community, and that any form of censorship, even self-imposed and with the best of intentions, was a bad thing. The chairman of the Gay Pride Committee said they were planning to ask Tom's superiors to okay Tom's being the Grand Marshall at the forthcoming Gay Pride Parade. There were a few hard-core activists also present who, like many activists for many causes, were firmly convinced that the sword was mightier than the pen, and that the way to right a wrong was to use the blacksmith approach—get a situation white hot and then use a sledgehammer to beat it into the shape you wanted it. They seemed to totally ignore the fact that since homophobia is not a tangible thing, it can't be eradicated by simply battering it into submission.

It was probably Glen O'Banyon, who had come in only about fifteen minutes late, who nudged the scale to a however-grudging consensus.

After everyone had had their say, O'Banyon came to the front of the room, still dressed in his court suit.

"Chief Black," he began—and it was instantly apparent why and how he became the successful lawyer he is—"is the best hope the gay community has for positive change within the police department. And regardless of how justifiably proud the community may be to claim Officer Brady as one of its own, the basic facts are these: Chief Black's opponents—the very same men who have hassled, harassed, and discriminated against the community all these years—are now looking to that very community for a specific reason to bring the Chief down. And the only way they can do this and succeed will be if the community hands them tacit confirmation that there *are* gays in the department in the first place."

He paused, and looked slowly around the room from face to face, before continuing.

"Of *course* there are gays in the department," he said; "they've been there for years. But they are there today only because no one can *prove* they're there. The only difference between Tom Brady and other gays on the force is that now the chief's enemies have a name, and a face, and an incident from which they can launch their assault on the chief. But their biggest problem, and Chief Black's strongest defense, is that no one…*no one*…in the department or out—" he paused for only a heartbeat, but it was long enough to make the point of the last two words, "—can *prove* that Tom Brady is gay. For Officer Brady to boldly step forward and admit to being gay, as some in the community would have him do, would do absolutely nothing but destroy his career, quite possibly drive Chief Black from office, and most definitely start a witch hunt for other gays within the department."

He paused yet again to give his message a moment to sink in.

Finally, he said: "The question each of you must ask yourselves, and every single member of the community you can talk to, is this: Is the gay community, by its reaction to this incident, going to hand the chief's enemies a loaded gun?"

The meeting broke up shortly thereafter, and I only had a quick moment to talk with O'Banyon and a couple other attendees before I had to head off for the Montero. The overall impression was that a concerted effort would be made to laud Officer Brady for his actions during the shooting incident, but to ignore as completely as possible his sexual orientation.

Everyone seemed greatly relieved, but no one expected it to be the end of the story.

* * *

I got to the Montero at 7:40—not too bad, considering parking was, as usual, a bitch. I walked through the lobby and into the cavernous dining room. A quick look revealed maybe 30 people, but none of them were Tom, Lisa, or Carol. I crossed the lobby to the cocktail lounge on the other side, thinking perhaps they were waiting for me there. Nothing. (Though the bartender was a real hunk; I made a note to return some evening soon.)

Back across the lobby to the dining room where the maitre d' was just returning to the podium from seating a family of four.

"One?" he asked.

"No," I said; "I was supposed to meet the Bradys...."

He gave me a classic "Ah" complete with raised eyebrows and a slight heads-up gesture. "Mr. Hardesty. The Bradys are expecting you: If you'll just take the last elevator to the left: The code is 244. It will take you to the President's Suite. I'll tell them you're on your way."

The President's Suite? You've arrived, kid! Hey, I admit it: I was impressed.

As I walked to the elevator, I realized that since the elder Brady owned the place and as far as I knew the President was occupied elsewhere, he could use any damned room he wanted to. Still....

The last elevator on the left did not have buttons, but a small numbered keypad; the same system used, I'd learned in an earlier case, to gain entry to the guest parking garage and from there access to the guest floors. I pressed 2, 4, 4 and the door swooshed open as though the elevator car had just been standing there, patiently waiting for me. I stepped in and, with a muted chime, the door closed and the elevator began its utterly silent ascent. It stopped at the 17th floor and the doors sighed open onto a small, richly paneled foyer; through the large open double door directly in front of me I could see a room about three times the size of my entire apartment.

Now try not to gawk, my mind cautioned, *and don't pick your nose.*

Yeah, yeah, I got it, I mentally replied.

Tom got up from a small semi-circle of chairs at the far end of the room and came over to greet me. He had on a powder-blue short sleeved shirt which appeared to have been tailor made to hug every contour of his body. And as he moved across that vast room, he truly looked "to the manor born". Beyond him another man rose from one of the chairs—I didn't have to be told who it was. Aside from having almost pure white hair, the resemblance to Tom was incredible.

Tom was still wearing his sling but otherwise looked to be in perfect health. We shook hands and went over to the semi-circled chairs. Lisa and Carol were seated on either side of the now-standing elder Brady, and looked truly beautiful. They'd obviously both just had their hair done for the occasion.

Mr. Brady, Sr. stepped forward and extended his hand. "Dick, it's a pleasure to meet you."

"Mr. Brady," I said by way of acknowledgment as I took his hand.

He smiled. "John, please," he corrected.

Good Lord, even his voice sounded like Tom's—or, I realized of course, more correctly it was the other way around. I could imagine that when Tom reached his dad's age, he'd look exactly like his dad looked now.

The women and I exchanged greetings, and I bent over to give each of them a peck on the cheek, then Tom's dad motioned me to the empty chair beside Carol.

Let the Breeder games begin! my little mind-voice said.

"Can I get you a drink, Dick?" Tom, who had remained standing, asked. I noticed that everyone else seemed to have one, so I said: "Sure, thanks."

"What would you like?"

As if you didn't know, I thought, but then caught just the trace of a smile that told me he was well aware of the games.

"Manhattan, I think," I said, then turned to Mr. Brady as

Tom went over to what appeared to be—and I'm sure was—a fully-stocked bar. "Congratulations on acquiring the Montero," I said. "It's a real landmark, and since its restoration...."

He looked at me and smiled. "Yes," he said, "and were I not so much a blatant capitalist I might very well feel a little guilty. The restoration nearly bankrupted the previous owners, and I got it for far below its true value. But now, with it back in pristine condition, it won't require major work for years."

"So how long will you be staying?" I asked.

He picked up his drink and took a sip, then set it back down onto the small table between his chair and Lisa's.

"Until these contract negotiations are taken care of...which may be quite a while, I'm afraid. I'd hoped that when Joe Giacomino was put away, it would make the A.H.W.A. more responsible and reasonable. But the leadership just switched around, it didn't change. And with Joey G. heading the local here, I'm sure he's going to be under a lot of pressure from Joe Sr. and the union leadership to prove he can be just as big an arrogant bastard as his old man." He looked up as Tom brought my drink, handed it to me with a smile, then went to sit beside Lisa. Tom's dad's eyes never left his son.

"But the longer the talks drag on," he said with a smile, bringing his eyes back to me, "the more time I'll have to spend with my son and my charming daughter-in-law." He reached over to pat Lisa's hand. Lisa smiled at him warmly.

The conversation moved on to and through a wide variety of subjects, with a great many questions from the elder Brady directed to Tom and Lisa, though politely phrased to include Carol and me, however peripherally. I was touched to see how obvious it was that the older man adored his son and was extremely proud of him.

A pleasant-looking, middle-aged waiter suddenly appeared from somewhere with menus in his hand. Brady Sr. smiled at him, nodded, and the waiter handed a menu to each of us. "Thank you, Walter," Brady said, then turned to Lisa, Carol, and me. "Walter has been on the Montero's staff for...?" he looked up at the waiter who was standing with his hands folded in front of his apron.

"Twenty-eight years, sir," Walter said, quietly.

"…twenty-eight years!" Brady repeated. "The Montero couldn't do without him," he said, and Walter, though trying to remain waiter-stoic, allowed himself a quick smile of pleasure. I was beginning to see how Brady had built his empire.

"I could have had the chef come up and use the kitchen here in the suite," he said, almost apologetically, "but didn't want to impose on him. And this way, we don't all have to have the same thing." He asked Walter to refresh our drinks while we looked at the menus and, after enquiring politely as to what each of us was drinking, Walter picked up the glasses that were empty and moved off to the bar.

* * *

Dinner, in the suite's formal dining room, was of course excellent. The wine, while I of course hadn't the foggiest idea of what it was, was very good, as was the Strega served with desert.

The conversation flowed smoothly, with both Lisa and Carol going out of their way to charm Tom's dad—and obviously succeeding. But I'd noticed throughout the evening, the senior Brady looking back and forth from Lisa to Tom and, more disconcertingly, from Tom to me. I wondered, somewhere in the back of my mind, if just perhaps the elder Mr. Brady were a lot sharper than any of us might have realized.

Over coffee, as we finished our desert—the Montero's staff included the best pastry chef in the city and his apricot-brandy cheesecake was pure heaven—the talk moved back to the upcoming labor negotiations, scheduled to begin in two days, and the bitter enmity between Brady and Joe Giacomino, Sr.

"Of course, Joe Senior and I don't have a patent on hating one another," he said, smiling. "Joey and Tom aren't exactly the best of buddies."

"You know Joey Giacomino ?" I asked.

"They grew up together," Brady senior said. "Well, same town, same school, though young Joey was two years ahead of Tom." He paused for a moment to take a small sip of his Strega, then a sip of coffee. "Joey is a real chip off the old block," he said, leaning back in his chair. "Every bit as much the blustering bully that his father was—and is. All the other kids were terrified of him, but not Tom!" His father's pride all but sparkled from his eyes. "Tell him about the Cracker Jack, Tom," he urged.

Tom looked embarrassed and quickly forked the last piece of cheesecake off his plate. Then he looked up and shrugged. "It wasn't anything much," he said.

But his father wasn't about to let a choice story go untold...not when it concerned his son. Although Tom was reluctant to tell it, his father was not.

"Tom had stopped after school at the candy store across the street. He was...what, eleven?" he asked, looking to his son for confirmation.

"Around that," Tom said, noncommittally.

"Anyway, Tom comes out of the store with a box of Cracker Jack: Tom loved Cracker Jack; and there's Joey Giacomino with a couple of his bully buddies. They see Tom with a brand new box of Cracker Jack, and Joey comes right up to him and says, 'Gimme the Cracker Jack, Stupid.' He's standing right in front of Tom, and he's a good half a head taller. Tom just looks up at him and says 'No, it's mine. Go get your own.'

"Well, Joey just stares at him, wide-eyed. No one except Joe Giacomino Sr. ever said no to Joey. Not ever—at least not more than once. Joey's eyes narrow, and he puts his face about two inches in front of Tom's and says 'I told you to give me that Cracker Jack!' and Tom doesn't bat an eye and says 'No.' Joey reaches out to grab it and Tom just punches Joey in the stomach with every ounce of strength he has in him. Joey goes flying backward, knocking over one of his buddies in the process, and just lies on the ground, crying like a baby. And Tom just walks away, with his box of Cracker Jack. Joey never messed with

Tom after that day."

I'm sure the older man embellished a little, but it was a story he obviously took great delight and pride in telling, and I was very glad to know that Tom had a father so proud of him.

Brady Sr. sat there, shaking his head in pleasure, grinning to himself.

"Yeah," Tom said, "I ate so many Cracker Jacks when I was a kid, I can't stand to look a them anymore. Seems like a long, long time ago. And I haven't seen Joey since he left school."

"Just as well," his dad said. "Although Joey hasn't forgotten about you. I ran into him today during a brief pre-talk meeting to lay out some of the details. Joey was there—he hasn't changed much since he was a kid, and he made some remark about 'I hear you've got a cop son.' The Giacominos are like elephants: They never forget, or forgive." Then a momentary look of sadness crossed his face as, I would guess, he thought of his dead son, Art. "But then," he added, "neither do I."

One of the things I found most interesting about the evening was that while Tom sat there wearing his arm in a sling, the one subject that was never brought up was the shooting. I knew full well the elder Brady was aware of what had happened, but whether he knew anything further than was reported in the papers, I had no way of knowing. And of course, Tom would never have brought it up. And so neither did the rest of us.

But all in all, it was a very pleasant evening. I really liked Tom's dad, as I had been sure I was going to. I'd forgotten what a great sense of humor Carol had, and she spent a good deal of time kidding with Tom's dad, who seemed to enjoy the attention. And I was greatly relieved that Mr. Brady made no open assumptions about Carol and me being a couple. I came away from the evening with a strong suspicion that Tom's father knew more about his son…and his daughter-in-law…than he let on.

* * *

I got to the office a little earlier than usual the next morning and was taking my time drinking my coffee and reading the newspaper when I heard what I thought was a knock at my door. "Come on in," I called, but no one turned the knob. I thought I could make out a figure on the other side of the opaque glass panel in the door, but wasn't sure. Then it came again, softly, tentatively. I set my coffee down and got up, moving around the desk toward the door. "I said 'Come on in,'" I repeated, mildly exasperated by somebody afraid to open a damned door. I opened it rather swiftly and saw…nothing. Nobody. Then I stuck my head out the door and saw someone with his back toward me, leaning against the wall about five feet from the door.

"Jonathan?" I asked, and he slowly pivoted around, his shoulders against the wall.

"Jonathan! Jesus! What happened?" I asked as I moved quickly to him. His shirt was torn, all the buttons ripped off; he had a badly cut lip and a deep bruise on his cheek. His left eye was black and swollen. He kept his head down and to one side and he wouldn't look at me. I put my hand under his chin and raised it up. He still wouldn't look at me.

"Jonathan, tell me what happened," I said.

Finally, his good eye moved to my face and his jaw began to quiver and his shoulders shake in silent sobbing. He was trying very hard to be brave, but he couldn't keep tears from running down his face.

I grabbed him by his arm and guided him into my office, closing the door behind us, and led him to the sofa. I made him sit down, then sat down beside him, our thighs touching. There was blood on his pants.

He took little shuddering gasps of air, still struggling to keep from sobbing audibly, though his shoulders still made small jerks as he fought to suppress them.

"Now tell me what happened," I said, calmly.

He kept his head turned away, but he shook it. I reached out again for his chin, turning his head toward me.

"I want you to tell me what happened," I repeated, slowly.

His chin and lower lip quivered, but he took a deep, rasping breath and said: "I'm sorry. I'm really sorry. I don't mean to bother you. But I didn't know where else I could go. I don't know anybody here, and you were nice to me and…I'm sorry."

I let him regain a bit more composure, then said. "Now tell me who did this to you."

Actually, I didn't have to know who. He probably didn't know, either, but I knew perfectly well *what* had happened. I was equal parts anger and sorrow, and some small part guilt.

Guilt? For what? my mind asked.

For letting this happen to him, I replied.

You can't save the world.

This isn't the world, it's one poor kid!

Ah, Hardesty….

"Do you know who did it?" I asked.

He nodded. "It was that man," he said; "that man who gave me all the money."

He looked at me now, hard, as if looking for an answer in my face. "Why did he have to do that? Why? I never did nothing to him." Then he raised up his right arm, as he had done at Hughie's to show me his new watch. But the watch wasn't there.

"He took my watch," he said, his voice almost dry with disbelief. "Why would he go and do that? And he took my money, too. All of it." He suddenly reached into his pants pocket and came up with a closed fist. "Except this," he said, and opened his hand to show me a nickel and a penny.

JEEZUS! My emotions were still in a close race, but the anger was surging ahead rapidly.

"He didn't have to take my watch or my money," he said, more to himself than to me. "He's a rich man. He doesn't need it."

I got up to get the coffee from my desk, and brought it back to him. "Here," I said. "Drink this. Have you eaten?"

He shook his head again. "I'm okay," he said, almost shyly.

"When did you eat last?" I asked, pressing him.

"Yesterday morning, I guess."

I got up again, went to the phone, and called the diner downstairs. "This is Dick Hardesty in 633," I said to whomever picked up the phone. "I want a breakfast to go: Three eggs, scrambled, toast, bacon, a large coffee, black, a carton of orange juice and two cartons of milk. I'll be down in five minutes. Thanks."

Hardesty, for chrissakes...my mind started to say.

Shut the fuck up! I told it.

I went back over to sit down beside Jonathan, who was sitting quietly, leaning forward, elbows on his knees, hands folded between his partly-spread legs, head down, looking at the floor.

"When did it happen?" I asked.

"Last night," he said. "Late. I went back to where he'd picked me up those other two times, and he came by in his van and we went where we went the other two times and we got in the back and then he went to get a rubber and he didn't have any and I told him I didn't either and that I couldn't have sex without him having a rubber and he told me yes I could and I damned well was going to and I told him no and that I wanted to go back to where he picked me up and I started to put my shirt back on but he grabbed it and tried to tear it off and then he held me down and he started to do it anyway and I pushed him away and then he just started beating on me and beating on me until I managed to get up and jumped out of the van and he stood there in the door and took all the money out of my pants and then he wadded them up and threw them at me and kicked my shoes out the door and then he slammed the door closed and just drove away. I didn't have chance to get my watch."

"Do you have any idea where this happened?" I asked.

He shook his head. "It was in the woods somewhere. There was a sign I saw when we drove in—Prichert Park, I think it was. It was a long way." Prichert Park was a forest preserve about fifteen miles from downtown.

"How did you get here?" I asked.

"I walked," he said casually.

"All the way?" I asked, incredulously.

He nodded. "I didn't have any other way. There weren't many cars out, and I didn't dare try to hitchhike looking like this. It took me from the time he drove off 'til now to walk here. I got kind of lost for awhile until I got to the top of a hill and I could see the buildings downtown here, so I knew which way to go."

"Didn't you try to get help?" I asked.

He shrugged. "While I was walking, just when it was starting to get light out, a police car pulled over to me and asked what I was doing and I told them what had happened to me and they just laughed and said 'Well, maybe you'll know better next time' and then they rolled up the window and drove off. And later on I came to a gas station that was closed but the outside bathroom door was unlocked and I went in there and washed myself off and I laid down on the floor for awhile and I think I went to sleep for a little bit, but I'm not sure."

Then he looked at me and asked, again: "Why would he do that to me? What did I ever do to him?"

I didn't have an answer for that, of course, but I vowed that if I were ever able to find that scumbag, I'd make damn sure he never did it again, to anyone.

I glanced quickly at my watch and got up from the couch. "You stay right here," I said. "I'll be right back." Just as I reached the door, I had a sudden thought, and said: "Since you were with the guy three times, did you by any chance find out his name?"

Jonathan looked down at the floor and shook his head. I reached for the doorknob and had the door halfway open when I heard him say: "I do remember his license plate number, though."

CHAPTER 5

While Jonathan was eating—and watching him made me wonder if it could only have been one day since he'd had any food—I dialed the City Building Annex and asked for Lieutenant Richman's extension. I'd been going to call him anyway, to let him know about the community meeting. But my main thought was of Jonathan. I knew what had happened to him happened a lot more than anyone knew, and that with everything else going on, Lieutenant Richman probably wouldn't have time for the problems of one unlucky hustler, but he was the highest ranking police officer I knew other than Captain Offermann and I was really, really pissed.

When Richman came on the line, I first told him about the meeting, and he seemed greatly relieved to hear it. Then I told him about Jonathan and about the police car that had just driven off without trying to help him. When I mentioned that Jonathan had gotten the license plate number of the van, and that I intended to find out who it belonged to, Richman asked for it and said he'd check it out. He didn't have to do that, but it was really nice of him to offer.

"And tell your friend I apologize on behalf of the department for how he was treated," he said. "He had every right to expect help from the police, and I will personally have the duty rosters and report sheets checked to see which cars were in the area of Pritchert Park. If I can find out which officers might have been involved, would your friend be willing to come down to the Annex for a personal apology from them?"

"I'm sure he would, Lieutenant," I said. Richman had definitely moved up another rung in my admiration. "Is there anything else I can do right now on...this other matter?"

"Not at the moment, I don't think," he said. "Just keep your ears open, and please call me right away if you hear anything we might need to know."

"I'll do that," I said. "And thanks again."

"Thank you, too, Dick," he said, and we hung up.

Jonathan, who had been sitting across from me using my desk as a table, had almost polished off everything on his plate—well, styrofoam tray—and had paused with plastic fork in midair to stare at me as I replaced the receiver on the hook.

"Wow," he said, with a look of little-boy admiration on his battered face. "You know some important people, huh?"

"I know some very *good* people," I said, and watched him finish eating. When he had taken the last morsel off the tray and finished the second carton of milk he got up, looked around for my wastebasket, and very carefully went over to put the empty containers in it.

"That was really good," he said. "Thank you."

"You're welcome," I said. He just stood there for a moment, not knowing what to do next, and I motioned him back to the chair. "So where are you staying, Jonathan?" I asked.

He looked a little embarrassed and he glanced up idly at the ceiling as though there were something of interest there. "Nowhere, really," he said.

"Nowhere?" I asked, and he shook his head.

"If I'd had a place to go, I never would have come here and bothered you," he said. "Usually when a guy takes me home I'll ask him if I can spend the night there. Sometimes they let me. I keep my stuff in a locker at the bus station. Sometimes one of the other guys from Hughie's lets me crash at his place. I went there first, but he wasn't home."

"Do you have any money in with your things at the bus station?" I asked.

He sighed and shrugged. "No," he said. "That guy took it all."

Shit!

"Did you check out that busboy job?" I asked, knowing the answer before I asked it.

He again looked embarrassed and dropped his head to look

at the missing buttons on his shirt. "I was going to," he said like a little kid caught doing something he shouldn't. "But then I thought of all the money I could make hustling, and…I'm really sorry. I should have." Then he gave me a sad little look that made me want to reach out and hug him. "I don't think I want to hustle any more," he said.

* * *

I called Reverend Mason at the M.C.C. to thank him for letting us use the room for the meeting, but with another purpose in mind, as well. I'd remembered that the M.C.C. had just started Haven House, a shelter for runaway and abused gay and lesbian teenagers, and I asked if there were any chance of getting Jonathan in. I explained his situation briefly, and the Reverend said the house was nearly full already, but that I should bring Jonathan by, to see what might be done for him.

Before we left my office, I reached into a drawer of my desk and got out my Polaroid. I wanted to document Jonathan's injuries just in case the bastard who did this to him was ever caught. I handed him the morning paper and told him to hold it up for the first photo as documentation of the date. When I asked him to take off his shirt, I saw he had bruises all over his upper body as well as his face. The guy had really done a number on him, and I was even more certain now that I definitely wanted to have a little private chat with the bastard who had done it.

* * *

I drove Jonathan to the bus station, asked him for his locker number and the combination to the lock, and told him to wait in the car while I went in. He'd gotten enough stares as we walked from my office to the car: He didn't need any more.

I then took him to my place…*okay, okay, you don't have to say it*…so he could shower and change clothes. He only had two other shirts and one other pair of pants in his small backpack, and I was too much bigger than him for anything I had to fit him.

"Can I use some of your aftershave?" he called from the bathroom.

"Help yourself," I said and shortly thereafter heard a couple short "Ow!"s as the alcohol touched his scraped and bruised face.

The aftershave came into the room before he did, but he looked a lot better than he had when I first saw him in the hallway. And battered and bruised as he was, he was still really cute.

Don't go there, Hardesty! my mind cautioned, and for once I agreed.

We drove to the M.C.C. and I noted as we got out of the car that the bungalow directly next door to the church had a small sign over the door saying "Haven House." Two teenagers, a boy and a girl, were sitting on the steps, talking. They waved to us as we walked up to the door to the church, and we waved back, then entered. No one seemed to be there, though we checked the office and even went downstairs to the Sunday School room where the community meeting had been held. Finding no one, we were coming back up the steps when we saw Reverend Mason…Tony…coming in the front door. He had on torn, paint-spattered Levi's and an equally paint-spattered Dallas Cowboys sweatshirt. I gathered he'd been working.

"Jack and Marie told me they'd seen you coming in," he said. "Sorry I wasn't here, but we're still doing a lot of work on the house." He smiled and shook hands with both Jonathan and me, and seemed to be totally oblivious to Jonathan's all-too-obvious bruises and black eye.

"Let's go into the office," he said, and we followed him into the small room just inside the front door, opposite the stairway. "Sit, please," he said, smiling, and we did.

"So how old are you, Jonathan?" he asked.

"Twenty-one…" he started to say, but caught me looking at

him and looked quickly away. "Nineteen," he amended.

Tony pursed his lips slightly. "You're just a bit older than most of our kids," he said. "How long have you been hustling?"

Despite the bruises that covered a good portion of his face, I could see Jonathan blush. "About a month," he said.

"Are you a runaway? Did your folks throw you out?"

Jonathan shook his head. "No, sir. I came here on my own. I'd never been away from home before and I figured it was time I got out and made something of myself."

Tony smiled, gently, then looked at me and sighed. "We are, as I told you on the phone, Dick, near capacity already. You'd be amazed at how many gay throwaway kids there are out there on the streets." Then he looked at Jonathan, who again was looking at the floor, anticipating being told there was no room for him at the inn.

"Are you willing to work, Jonathan?"

The youngster lifted up his head immediately. "Sure," he said. "There's a place in Dick's building that's looking for a busboy, and…"

"Good," Tony said. "All our kids, even the very youngest, are expected to find some kind of outside work. But I meant are you willing to work here, too, to help us finish Haven House? We're in the process of converting the attic into two more bedrooms, and…"

"Sure!" Jonathan said, eagerly. "I helped a guy back home fix up his place and we even built a game room in his basement and I put up paneling and helped him build a couple walls and…"

Tony gave me another quick smile and a quick but gentle hand-raise to turn off Jonathan's motor.

"Well, then, if you don't mind living in an unfinished attic until we get the rooms done, we'd be happy to have your help."

Jonathan, boy puppy-dog, was back. "Wow!" he said. "That's great! Thank you!"

Tony looked slowly from Jonathan to me and back again. "Now you understand, particularly since you'll be the oldest of our kids, that this arrangement is only temporary, until you can earn enough money at an outside job to get your own place. And even with an outside job, you'll have work obligations here as well, and we can't accept excuses for not meeting them. Is that agreeable to you?"

"Sure!" Jonathan said. "Anything!"

I could tell that Tony could see in Jonathan pretty much what I did—a nice kid who was not only in need of help, but who could appreciate it when it was offered to him.

"And of course," Tony said, "we do have some rules which cannot be broken: No drugs, no drinking; no fights—you have a problem, you bring it to me. Understood?"

Jonathan nodded eagerly.

Tony slapped his hands on his knees, got up from his chair, and said "Okay, then, let's go get you settled in."

Jonathan practically leapt from his chair and, having momentarily forgotten his bruises, winced in pain.

I got up, too, soaking in a bit of the glow that was practically radiating from the young man. We all left the office and, outside the door to the church, I shook hands with Tony and offered my hand to Jonathan. He looked at me questioningly. "Aren't you coming?"

I shook my head, oddly touched that he'd expected me to. "No, Jonathan, I've got to get back to work. You'll be fine. You let me know when you get that job, okay?"

Tony put his arm around the young man's shoulders and gave him a quick—but not too rough—squeeze. "We'll see to it," he said.

I started down the steps and heard Jonathan say "Dick?"

I turned back to him. "Yeah?"

"Can I hug you?"

I moved up to him, open-armed. "Sure," I said, and he grabbed me in a bear hug which surely must have hurt his sore chest. Then he backed away.

"Thanks again, Dick!" he said happily. "I'll come see you."

"You do that," I said, and turned again to walk to my car.

For some reason, I almost had a lump in my throat.

Oh, Hardesty, my mind sighed *...you are <u>such</u> a marshmallow!*

* * *

There was a message waiting for me when I got back to the office: Lieutenant Richman. I returned his call immediately.

"Lieutenant," I said when I heard his voice, "it's Dick Hardesty. What did you find out?"

There was a very slight pause and then he said: "I tell you what, Dick," he said, "I've got some work on my desk I've really got to get to. Are you going to be home this evening? Maybe I could give you a call there, if you don't mind."

Mind, hell! I thought. *Don't bother to call, just on come over and wear your cellophane pants!* "Sure," I said. "I'll be home around 5:30."

"Fine," he said. "I'll probably give you a call sometime later then."

We exchanged goodbyes, leaving me with a definite feeling that something was very strange about that call. Of course, my crotch was all in favor of its having some subtle sexual meaning, but the rest of me just thought it was unusual, somehow.

I tried to devote the rest of the day to the things I was being paid to do, like tracking down the source of a letter a client's boss had received accusing my client of being a child molester. The boss hadn't believed it for an instant, and had handed it over to the client, who wanted the source rooted out so he could sue whomever it was for slander (and, having the letter in hand, he'd probably have a good case). I'd pretty much narrowed it down to the client's lover's ex, who apparently blamed the client for stealing his lover, though they'd not been together for about two years before the client even met the lover. Some people just don't know when it's time to put out the torch.

* * *

I got home at about 5:20 and had just fixed myself a Manhattan when the phone rang.

"Dick Hardesty." I said.

"Dick, it's Mark Richman. Am I interrupting anything?"

I wish! I thought. "Not at all, Lieutenant," I said. "I just got home a while ago."

"Good," he said. "Look, we really have to talk."

"Name the time and place," I said.

"Well," he said, "my wife and kids are out of town again…" *Whoopee!* my crotch shouted "…so I was just going to stop somewhere and grab a pizza, then maybe we could meet somewhere a bit later."

"You're welcome to come over here," I said. He had, after all, been to my apartment once before, on another case. *Yeah! Yeah! Good idea!* my crotch panted.

"I'm glad you offered," he said. "Actually, under the circumstances, it's probably not a good idea for us to be seen in public together too often—no offense, which I'm sure you realize."

I did, completely. With a virtual civil war developing inside the department, discretion was indeed the better part of valor. Richman had to maintain at least the appearance of neutrality for as long as he could, and for him to be seen too often with a card-carrying faggot might threaten his neutral image.

"Let's go one farther," I suggested. "I haven't even begun to think about dinner, but pizza sounds good. Why don't I order one in and we can talk while we eat."

There was only the slightest pause, and then: "…Uh, sure; that sounds fine. Do you drink beer? I'm off duty and on my own time, so…I can stop and pick some up."

I'm not saying a word, my crotch whispered.

"That'd be great," I said. "Have any preferences in your pizza?"

"I like everything," he replied.

I'm still not saying anything.

"Okay. I'll call now. About how long before you get here?"

"I'm just getting gas, and calling from the station. I see a liquor store across the street, so I can just run over there now. Maybe 25 minutes?"

"Good," I said. "You know how to find the place, right?"

"I remember. See you shortly, then."

He remembers, my crotch snickered.

Oh for the love of God, drop it! my mind commanded. So I did.

*   *   *

I called Momma Rosa's and ordered a large Supreme with everything (I had a can of anchovies in the kitchen, just in case), and when the bell rang almost exactly 25 minutes later, I didn't know if it was Richman or the pizza. I buzzed whomever it was, took a bill out of my wallet so I wouldn't have to fumble for it later, and walked to the door, anticipating the knock. When it came, I opened the door to find Lieutenant Richman standing there in his civies, holding a six-pack of imported bock beer in his left hand. He offered his right for a handshake, then came in and I closed the door.

"I figured you for a bock man," he said. "Hope I was right."

"On the head," I said. He handed it to me and I took it into the kitchen, with him close behind me. "Want one now, or wait until the pizza comes?" I asked.

"Now's fine," he said. I took out two bottles, opened them, and put the rest back in the fridge; I led the way back into the livingroom.

We'd just sat down when the buzzer rang.

"Good timing," Richman said as I got up to buzz the delivery man in. Rather than return to my chair, I just waited by the door until I heard the knock. I opened it, mildly surprised to see young Jeff, the kid from the laundromat, once again standing there.

"Hi, Jeff," I said, glad to see him. Tom had a point about Jeff being old enough to know what he wanted, but much as I'd have enjoyed it, my mind wouldn't let me get beyond the "legal age" thing. Jeff grinned broadly at me, then looked over my shoulder at Lieutenant Richman seated on the couch. His grin broadened even further.

"Where do you *find* these guys?" he asked in a conspiratorial whisper.

I returned the grin. "Fate," I said, and handed him the bill I'd put in my front pocket. "Keep the change."

"Thanks," Jeff said, pocketing the bill. He then leaned toward me, head down but eyes on mine. "I do three-ways," he said.

"I'm sure you do," I said with a laugh, putting my hand on his shoulder and giving him a friendly push. "Now get out of here."

Jeff, still grinning, waved at the Lieutenant, winked at me, and left.

I carried the pizza into the kitchen and, pulling out two pieces for each of us, I put them on plates and took them to the living room.

"Want a TV tray?" I asked.

"Lap's fine," he said.

It occurred to me that as often as I had seen Richman, we'd never really had a person-to-person conversation. It had always been about work. I had absolutely no idea of who Mark Richman was. He was sharp as all hell, that I knew; he was very good at his job, or he wouldn't have gone as far in the department as he already had; he was a very good looking man, and he was, from everything I could tell and despite all my crotch fantasies, totally and completely straight. But he was obviously not threatened by being around gays, and he had done me and the community a lot of favors. I wished all straight men were like him.

"So tell me, Lieutenant," I said, deciding to venture out into conversational terra incognita, "how many kids do you have?"

He took a swig of his beer and a large bite of pizza. "Three," he said: "Craig, Ken, and Marcie. Craig's 15, Ken's 13, and

Marcie's 9. Good kids, though Craig's getting to that 'I know more than you do' stage. And I wouldn't be surprised if he turns out to be gay."

That got my attention. "How do you know?" I asked. "And how would you feel if he is gay?"

Richman grinned and leaned forward to put his beer on the coffee table. "I'm his dad," he said. "I know that something's going on, but I haven't pressed him on it. He knows he can talk to me, and when he's comfortable with it, he will." He took another bite of his pizza. "As to how I feel about it…" he shrugged "…he's my son; I sure won't love him any the less. I've got two other kids who can provide the grandchildren. Now, if all *three* of them turned out gay, it might be a problem. I do want to be a grandpa. But for Craig, I just want him to be happy and comfortable with who he is. And if he is gay, I sort of hope he turns out a lot like you."

Wow! I was glad I had a firm grip on my pizza, or I probably would have dropped it. That was probably one of the nicest compliments I'd ever been paid in my life, and I was so surprised by it, I don't think I even blushed. And to think it came from a straight guy….

"Thank you, Lieutenant," I said. "That means a lot, coming from you."

Seeing he'd just about finished his second piece of pizza, I got up quickly and went into the kitchen for the box. "Another beer?" I called into the living room.

"Sure, thanks," he said. I opened he refrigerator, got out two more beers, opened them and then, beers in one hand by the neck and pizza box in the other, I returned to the living room.

"To hell with formality," I said as I handed him his beer, put the pizza box down on the coffee table, and took my seat.

"Speaking of formalities," he said as he leaned forward to open the box and extract another large slice of pizza, "we're both aware that we're in a grey area here." He was smiling, but I knew he was serious. "By getting together outside of our professional roles, we're walking a very fine line that could have conflict of interest implications. But I'm pretty sure we both know where the line is, and can avoid crossing it. So, when we run into one another outside of the office, I'd be more comfortable if you just called me Mark. Hell, I've been calling you Dick for quite awhile."

"Hey," I said, "I don't mind 'Lieutenant'—I almost consider it a first name, by now. But I do appreciate the conflict problem, and agree that we can avoid it. If I ever do cross the line, I'm pretty sure you'll let me know."

"Count on it," he said with a grin.

The phone rang and I excused myself for a moment. As I was reaching for the phone, Richman…Mark…stood up and, with a raised eyebrow and a gesture, indicated he had to use the bathroom.

"Dick Hardesty," I said, picking up the receiver while pointing the way to the bathroom.

"Dick, it's Tom," the voice said.

"Tom!" I said, glancing down the hall toward the bathroom and keeping my voice down. "I was going to call you. Lieutenant Richman is here; we're having pizza and talking about the situation. He just went to the bathroom, so maybe it would be wisest for me to call you back later?"

"Sure," he said, but there was something in his voice.

"Is something wrong?" I asked. "We can talk now if you want."

"No, no, later's okay," he said.

"*Is* something wrong?" I repeated.

"Nothing major," he said. "We can talk about it later."

I heard the toilet flushing, then saw the bathroom door open and Richman enter the hall.

"Okay," I'll call as soon as I can." "'Bye."

* * *

We finished the pizza and were sitting with the last two beers when apparently he decided it was time to cross from socializing to the business that had brought him here in the first place.

"Do you fish?" Richman asked, by way of segueing between the two.

I didn't recognize the question for what it was at first, and was confused.

"Uh…not really," I said. "Why?"

"Because you are better at opening cans of worms than anyone I've ever met," he said.

Oh, oh! What now? I wondered. "Meaning?" I asked.

"Meaning that I checked the license number of the van that picked up your hustler friend. I hope he got the numbers wrong."

Talk about fishing! He had me hooked and was reeling me in slowly. "It's possible," I said, still confused. "Why?"

"Because the plates matching those numbers belong to one Joseph G. Giacomino, who just happens to be…" He might as well have gotten off of the couch, shuffled his feet on the carpet, and touched my nose with his finger: It was that kind of shock!

"…president of the local Amalgamated Hotel Workers of America." I finished for him.

Little Joey Giacomino! Well, what d'ya know?

"Definitely *not* good," Richman said. "Joey's got a wife and three kids and is a close golfing buddy with Deputy Chief—former Interim Chief—Cochran. And he's got labor contract negotiations starting tomorrow. So here we are with exactly what the department doesn't need right now: Another ticking time bomb!"

"Ah," I said, as a little light bulb came on in my head, "but this one is *our* ticking time bomb!"

Richman looked at me with knit brows for a second, then I could almost see the light coming on behind his eyes. "You're right! I must be having one of my stupid days! I was just concentrating on the ramifications of having to toss a powerful labor boss in jail just at the start of the labor talks. But now that you mention it, this could be the best thing that could have happened..." he cut himself off abruptly, realizing what he'd said. "I'm sorry," he said, "of course I didn't mean..."

"I know you didn't," I reassured him. "But now Chief Black's got some ammunition of his own: If Cochran and his cronies try to use the fact of Tom's being..." now it was I who caught myself just in time. "...I mean, the circumstances surrounding Officer Brady's being at the scene of the shooting, Chief Black can trump it with this sick sadistic buddy of Cochran's."

There was another moment of silence while we were each lost in our own thoughts, until Richman said: "Of course, if it's *not* Giacomino ...if your friend did get the numbers wrong, though since the plates are for a van that's not likely...or if Giacomino comes up with a story of having lent it to a friend, which he very well might try...."

"There's one way to be sure," I said. "This morning's paper had a big story on the talks, and Joey G.'s photo was right there on page 1. I know I didn't throw it away, because I hadn't had a chance to finish it when Jonathan showed up at my door. He had the paper right there in his hand when I took Polaroids of him, but of course he wasn't in any condition to pay attention to what was in it. I can show it to him, and if he can identify Joey G. as the guy who beat him up..."

"...then we have yet another problem," Mark not so much interrupted as picked up the ball. "We can arrest the bastard right then and there, blow the contract talks out of the water, or..."

Now it was my turn to catch juggler's pin: "...or just sit on it until after the talks or until we see what Cochran and Company is going to try to do about Tom."

We sat silent for a moment, then I said: "I promised Jonathan I'd get—*we'd* get—the guy who did this to him, and it galls me to think of that sonofabitch being out there on the streets one second longer, maybe doing the same thing, or worse, to some other poor kid. From what I've heard about this asshole, I'd guess he goes for the ones he thinks won't fight back."

Mark nodded. "I agree. But first things first: First let's be sure it *was* Giacomino. Then we'll take it from there."

He paused for a moment, then said: "And speaking of your friend, I think I found the officers who left him out there—there was only one car in the area around sunrise: It's a pretty quiet area, so we don't feel it necessary to have too many cars covering it. They work the 11-7, and I've told their squad captain I want them in my office at 7:05 sharp tomorrow morning. I know it's short notice, but can you bring the kid down to Annex around 7:15? I want to talk to these guys alone for a few minutes. If they admit to it, and they're willing to apologize, I'll drop it there. But if they deny it and your friend can identify them, he may have to wait for his apology, but I'll have them up on charges so fast they won't know what hit them. They're both long-termers and from what I know, I suspect they're on Deputy Chief Cochran's team."

"Sure," I said. "I'll have him there." I was pretty sure Jonathan wouldn't be able to do any serious job hunting until his face looked a little less like it had been used as a punching bag; and I suddenly got another rush of anger thinking of what had happened to him.

Joey Giacomino, huh? I thought.

* * *

Richman…Mark (that was going to take some getting used to)…left around 9:30. An interesting night, and I decided I really liked the guy. What was perhaps the most surprising, and I think positive, aspect of the evening was that my crotch had not been heard from at all. I think it finally had come to the same realization I had: That some people are simply the way they are and all my fantasizing isn't going to make them change. Mark Richman was an extremely handsome, sexy guy who I'd have gone to bed with in a heartbeat. But that just wasn't going to happen and it was really unfair to both of us to think that it was. And friends last a lot longer than tricks.

As soon as he left, I called Tom and was rather surprised to hear him answer the phone—and by the sharpness and anger in his voice when he said "Hello!"

"Sorry we couldn't talk earlier," I said. "What's up?"

He sighed. "Oh, Dick…sorry," he said, "I thought it might be…" There was a slight pause, and then: "I know this shouldn't bother me but I'm afraid it does. We got—or rather Lisa did, since she's been answering the phone—three calls tonight; one just a few minutes ago."

"What kind of calls?" I asked, though the knot in my stomach told me I knew full well.

"The first one said he wanted to talk to 'the queer.' Lisa hung up on him. The second, the guy just yelled: 'No fags on the force!' and hung up before she could. The third, well…you get the picture."

"Jeezus!" I said. "Some psycho idiot, I'll bet. Don't let it get to you."

"*Three* psycho idiots," he amended. "Lisa says they were all different voices. I'm not going to let her answer the phone anymore. These assholes have a problem, I want 'em to talk directly to me. But they haven't got the guts, of course."

I didn't even ask him if he planned to report the calls. I knew what his answer would be: "I can handle my own problems." That might not be considered reasonable for a cop, but it's what I would expect from Tom.

"Well," I said: "Some people are just pathetically desperate to prove to themselves that they're superior to somebody—anybody."

"One thing we're going to do is to stop answering the phone. Period. We'll let the answering machine pick up the calls. I suspect that will cut down on a lot of the messages if the caller thinks I might be getting their voice on tape. And I'll be saving the tapes, that's for damned sure."

Well, that told me without doubt that Tom thought the calls were coming from his fellow officers, and I felt both angry and sad by what that implied.

"So how did it go with Lieutenant Richman?" Tom asked, obviously wanting to change the subject.

"Ah, I'm glad you asked. Speaking of lowlife scum, I think I have some news you'll find pretty damned interesting...." And I told him everything about Jonathan, what had happened to him, his encounter with the two cops, and everything Richman had done to help. "I'm taking Jonathan down to City Building Annex first thing in the morning to confront the two cops. But the frosting on the cake," I said, "is that when Richman traced down the license number of the van, it belonged to..." I couldn't resist pausing for a mental drum roll... "your boyhood chum, Joey Giacomino!"

"Jesus!" he said. After a short pause, he continued. "I almost started to say 'I don't believe it,' but I do. It sounds exactly like that bullying sonofabitch!"

A glance at my watch showed it was getting close to ten o'clock and I still hadn't gotten in touch with Jonathan to let him know about tomorrow.

"I'd better go if I want to catch Jonathan before curfew, if they have one at Haven House. You try to get some sleep and ignore those crackpots."

"I will," he said. "But I don't think we're going to answer the phone any more tonight."

There was a slight pause, and then he said: "Thanks for being there for me, Dick. It means a lot."

"For me, too," I said. "We're in this thing together, remember."

"Yep," he said. "Talk to you tomorrow."

"'Night, Tom." And we hung up.

I knew both Tom and I realized the calls he'd gotten would not be the last, but neither of us wanted to worry the other. Well, I was worried enough for the both of us. And not just a little afraid, for Tom.

To force my mind back to the things I could have some control over, I realized that if I didn't call Jonathan right now, I would have to just go over there at 6:30 in the morning and pound on the door to wake him up. Not a good option, so I immediately dialed the M.C.C., knowing there was usually something going on there until at least 10, and I wanted to be sure Reverend Mason would have no objections to Jonathan going off with me first thing in the morning. Whoever answered the phone said Reverend Mason was next door at Haven House, and gave me the number.

I dialed the number and asked the girl who answered if I could speak to Reverend Mason. There was a momentary silence, then Tony's voice: "Reverend Mason; can I help you?"

"Tony, hi, this is Dick Hardesty," I said—he didn't know me well enough that I could expect he'd automatically recognize it. "How's Jonathan doing?"

"Just fine, Dick. I think he's going to fit in very well. He's up helping to put the wallboard up in 'his' room. Would you like to speak with him?" Before I had a chance to say anything I heard a hand covering the mouthpiece and a muffled voice calling: "Jonathan! Telephone."

Well, I hadn't really intended to talk with Jonathan, but it was too late now, and I figured I could explain what was going on.

"Tony?" I said, hoping he'd hear and come back on the line.

"Yes, Dick?"

"Do you have any policies about when the residents have to be in or when they can leave? I have a friend at the police department who says he has tracked down the officers who left Jonathan out there on the road, and he'd like Jonathan to come down so the officers can apologize."

"I can't see a problem," he said. "About what time?"

"We have to be at City Building Annex by 7:15," I said.

"Well, he only has to sign out and say where he's going. That'll be fine." There was a pause, and then: "Here's Jonathan." and the sound of the phone being passed from hand to hand.

"Hello?" Jonathan said, tentatively. I don't suppose he was expecting any phone calls.

"Jonathan, it's Dick. How's it going?"

"Gee, Dick, it's nice of you to call!" he sounded really pleased. "It's going swell! I've got my own room—or it will be when it's done and I'll have a roommate Skip who's a real nice guy and there's a bathroom right next door and there are some really nice kids here and Reverend Mason is really a nice guy and..."

"Uh, that's great, Jonathan," I said, breaking in to his stream-of-consciousness chatter. "I want to come by tomorrow morning really early and pick you up to go down to the police station with me. I think the officers who left you out there might want to apologize to you."

"Wow, that's nice of them," Jonathan said, not a trace of irony in his voice. "What time?"

"I'll pick you up at quarter to 7," I said.

"Quarter to 7 in the *morning*?" he asked, then quickly added: "Okay. Sure. I'll be ready. I'll meet you out in front, okay? I'd really like to show you around here, but that's pretty early and most of the kids will still be sleeping, and..."

I hated to cut him off, but was pretty sure if I didn't, neither of us would get to bed before midnight. "I'd like to see it sometime," I said. "But I'll meet you out in front at quarter to 7." Realizing that he had had very little sleep in the past 24 hours, I said: "You get some sleep now."

"I will," he said, brightly. "We've got our beds in the room already and we have to keep them covered up with a drop cloth during the day when we're working there, but..."

"Good night, Jonathan," I said with a smile.

"'Night, Dick!"

* * *

Sure enough, when I pulled up in front of Haven House, Jonathan was sitting on the stairs, leaning forward, elbows on knees, hands folded. When he saw me, his face broke into a big grin, and he got up immediately and hurried over to the car.

He looked a lot better this morning than he had the morning before when he'd come to my office. The swelling had gone down considerably, the angry red abrasions had dulled a bit and softened in shade. He had a small band-aid over the cut just above the left-side corner of his mouth. His black eye was still puffy and bloodshot, but at least he was able to open it a bit. He was wearing an (obviously) old but clean and unwrinkled ABBA tee-shirt that one of the other kids must have loaned or given him, and I think the same pair of pants he'd been wearing the day before. I assumed Haven House must have a washer and drier, because I couldn't see the bloodstains.

I headed the car for downtown, and sat back with a bemused smile to listen to everything that had happened to him since I'd left him the day before, a roster of the other kids in the house, their names, their ages, what he'd found out about them, which ones he liked more than others and why, what his room was going to look like when it was done, etc.

We all know people who ramble endlessly, and normally it's a trait that drives me up the wall, but with Jonathan I got the feeling that all this was somehow important to him and that he really wanted to share it with me, so I didn't mind at all.

* * *

We parked in the public garage under Warman Park and walked the two blocks to the City Building Annex. Jonathan got quite a few discreet stares, but didn't seem to notice. He did appear to be slightly apprehensive as we walked up to the main entrance of the Annex. Probably because it was shift-change time, the alley beside the building was lined with police cars and there seemed to be an inordinate number of uniformed officers walking around entering and leaving the various side doors and even the main entrance.

We found our way to the elevators and went up to Richman's floor. One officer in the car with us stood looking straight ahead at the door, but I could see him looking at

Jonathan out of the corner of his eye. While I have an absolute obsession with not being late, I'd deliberately slowed our arrival so that we got off the elevator at, my watch said, 7:17. I wanted to be sure that the officers had gotten there before we did, and had had a chance to either confirm or deny that they were the ones to leave Jonathan standing in the road. It would be very unlikely, if we were there first, that they would be stupid enough to deny it. But if they thought a denial would get them off the hook, and Jonathan then came in and identified them....

I could hear voices as we approached Richman's door. Jonathan had been quiet all the way up on the elevator and apparently was a little intimidated by the surroundings and not really knowing what to expect next. I couldn't really blame him.

I knocked and heard the Lieutenant's voice: "Come in."

I opened the door and held it for Jonathan to go in first. The two officers seated in front of Richman's desk turned slightly, and the look on their faces made it fairly clear how they had responded the Lieutenant's question.

Richman got up from his chair, and walked over to shake hands. "Mr. Hardesty," he said, taking my hand, then turned to Jonathan, whose eyes moved back and forth between the two officers. "Mr....?" he asked, taking Jonathan's hand. I realized I didn't know Jonathan's last name either.

"Quinlan," Jonathan replied.

I noticed that the two officers had turned back to their original positions, and were staring out the window behind the Lieutenant's desk.

"Mr. Quinlan," Richman said, "this is officer Kerr and officer McGinnis. Are these the two officers you met on the road yesterday morning?"

The two officers reluctantly turned again to face Jonathan, expressionless.

"I think so," he said. "I didn't get a good look at the officer in the passenger's seat, but this officer..." he nodded toward the one in the chair closest to us..."was driving."

Richman didn't so much as look at the two officers. "I see," he said. "Well, I just wanted you to meet Officers Kerr and McGinnis personally, to express our regrets for the incident, and to assure you that it will not happen again. Thank you, gentlemen, for coming in," he said as he extended his hand again to Jonathan, then me. Then, without another word, he turned and went back to sit down behind his desk, facing the officers. Recognizing an exit cue when I saw one, I turned and went to the door, Jonathan close behind.

As we rode the elevator down to the lobby, Jonathan said: "Are they going to be in trouble?"

I gave a small smile. "I wouldn't be surprised," I said.

* * *

As long as I had Jonathan with me, I decided to take him by my office to check out the paper with Giacomino's photo. It was, as I'd said, the same paper that Jonathan had held in front of him when I took the Polaroids, but again, neither of us was paying much attention to the paper itself at the time. When we got to my building, we stopped in the ground-floor coffee shop to get Jonathan something for breakfast—I was pretty sure he hadn't had a chance to eat before we left Haven House, and all I'd had was a quick cup of coffee while I was getting dressed. I noticed, as we walked into the diner, that the Help Wanted sign was gone. Actually, it was Jonathan who noticed it. "Darn it!" he said.

Eudora and Evolla, the identical-twin waitresses, were on duty as they had been just about every single time I'd ever been in the place. Eudora had had a mild stroke some time before, but it didn't seem to have done any serious damage. They had to have been in their mid-seventies by this time—probably fifty of those years spent behind the same counter—but if that fact ever even occurred to them (and I rather hoped it didn't), they never let on.

It was too early in the day for soup—hearing either one of the sisters yelling "BAW-el!" to the cook behind the service window was one of my life's little pleasures—so we each had a ham and cheese omelet, with a side order of French toast and a large orange juice for Jonathan.

I saw him casting a rueful look at the spot in the side window where the Help Wanted sign was located. "There are other jobs out there," I said.

Jonathan sighed. "Yeah, I know. But...."

Evolla—or whichever one of them was wearing Evolla's name tag that day—brought Jonathan's orange juice and French Toast, set it in front of him, and moved away without a word. I knew they could talk, of course, from their calling out orders to the cook, but I wondered if, even at home, their vocabulary included words not found on the diner's menu.

Jonathan reached for the pancake syrup and emptied about a quarter of it over his toast.

"So what kind of work would you like to do, Jonathan?" I asked. "If you could do anything you wanted."

He cut a large piece of toast, swirled it around in the lake of syrup, and somehow managed to convey it to his mouth without having syrup dripping all over him. He was obviously hungry and so concentrated on the food in front of him he did not look up from it. "Anything I can get," he said. "I can't afford to be choosy."

I took a sip of my coffee. "Yeah, but if you could," I prompted.

He put his fork down and looked at me. "Plants," he said. "I like plants."

"You mean like a florist shop?"

He shook his head, looking just mildly disgusted. "No, not roses in a box or corsages or funeral arrangements: I think it's wrong to kill flowers like that. I like flowers that stay right where they grew. I like plants, and trees—especially fruit trees, and shrubs and bushes...stuff like that."

"Well, maybe you can check out the nurseries when you're ready."

He gave me a quick, sunrise-smile. "Yeah, I could, couldn't

I? I thought about it when I first got to town, but I didn't see any anywhere. I guess they're all out in the suburbs, and with me not having a car…but I think I'd really like that!"

Evolla (?) brought our omelets, and we ate.

* * *

When we got to my office, I first checked the answering machine, not really thinking I'd have heard from Lieutenant Richman/Richman/Mark—I didn't know if I was ever going to be able to settle on which one—and I hadn't. There was a message from Tom, asking me to give him a call when I had the chance. I'd thought of calling him even before I'd gone to pick up Jonathan, but didn't want to wake him, and for some reason I didn't want to return the call with Jonathan there. I also had a message from a client checking on the status of his case, and I felt a flush of guilt at not devoting full time to what I was being paid for rather than wandering the landscape looking for new windmills to tilt at.

I dug the newspaper out of my desk and there, sure enough, was Giacomino's photo on page 1 under the headline "Rough Talks Ahead." I handed the paper to Jonathan and his eyes instantly locked on Giacomino's photo.

"That's him!" he said. "That's him right there! Shouldn't we tell the police?"

"They already know," I said.

"Are they going to arrest him?"

Good question. "I hope so," I said, "but…"

Jonathan's face fell, and he continued to stare at the picture. "Oh," he said, his voice flat. "I know. He's rich and he has his picture in the paper and I'm just some stupid nobody from Wisconsin."

"Don't talk like that!" I said, maybe a little more harshly than I'd intended. "I promise you that this guy is going to get exactly what he has coming to him. Trust me, okay?"

He gave a shrug and his voice reflected his doubt, but he said: "Okay."

* * *

As we were getting off the elevator on the ground floor I stopped to say something to a woman from the office next to mine, who was just getting on. As the doors closed between us, I turned to see Jonathan, who was a few feet ahead of me, standing there with a look of mild surprise on his face.

"I wonder what he's doing here?" he asked.

"Who?"

"That cop," Jonathan said, pointing toward the front entrance. "The one who was driving the squad car."

"Where?" I asked. I didn't see anybody.

"He was standing right there," Jonathan said, pointing. "Looking at that list." He indicated the building registry. "Then he saw us and turned around real quick and left."

"Are you sure it was him?" I asked as I started walking a little faster than normal for the door.

"Sure I'm sure," he said. "He wasn't wearing his uniform, but I recognized him right away."

We reached the door and went out into the street, each of us looking up and down the sidewalk, but there were just too many people to be able to spot one guy I'd only seen once.

Very strange, I thought…and it was far from a happy thought.

CHAPTER 6

I drove Jonathan back to Haven House, and he asked me if I'd like to come up and see his room. I told him I had to get right back to the office to take care of a few things, but said I'd like to have a rain check. He just smiled and said "Okay!"

He got out of the car and headed up the sidewalk toward the house as I drove away.

I was going to wait until I got back to the office to call Tom, but though I'd tried to kid myself that the calls he'd gotten were no big deal, it just wasn't working. When I glanced down at my fuel gauge and saw I needed gas, I used it as an excuse to pull into the next station I came to. I drove to a "full service" pump—another indication of my hurry to get to a phone—and, getting out of the car while fishing in my pocket for change, went directly to the outside pay phone. I dialed Tom's number, and was glad to hear his "Hello?"—though I could tell it was a guarded "Hello."

"How's it going, Buddy?" I asked.

"Oh, hi, Dick. Glad it's you."

I wondered what that meant, but let it slide for the moment.

"Did you get some sleep?" I asked, then immediately added: "Sorry, I wasn't going to do my Mother Hen number."

Tom laughed. "That's okay. It's nice having someone of the same gender who isn't a relative make a fuss over me. I talked Lisa into going to work today, and I decided I'd answer any phone calls myself. Glad I did, because the department called. They want me back to work Monday, if the doctor okays it. I'll be on a desk for a week or so, maybe, but it'll be good just to get back."

"No more harassment calls?" I asked.

"I heard the phone ring a couple times during the night, but nobody left a message. I guess they didn't want their voices recorded for posterity. I think guys like that are pretty much nightcrawlers, anyway."

"Well," I said, "I guess we both knew something like this was almost inevitable. There are too many sickos out there for it not to. The main thing is not to let it get to you."

"Oh, I won't," he said. "We Bradys are pretty thick-skinned."

"Speaking of which," I said, suddenly remembering the elder Brady and the labor negotiations, "have you talked to your dad?"

"I called him this morning just before he left for the talks. He's ready, and he's sure not going to let that sick bastard Giacomino walk off with the farm. I wanted to tell him about the incident with that kid, but decided against it. He's got to stay focused, and if he knew what that bastard did, he'd beat the shit out of him…he's a tough old bird, and he could do it, too."

I had no doubt.

"So you're going to be home all day?" I asked.

"I've got to be at the doctor's at ten thirty, but I'll be back a little after noon, probably," he said.

"Good," I said. "Maybe I'll give you a call later and see if you'd like some company."

"Gee, I don't know," he said. "Lisa won't be home until about 6, so we'd have to be here all by ourselves. I can't imagine what we might find to do to keep ourselves busy…."

"We could always improvise," I said.

He laughed, and we exchanged good-byes and hung up.

* * *

I let myself relax for the rest of my drive downtown, but the minute I walked up to the main entrance of my building, I flashed back to Jonathan's claim to have seen one of the cops from Richman's office. I didn't question for a minute the fact that Jonathan sincerely thought he saw him, but it was really pretty unlikely. Still….

I stopped at the lobby newsstand for the paper, noting the headlines: "Labor Talks Underway," and mentally wished Tom's dad and his team well. I forced myself not even to think about that scumbag Giacomino.

The phone was ringing as I opened the door and I hurried to the desk to pick it up.

"Hardesty Investigations."

"Got a pencil?" the voice—I recognized it as Mark Richman's immediately—asked.

"Yeah..." I said a bit hesitantly as I opened the top drawer of the desk to find one out of the 34 in there that might actually have a sharpened point.

"Take this number down, then go to a payphone and call me there in five minutes."

Thoroughly confused, I reached into the wastebasket for an old envelope, and wrote down the number Richman gave me.

"Five minutes," he repeated, and hung up.

I noticed the light on my answering machine blinking, but decided to wait until I got back to check on it. I left the office, and took the elevator to the lobby, which fortunately had a bank of payphones, only one of which was unoccupied. I glanced at my watch and dialed the number.

"Dick?" Richman's voice asked.

"Yeah," I said. "What's going on?"

"Sorry for the cloak and dagger business," he said, "but I have very good reason to believe your phone—your home phone, too, probably—is being tapped. All hell is starting to break loose around here, and this Brady incident is becoming the focus. They know you and Tom Brady are friends, and since they know you're gay: They're hoping to catch either you or him saying something incriminating."

Jeesus H. Kee-ryst! My mind yelled *What the hell did you just do, Hardesty? If they're tapping Tom's phone and got that last little exchange between you two...! Shit! Shit Shit Shit!!!*

God, I didn't dare say anything to Richman!

He, of course, was oblivious to what was going on in my

head.

"But don't feel too bad;" he was saying; "I found out this morning that my office phone, at least, is being tapped, too."

No good! No good! I thought. *If anybody heard Tom and me talking, the shit has hit the fan for sure!* I decided I had to tell Richman; there was too much at stake not to.

"Uh, Lieutenant…" and I used his official title very deliberately "…we have a big problem…." And I told him of my conversation with Tom, as close to verbatim as I could remember it. Up until that moment, Richman had known Tom was gay without *knowing* he was gay, if you can follow that one.

"We didn't actually *say* anything," I said, lamely.

Richman sighed. "You didn't have to," he said. "I think my grandmother could have read between the lines on that little exchange."

"So what can we do?" I asked.

"Let me talk it over with Captain Offermann and see if we can meet with the chief. This is really bad, I'm afraid, but we just might be able to do some damage control."

He was silent for a moment while I mentally kicked myself around the block several times. Finally, he said: "Is your friend Jonathan somewhere safe?"

"Yes," I said, somehow vaguely disturbed by the question. "For the moment, anyway."

"Good," Richman said without further explanation. There was another long pause while I continued on my mental-masochist marathon, but trying to calm myself down.

"The only thing I can think of in regards to the current situation," Richman said, "is to take the offensive. We'll lay everything out to Chief Black—assuming he'll listen—and maybe we can offer Cochran a trade: No action on Tom Brady for no action on Joey Giacomino. I know the chief's going to hate like hell to do it, but the only other alternative is for both sides to come out with cannons firing, and everybody loses. At least this way we can gain some time. I hope we can count on the fact of Deputy Chief Cochran's having too many skeletons in his closet to risk his association with Giacomino's shaking them all loose. Keep your fingers crossed. If you're going to be home tonight, I'll try to stop over and give you any news."

"I'll be there," I said. "And I'm so fucking sorry I…"

He cut me off. "You've got nothing to be sorry about: You had no way of knowing any of this. So I'll talk to you later."

We exchanged good-byes and hung up.

I was feeling like a ten pound bag of dog crap but was able to put the mental whips away and focus on the anger against Cochran and his entire crew. And as for Tom…well, whatever happened, he could handle.

* * *

My first reaction was to get over to Tom's immediately and warn him, and then I realized: *About what?* I was the only one to whom he was at all likely to be saying anything that might give any listeners-in even a hint that he was gay, and we'd already neatly handed them that one on a silver tray. It had occurred to me, too, as I tried to calm myself down, that to do a 24-hour phone tap on someone would require a lot of manpower and effort—and multiply that by three if Tom's, my, and Lieutenant Richman's were the only ones being tapped. Maybe it was just sporadic; maybe they hadn't heard that particular conversation.

Uh huh, my mind said.

Hey, it's my straw and I'll cling to it if I want, I replied.

By the time I'd returned to the office, I'd managed to hand over control to my stoic side: What was done was done, and there was little point in getting too worked up over it. (I was getting pretty good at that, I must admit, and was pretty proud of myself for it.)

Then I checked the message on the answering machine.

"Dick, this is Tony Mason at Haven House. Could you call me right away, please?"

Double Shit!
My stomach immediately knotted up, and when I saw my hand automatically reaching for the phone. I yanked it back and headed back out the door. This was going to get very old, very fast, I told myself.

I stopped at the lobby newsstand and asked Charlie, the proprietor, for five dollars worth of change. I was going to need it, I suspected.

I dialed Haven House's number.

"Hi," a voice I didn't recognize answered.

"Hi," I repeated. "Is Reverend Mason there?"

"Sure, just a sec." The phone was put down, and I could hear several voices in the background, and music, but no call "Hey, Reverend," so I assumed whomever had answered had gone to get him. A minute later, the phone was picked up.

"Reverend Mason."

"Tony, it's Dick, returning your call."

"Ah, Dick, thanks. Jonathan didn't want to call you, but I thought I'd best."

The knot was still in my stomach. "Is something wrong?"

"I'm not really sure, but when he came into the house, he was acting…a little strange. I thought at first maybe you and he had had some sort of argument, but he kept going to the front window and looking out to the street. And he seemed nervous. I asked him if anything was wrong, and he said 'no,' but I'm afraid I didn't believe him. Since he'd been with you, I thought perhaps you might have an idea."

"No," I said honestly. "When I dropped him off he was fine. Maybe I should talk to him. Can you put him on?"

"Sure. Just a moment." And I heard the phone being laid down, then only the background voices and music, and a couple kids laughing.

What the hell could have happened? I wondered. *I just left him not forty-five minutes ago.*

"Hello?" I heard Jonathan say.

"Jonathan…did something happen?" There was a long

pause. "Jonathan?" I repeated.

"They followed us, Dick," he said.

"Who?" I said, but the knot got bigger.

"Those cops. As soon as you drove off, and I started up the stairs and into the house, I turned around and this car pulled up to the curb…just for a second, but I saw this guy lean toward the passenger's window just far enough so's he could see me, then he drove off. It wasn't the one I saw at your building; it was the other one." There was a pause, and then he said: "I don't think I like this, Dick. Why would they follow us?"

To find out where you live, my mind said. And I didn't like it, either.

"Tell you what, Jonathan," I said, trying to sound casual, "you just stick around there for a while, and I'll call you back, okay? I want to check on something."

"Okay," he said.

"Don't leave the house. And don't worry about anything. I'll get back to you in just a bit. 'Bye."

* * *

Oh, I *didn't* like it! Not one bit! Under normal circumstances, I could probably have chalked it up to my just being my usual mildly paranoid self, but after my conversation with Richman…and my phone was being tapped, for Chrissakes! And little puzzle pieces of information were falling into place and starting to form a very ugly picture. I'd just paraded Jonathan in front of two guys who not only looked very much like they could hold a grudge, but who wouldn't be averse to currying a little favor with the anti-Black team by reporting Richman's taking the side of a fag hustler over his fellow officers'. I remembered what Richman had said about the two officers being in Cochran's pocket.

Everything that had happened thus far—our meeting with the cops, the one cop showing up at my office building, Jonathan seeing the other one in front of Haven House—had happened in too short a time-frame to think Cochran was even aware of it…yet. But the two cops were certainly aware that Cochran was looking for anything at all to paint Chief Black as being soft on fags. I was sure they considered keeping track of Jonathan a way to gain a few points with Cochran. I doubted they had any idea of the link between Jonathan and the van and Giacomino.

But I'll bet *Cochran* would know where the links led, and that he'd be very happy to know where Jonathan was. If Richman could trace the van numbers I'd given him over a tapped line, so could whoever might have been listening in. I think I realized for the first time just how much of a threat Jonathan might be perceived to be. And if he was considered a threat—most directly to Joey G. but by extension to the anti-Black forces in the department—Jonathan could be in real danger.

The only thing I could think of was to get Jonathan out of Haven House, and fast, before the two cops could pass on their information to Cochran. My mind was apparently a couple steps ahead of me, for I found myself reaching for my billfold and looking for Tim and Phil's new phone number. Hoping against hope that Phil might be home, I dropped some more coins in the payphone and dialed.

"Hello?" Phil's voice said.

Thank you, God!

"Phil! I didn't think you'd be home, but I'm glad you are!"

"Hi, Dick," he sounded just a bit hesitant and I could tell he probably read something in my voice. "I've got the day off. What's up?"

I knew what I was going to ask was a huge imposition—he and Tim had just moved in together, and were still just getting to know one another, really—but if you can't impose on your friends…?

"Phil," I began, "I need a favor—a really big one…."

* * *

I was sitting by a window at Denny's, on my second cup of what the menu laughingly referred to as coffee, when a car drove up to the front entrance and Jonathan got out, carrying his battered little backpack. He put it on the ground and turned back to offer his hand to Reverend Mason, who had leaned across to the passenger's side to shake it. I was keeping my eye on the street, to see if there were any evidence that they'd been followed. I kept looking while they exchanged a few words, then Jonathan closed the door and waved as the car drove off. He watched it go, then picked up his bag and headed for the door of the restaurant. No other cars had passed or, within line of my sight, pulled over to the curb, so I relaxed a little.

Jonathan came in, looked around, spotted me, and came over, putting his backpack on the seat nearest the window. He did not look particularly happy.

"I really liked it there," he said wistfully, obviously referring to Haven House. "Did I have to leave?"

I nodded. "At least for awhile," I said. I didn't want to worry him any more than I had to. "Now that those cops know where you live, I didn't want them coming around to hassle you or anybody else at the house."

The waitress came over and Jonathan ordered coffee and, at my insistence that he get something to eat if he was hungry, an order of French toast.

"But why did I have to tell everybody I was going home?" he asked. "I'm not going back to Wisconsin; not right now."

I tried to give him a reassuring smile. "Well, that way if anybody asks where you are…"

"You mean the cops," he said, and I nodded…

"…Everybody at the house can tell them you went back to Wisconsin and they won't know they aren't telling the truth."

The waitress brought his coffee and we sat in silence for a minute or two.

"So how come you didn't come to the house to get me?" he asked.

"Because I didn't want anyone to see you driving off with

me," I said. "I want everyone to think you've really gone."

Jonathan took a sip of his coffee, made a face, and emptied two packets of sugar and three little packets of dry dairy creamer into the cup. "So where *am* I going?" he asked, stirring the floating mound of powdered creamer to dissolve it.

"I have two really good friends, Phil and Tim, who have an extra bedroom you can use until things calm down. They're great guys, and I know you'll like them. Phil used to be a hustler, so he can understand where you're coming from, and it might be good for you to have someone who's been where you have to talk to."

Jonathan's French toast arrived and he asked for another little pitcher of syrup. When the waitress went off to get it, he poured the syrup she'd brought with the order over one piece, then looked up at me.

"How come you're doing all this for me? Why should you care what happens to me?"

I smiled and carefully looked him in the eye. "Because I do," I said.

"Then how come you never want to have sex with me?" he asked.

Good question, kid, I thought.

I had to think about how to answer that one. "Because," I said, "I think it's important for you right now to know that there are people who can be your friend without expecting sex in return."

You talk a good game, Hardesty, my mind said skeptically.

"What if I really want it?" he asked.

Got'cha! my crotch chimed in.

Luckily, the waitress showed up just then with the extra syrup and to ask the mandatory: "Everything okay?" We both nodded.

I'd rather hoped the distraction would have sidetracked his thought, but I saw his eyes were still on me, expecting an answer.

"Let's talk about that after all this is over, okay?" I said.

He must have seen something in my eyes that I didn't know was there, because the corners of his mouth curved up into a very Mona Lisa type smile.

"Okay," he said, and picked up the extra syrup.

* * *

On the drive over to Phil and Tim's, I told Jonathan about how I'd gotten to know each of them, and how they'd gotten together. He seemed especially intrigued about Phil's past—which was hardly surprising—and I really hoped Phil could be something of a role model for Jonathan.

I'd made sure, of course, when I'd called Phil, that he would get Tim's okay on having an unexpected houseguest before I brought Jonathan over. Since they were still in something of a honeymoon stage, I knew Tim called Phil several times a day whenever Phil wasn't working. Phil never called Tim at work, of course, since Tim was one of the thousands of not-closeted-but-not-open-at-work gays working for local government agencies. And not surprisingly, the Coroner's Office, for which Tim worked, was a rather by-the-book group. Tim was sure almost everyone he worked with knew he was gay, but he was out to only a couple of them. And Tim always called from a pay phone.

Anyway, Tim had called Phil shortly after I did, they discussed it and, as I knew he would, Tim said "Sure!" I'd waited at the office until Phil called me back to let me know—without mentioning Jonathan or referring to house-guests, of course, and that set off the chain of events that led us to heading for their apartment.

Jonathan had regained some of his puppy attributes on the drive, apparently having been reassured that he might be able to return to Haven House before long, and alternated questions about Tim and Phil with accounts of how his room at Haven House was coming and what color he was going to paint it and the posters he wanted to get for the walls and…well, Jonathan-talk.

I'd never been to Tim and Phil's new place myself, yet, but was pleasantly surprised to find it was in an almost-new, three-story apartment building not too far from The Central. It had, Tim told me, in fact been built and was run by a gay-owned management company, which probably accounted for the fact that it had some character.

Jeezus, what a heterophobe! my mind snorted.

We walked through the small courtyard, Jonathan commenting approvingly on the small trees and plantings, and entered the small, enclosed foyer, where I found "P. Stark/T. Jackson: 314" and pressed the button beside it.

"Dick?" Phil's voice asked from somewhere I couldn't identify. There was no button for me to press to respond, so I just said: "Yeah, it's us" to no one in particular, and there was a soft click as the door unlocked. We entered a small lobby with an open stairway on either side and directly in front of us an elevator. I pressed the button for the elevator, and the doors opened immediately.

"Nice place," Jonathan said.

The doors opened again on the third floor, and I faced four floor-to-ceiling narrow windows that I'd noticed as we'd come through the courtyard. About ten feet to the left and right of the elevator, were hallways running back into the building. The wall of the hallway to the left of the elevator had a neat but decorative arrow beside the numbers "301 - 315", and on the right hallway "302 - 314". We wisely chose the right hallway.

314 was at the far end of the hall, and Phil was standing at the open door to the apartment when we arrived. We exchanged hugs and then I motioned Jonathan forward and introduced them. I could see Jonathan was notably impressed. Phil appeared completely oblivious to Jonathan's still-all-too-obvious cuts and bruises, and guided us into the apartment.

"Wow, this is really nice," Jonathan said. "You've got goldfish!" he said, spotting a large aquarium in one corner of the living room.

"My God, you've turned domestic on me!" I said, approvingly.

Phil grinned. "Sort of, I guess. We found out we both like fish, so we went for it. We've only got a few—those little buggers are expensive. We saw a couple we really wanted, but we're going to have to wait awhile on those. But, hey, you only live once."

The apartment wasn't large, but it was very comfortable. I recognized pieces from both Phil's old apartment and Tim's, and a few new things, including the aquarium. There was a small semi-open dining room, through which I could see into the kitchen through Dutch doors. A short hallway, one wall of which was shared with the dining area, revealed two doors on the right, and a good-sized bathroom at the end.

Noticing Jonathan still holding on to his backpack, Phil said: "Come on, Jonathan, I'll show you your room."

* * *

I left Jonathan in Phil's capable hands at around 11:30. Before I left I cautioned both of them that, because my office—and quite probably my home, for all I knew—phone was tapped, Jonathan was not to call me at any time, either at home or at the office. I promised I would call him frequently from pay phones. Phil and I agreed that it was probably advisable for Tim not to call me at all, either. I did not want to get him into any trouble with the city bureaucracy. And with Phil as my only direct contact, we agreed that when one or the other of us did call using my home or office phone, neither of us was to mention Jonathan.

It occurred to me that all this cloak-and-dagger stuff, as Richman had called it, may have been a little excessive, and I fervently hoped so, but I figured it was infinitely better to be safe than sorry.

* * *

Since I wanted to make sure Tom had had enough time to get home from the doctor's, I made a quick swing by the office to deliberately make a few phone calls. I didn't want whomever had planted the tap—as if I didn't have a pretty good idea—to know I was aware of it. Though it never would have occurred to me under normal circumstances, I carefully listened during pauses in the conversation and, sure enough, I could here an odd little "click" every couple seconds—proof positive, if I'd needed any, that the line was tapped.

After I'd made the last call, I headed out again. I'd thought about stopping at the payphones in the lobby to call Tom, then thought better of it. I'd just go right over to his place and if he wasn't home yet, I'd wait.

On the way over, to kill a few extra minutes, I took a drive down Beech. I don't know, maybe I just wanted that sense of security that being in the heart of The Central gave me; knowing that three out of any four people I passed were my own people. I noticed, as I passed Beech & Ash, that the new police substation was nearly finished, and they'd begun excavating for a parking garage directly across the street. The substation was scheduled to open the week following the upcoming gay pride festival. The initial strong objections to the station had largely waned as the community's trust in Chief Black's desire to make positive changes grew. And the incident involving Tom certainly helped. A gay cop! One of our own! On the force!

If only they knew....

* * *

I decided to leave the car at my place and just walk over to Tom's—I figured that since I was sure the cops knew what kind of car I drove, it might not be a good idea for any of Cochran's boys to see it on the street near Tom's. I had the radio on as I pulled into my garage, and heard a news bulletin announcing that the A.H.W.A.'s local president, Joseph Giacomino, Jr. had called a strike against the city's hotels, to begin at midnight. It struck me as a little too early in the game to be calling a strike, but obviously Joey G. was definitely playing hardball.

I spent the afternoon with Tom. We talked…a lot…about the strike and his situation at work, but tried very hard to avoid speculating, other than to reassure each other that things would work out. I felt really bad for Tom because I knew he was almost certain to lose the job he'd wanted all his life—a job he was damned good at. He felt somehow responsible for the civil war brewing within the department, but I assured him that if it hadn't been the shooting and the gay issue that had triggered it, it would have been something else. He was just the match that set off the explosion: The gas fumes had been building steadily ever since Chief Rourke had left office.

The doctor had okayed Tom's return to duty, and we talked a bit about what he might expect when he did go back. Chief Black would never tolerate any overt acts from other officers, but we both knew Tom could expect some pretty rough treatment from his peers. He said he was up to it, and I hoped he was right.

All we—which really boiled down to just Tom in the long run—could do was try to ride out the storm and deal with things one at a time as they came up.

And, yes, we spent a lot of the time in bed. Don't kid yourself: Sex can be as effective a means of communication, and of mutual comforting, as anything I can think of. Touch is one of our most underrated senses, and just to know, by simple full-body skin-on-skin contact with another human being you care for, that you are not alone can do wonders.

And, yes again, Tom and I did care for one another: We always had. I'd deliberately, since he reentered my life, avoided speculating on just how much I might care, and at the moment, it really didn't matter.

I was glad to see his shoulder was apparently pretty much back to normal and did not seem to be bothering him.

I did caution Tom, before I left, to make his dad aware of the line tapping, and to avoid discussing any specifics of the labor talks over the phone. I didn't know just how close Cochran was to Giacomino, but there was no point in taking chances. I also had no real idea of how much Tom's dad knew about what was going on. I did know he wasn't stupid.

* * *

Unsure of exactly when Richman might be coming over, I decided not to go back to the office. I did stop at a pay phone to make a quick call to Phil, to see how he and Jonathan were getting along—I was sure Tim wasn't home from work yet. And I did feel a little guilty for imposing on them, especially since I really didn't know Jonathan all that well. I knew, of course, that he had found a kitten while on the way home from school when he was in the second grade and his mother had let him keep it and he named it "Oscar" and that he'd had it for ten years until it went out one day and never came back and…things like that. I found his eagerness to share every single aspect of his life oddly charming, but couldn't expect others to see him the same way, especially when exposed to it all day long.

Phil answered on the second ring.

"How's it going?" I asked.

"Fine," he said, with a grin in his voice. "He's quite a kid."

I found it interesting that Phil, who wasn't in actual fact all that much older than Jonathan when I'd met him, and still was quite a few years away from collecting Social Security, thought of Jonathan as a kid. So did I, pretty much. Sort of like a kid brother….

Oh, sure, my crotch said. *Who the hell do you think you're kidding?*

"Has he talked your arm off yet?" I asked, bringing myself back to Phil.

"Just to the elbow," he said, good-naturedly. "I keep wanting to offer him some milk and cookies. You want to say 'hi' to him? He's feeding the fish."

"Sure," I said.

I heard Phil say something and a moment later Jonathan came on.

"Hi, Dick!"

"You doin' all right there?" I asked.

"Oh, sure!" he said. "Phil sure is a nice guy." He then lowered his voice to just above a whisper and said: "And *hot*, too! Is his lover half as hot as he is?"

"You'll see," I said. "But don't go getting any ideas, hear?"

He sounded crestfallen. "Of course not!" he said. There was a slight pause, and then: "I'm waiting for you." Four simple words with two very different meanings, and I didn't have any doubt which one he meant. Most of me hoped he was teasing, but some of me…care to guess which part?…was more than a little flattered.

He's 19, chicken hawk! my mind said, disgustedly. I realized that I was being a tad hard on myself: 19 was hardly chicken, but it was still under my 'not-til-they're-21' rule, no matter how stupid that rule might seem to other people. And I realized, too, that with all that had happened to him in the past few days, he very well might be confusing gratitude with, well, something else.

I asked to speak to Phil again, thanked him again for taking Jonathan in, and told him to give my best to Tim and if he needed me for anything, to call and ask if I'd talked to Jared recently—I'd know to get back to him right away.

CHAPTER 7

Though I knew Richman's visit wasn't going to be a social call, I stopped and picked up a six-pack of bock beer, just in case, and was home by 5:15. I had a couple messages, from Jared and Bob Allen but didn't dare return them until I'd had a chance to call them from a pay phone and let them know my line was tapped.

At almost exactly 5:30, the buzzer rang and I pressed the entry door unlock button and waited for Richman's knock.

We shook hands at the door and he came in and took a chair. I offered him a beer but, as I expected, he passed.

"My wife's expecting me for dinner, so I can't stay long," he said.

I took a seat on the couch across from him and leaned forward, elbows on my knees.

"So what happened?" I asked.

Richman sighed and sat back in his chair. "Well," he began, "I first talked to Captain Offermann, who is one of Chief Black's strongest allies—and who, I can assure you, was far less than happy to have Officer Brady's homosexuality confirmed—and he got us in to see the chief almost immediately. The upshot is that the chief called Cochran in for a private meeting, and apparently they've reached something of a standoff, if not exactly a truce. If your friend Jonathan agrees not to press charges against Giacomino—he can always do that later if he wants to, after things settle down—Chief Black has agreed to not pursue it and Giacomino's links to Cochran, in exchange for Cochran's agreement not to press the Brady issue. I suspect those links go a lot deeper than we know."

He sighed, and I knew it was a precursor to something I didn't want to hear. "But this is a pretty shaky standoff, and I'm not sure it will hold. Cochran may not use a frontal assault on

Brady, but you can be damned sure he's not finished. Cochran's a rabid homophobe, and he sees this Brady affair a golden opportunity, not only to discredit Chief Black by his association—however loose—with Brady through his wife, but to rid the department of gays and anyone else who thinks the department needs to move forward.

"The minute Cochran heard that Brady'd been in a gay bar prior to the shooting, he wanted him out. He wanted to put Brady on suspension immediately pending an inquiry into the 'circumstances of the shooting'—which means the probability of Brady's being gay. When Chief Black vetoed that idea, knowing full well that he'd have the entire gay community up in arms, Cochran was furious. Suspending Brady would have given Cochran and his boys a pulpit and a theme for their attacks on what they see as the undermining of the 'moral foundations of the force'—which is to say, the status quo that has kept the good ol' boys in power all these years."

"And the phone taps?" I asked.

Richman shrugged. "Another 'iffy' area. Cochran of course vehemently denied having any knowledge of it, but Chief Black made it clear that if they didn't stop immediately, he would have no choice but to do whatever it takes to root out the responsible parties and have their jobs. I think Cochran got the message, but we'll have to see on that one, too."

He was silent a moment, looking at me steadily.

I told him about the two cops following us, and that I had taken Jonathan out of Haven House and led everyone there to believe he had returned to Wisconsin. I didn't tell him where Jonathan was now, other than that I was sure he was safe, and he didn't ask.

"Those two are poster boys for the way the department used to be run," he said, "and the way I'm afraid it's likely to be run again if Cochran is able to force Chief Black out. I just hope they were trailing Jonathan looking for an excuse to pick him up, or at least to know where to look for him. I wouldn't imagine that Joey G. would have told Cochran about his encounter with

Jonathan: He sure as hell wouldn't want Cochran to know he picks up male hustlers, but if Cochran finds out about the plates and makes the connection between Jonathan and his golfing buddy, Joey G., he'll readily be able to spot the implications for himself."

Shit! I remembered that Tom and I had mentioned Giacomino's link to Jonathan and the van over the phone! If Cochran hadn't known about it before, and if he was behind the phone taps, he sure as hell did now! I told Richman what I'd remembered about that part of our phone conversation, too.

He shrugged. "Well," he said, "I'm sure Cochran would have put the pieces together on his own eventually. But if I were you, I would urge your friend Jonathan to stay off the streets. Hustling can be a dangerous occupation under any circumstances, but right now, for him in particular…."

He didn't have to spell it out.

"He will," I said. I was once again painfully aware of the threat Jonathan posed to both Cochran and Giacomino and therefore the potential danger he might be in. Without Jonathan, Giacomino was off the hook and so, by extension, was Cochran.

"So," Richman said with a long sigh, "all we can do now is sit back and watch what happens. Officer Brady is returning to work Monday, I understand. We'll see what happens then."

He left a few minutes later, leaving me to try to convince myself that everything would work itself out in time, and that the worst was over. But I didn't believe it for a second.

* * *

The rest of Thursday night and most of Friday was half a jumble, half a blur. I'd determined, shortly after Richman had left Thursday night, that apparently the phone tap was off—I'd called Bob Allen to ask if he'd like to run out and grab a quick dinner, and listened for the telltale "clicks." There were none. Still, I determined to be a lot more careful of what I said over the phone in future.

Any illusions I'd had about things calming down were pretty much shattered Friday morning when I got to work to find a phone message from Reverend Mason. It seems that just after breakfast that morning he had a visit from the police, looking for Jonathan. They told the good reverend that a hustler fitting Jonathan's description had robbed a john late Thursday night and they wanted to take him in for questioning. *Uh huh.* They did not explain how they knew where to come looking for him. The description of the two cops did not fit what I remembered about the two from Richman's office, which made me even less happy, since it meant it was no longer just the original two cops who were looking for Jonathan.

When Reverend Mason told them Jonathan had returned to Wisconsin, the cops asked to speak with a couple of the other kids, all of whom told them the same thing. Whether they believed it or not, I didn't know. But they went away.

I'd talked to Jared Friday—from a pay phone—to sketch in what had been going on. He said he had to run up to Mountjoy for the day, but that he'd be at Tim and Phil's party. One of the reasons I'd called, I realized, was that it suddenly occurred to me that Jared and I had not gotten together for a little…uh, socializing…in far too long, and I was hoping to remedy that. As a matter of fact, my crotch reminded me, now that Tim and Phil were together, my little 'stable' of regular tricks had dwindled dramatically. I'd have to do something about that as soon as this whole thing was over with.

I hoped Tom would be around to provide frequent…uh…social opportunities, but I knew his life was pretty hectic right now, and since I knew our relationship would never be more than it was now, I couldn't see any point to limiting my sex partners to just one.

Friday night I determined to go out and pick up a trick, just so I wouldn't forget how. Not the best of ideas, since because while my crotch was all for it, the rest of me was too distracted to really enjoy it. I walked into the Cove, had two beers, started talking to the guy next to me and…well, you know. We went to his place, and I was back home by shortly after midnight. I was more than a little ashamed of myself, Saturday morning, to realize that I couldn't even remember his name. I decided that sex is a lot more fun when you really want it rather than when you just go through the motions from habit or some vague physiological urge.

* * *

And then it was Saturday. I spent the morning doing Saturday things: Paying bills, doing the dishes that magically pile up until there's no room in the sink, grocery shopping, etc. I stopped off at the laundromat and was oddly glad to see Jeff behind the counter. He gave me a very sexy smile—*Does he have any other kind?* I wondered—as I hoisted my full duffel bag onto the scale in the little alcove beside the cash register.

"Can I leave these and pick 'em up later?" I asked.

"Sure," he said, still smiling. "Can I play with them first?"

"Be my guest," I said, laughing.

"Still holding to that '21' thing?" he asked as he wrote out a receipt for me.

I was a little surprised at myself to realize that while Jeff and Jonathan were only a little over a year apart in age, having met Jonathan had somehow rather weakened my resolute stand on the age issue. Still, there was a considerable difference between 18 and 19—well, nearly 20.

"Alas, yeah," I said.

"Pity," he said, handing me the receipt.

We exchanged grins and a wave, and I walked out feeling somehow mildly frustrated.

After leaving the laundromat, I headed for Reef Dwellers, a big new tropical fish store which had just opened a branch in The Central. I was pretty sure that's where Tim and Phil had gotten their aquarium, and since I had no idea what specific fish they were looking for, I got them a gift certificate for whichever one(s) they wanted. I had to practically drag myself out of the place, having become mesmerized by the incredible number and variety of the specimens gliding serenely through the water of the variously sized and shaped tanks. I'll bet they didn't have to worry about having their phones tapped.

A quick stop at the card shop next door, and I was ready to party.

I'd thought, as Tim had suggested, of asking Tom, Lisa, and Carol if they would like to come to the party, and had in fact broached it while Tom and I were getting dressed after our last meeting, but he indicated that they'd probably better pass, and I understood. I really would have liked to spend more time with Tom over the weekend, but realized that probably wouldn't be a very good idea under the circumstances.

I did give Phil and Tim a call from a pay phone, to see if they needed anything for the party or if there was anything I could do to help, but Tim, who answered the phone, assured me that they had plenty of help from their houseguest, who had volunteered to serve as bartender for the party as well. I was relieved, since it had occurred to me that perhaps Jonathan's being there might be even more of an imposition while they were trying to get ready for a party. But I got the impression Tim was favorably impressed by Jonathan, though of course neither of us mentioned him by name. Still, I realized that since this whole mess didn't show signs of being resolved any time soon, I was going to have to think about making other arrangements for Jonathan. I was beginning to feel a little bit like Harriet Tubman working on the Underground Railroad.

* * *

The party was scheduled to start at 7:30 and knowing Tim, I was sure he'd have enough food for the Spanish army, so I just had a grilled cheese sandwich and a small salad before I left the apartment. I was, of course, ten minutes early, and forced myself to walk around the block twice before going in. Even so, I was still the first guest there.

Phil greeted me at the door, looking even more spectacular than ever. Married life obviously agreed with him. Tim came out of the kitchen with a small bowl of something that he was somehow able to find space for on the dining room table which, even with a leaf in, was covered in plates, platters, bowls, and chafing dishes. He carefully adjusted the rheostat to dim the lights over the table, then came over to greet me and give me a hug. Seeing him and Phil standing together made me think that the fates can sometimes be very kind. I handed Tim the card, for which they both thanked me, and which Tim laid on the lamp table beside the door for opening later.

Noticing me looking around for any sign of Jonathan, Phil grinned and said: "Oscar is in the kitchen."

I looked at him with a slightly raised eyebrow, and Tim said: "He knows why he's here, and he thinks he should tell everyone his name is Oscar so they don't make any connections to anybody named Jonathan. He thinks he's protecting you. He's really a sweet kid."

I nodded, just as the buzzer rang announcing the arrival of other guests.

"Go in and get a drink, why don't you?" Phil said.

I made my way toward the kitchen, where I could see Jonathan, his back to me, taking a bag of ice out of the freezer. When he turned around and saw me, his face breaking into a huge grin, I had to do a double-take. He was wearing a white dress shirt and black pants, apparently borrowed from Tim who, I realized, was almost the same size as Jonathan. But his bruises and cuts were completely gone, and it took me a moment to remember that Tim had been known to dabble in a bit of cosmetic enhancement on special occasions, and apparently had worked his magic on Jonathan. But whoever had done whatever, he looked better than I'd ever seen him. And sexy as all hell.

"Hi, Dick!" he said, happily.

"Hello, Oscar," I said, and he set the ice in the sink and made a gesture to come toward me, then apparently thought it might not be a good idea. I walked over to him, instead, and gave him a hug which obviously pleased him and which he returned with surprising strength. I noticed he'd borrowed some of Phil's after-shave, but not too much, and he smelled as good as he looked.

Hardesty...my mind cautioned.

What? I mentally replied, feigning innocence.

You know damned well 'what', it said. *Just cool it!*

"You look good, Oscar," I said as we broke the hug and moved away from one another. "Are you behaving yourself around Tim and Phil?"

He gave me a quick look of surprise before he apparently realized I was kidding, then he grinned broadly and said: "Oh, sure! They're really great guys, and they let me help them do things around here, and I get to feed the fish, but not too often so they won't get too fat, and I've even got a TV in my room so I can let them be alone when they don't have something they want me to do." Then his smile softened, and he said: "You look good, too."

Har-des-ty!

I know.

Fortunately, we heard the sounds of other people in the dining room. "So what would you like to drink?" Jonathan asked.

"Bourbon and seven," I said.

The smaller kitchen table had been set up with bottles of gin, vodka, bourbon, scotch, sweet and dry vermouth, rum, and several bottles of various mixes. A large cooler on a chair beside the table was filled with ice and several different kinds of beer.

Jonathan swiftly and smoothly moved to take a glass from several rows of different sized glasses on the counter to one side of the refrigerator, took ice out of a rather elegant-looking ice bucket with a small silver scoop, replaced the lid, dropped the ice into the glass, and reached for the bourbon. "Strong or weak?" he asked.

"Medium," I said, then turned to see Jared entering the kitchen.

We exchanged a handshake and a hug, which wasn't lost on Jonathan, who had been staring in wide-eyed wonder at Jared.

"Jared," I said by way of introduction, "this is…Oscar."

Jared gave me a quick, raised-eyebrow look, and I just nodded.

"Nice to meet you…Oscar," he said as they shook hands.

More people were coming in, now, and after Jonathan had given me my drink and gotten a beer for Jared, Jared and I decided to make room for the new arrivals, and moved back out into the living room. For somebody who didn't drink, Jonathan made a pretty good bartender.

There were several people I knew, and several more I didn't. Tim and Phil were natural hosts, and made sure everyone met everyone else. There was a nice woman from Tim's work—the only one of his coworkers to whom he was out—and her husband, a few of Tim's other friends, and a few guys Phil used to work with in his ModelMen days: Aaron Aimsley, who radiated so much sexual heat he would never be allowed in Madam Toussaud's Wax Museum lest he melt the figures, was as usual all in black. Mark Neese, another ModelMen alum, as usual looked as though he'd just stepped off a magazine cover, and the androgynously beautiful Steve Thomas came in with his wife, a very attractive blonde named Cindy.

And I was delighted, a little later in the evening, to see Iris and Arnold Glick, the founders of the ModelMen agency which had gotten Phil off the streets, come in. I'd not seen them in quite a while, and we managed a few minutes of conversation between the usual party interruptions.

All in all, a very pleasant evening. Aaron, I noticed, spent quite a bit of time in the kitchen talking with Jonathan. I was only mildly concerned, since while Aaron could easily eat Jonathan alive, he was basically a nice guy. He liked to play rough, but always respected his partners' limits. And I knew full well that Jonathan wouldn't be leaving with him even if he wanted to.

And why should you care if he wanted to? my mind asked.

I nipped that little line of thought in the bud and forced myself back to enjoying the party.

* * *

I stayed after most of the guests had left, to help with the cleanup. I'd been hoping that maybe Jared would want to get together afterwards, but he had a date with some biker number he was meeting at the Male Call, and had to leave around ten. We did arrange to meet for brunch on Sunday and I knew that if we followed our usual Sunday Brunch pattern, the afternoon would pretty much take care of itself.

Phil and Tim were picking up the living room while I helped Jonathan wash the dishes. I'd really been quite impressed with Jonathan, what little of him I'd seen during the evening. He really worked his little tail off. I knew Tim and Phil obviously appreciated it, since it took a lot of the pressures off them.

"Well," I said when we'd put the last of the glasses in the cupboard, "I guess I should be getting on home."

Jonathan looked disappointed. "Can't you stay?" he asked. "I've got a big bed."

I smiled. "Thanks, Jonathan," I said, "but I don't think that would be such a good idea."

"Tim and Phil wouldn't mind," he said. "We could ask them."

"Well, I really wouldn't feel comfortable doing that," I said, feeling doubly *un*comfortable for being put in an awkward position and for being tempted.

Jonathan's face became very sober. "I understand," he said.

I reached out and took him by the shoulders. "No, Jonathan, I don't think you do." Well how the hell could he understand when I didn't myself? But I gave it the old college try. "We haven't known one another for a week yet. As I told you at the restaurant, I want you to understand that someone can want to be your friend without expecting you to pay for it with sex. Let's just work on the friends part right now, okay?"

He picked up on that one like a shot. "And later?"

I sighed. "We'll see when later comes," I said.

As if someone had turned on a light switch, his face brightened again.

"Okay," he said, and closed the cupboard door.

* * *

I said good night to Tim, and Phil walked me to the door while Tim and Jonathan finished cleaning off the dining room table.

"You've got a fan," Phil said with a warm smile, nodding to Jonathan.

"Yeah, I gather," I said, mildly embarrassed. "Puppy love."

We'd reached the door, but Phil hesitated with his hand on the knob. "Probably, but he's a pretty cute puppy. And I've noticed that he talks about everything and anything, as you've noticed. Except you. I suspect Jonathan talks about surface things, not things that are inside. And you *are* something of his knight in shining armor, after all."

I sighed. "Yeah, I guess maybe he does see it that way. Well, give him time."

* * *

Jared and I had arranged to meet for brunch at Rasputin's at 12:30, and while I'd fully intended to sleep in—a pathetic little game I play with myself, since I always *intend* to sleep in on Sundays and never do—I was up and working the Sunday paper's crossword puzzle by 7:30.

I'd just gotten up from my chair to start another pot of coffee when the phone rang.

"Dick Hardesty," I answered, wondering for the 4,000[th] time why I never just said "Hello."

"Good morning, Dick. It's Lisa." Even if I hadn't recognized her voice instantly, it wasn't as though I'd have to go through a long roster of what women might be calling me.

"Hi, Lisa, what's up?" I found myself straining to hear any tell-tale 'clicks' indicating the tap was back on, but there were none.

"Carol just came by" *uh huh* "and we were wondering if you'd like to come over for coffee."

"Sure," I said. "Want me to stop by the deli and pick up some rolls?"

"That would be great," she said. "Could you get me an apple fritter? I love their apple fritters!"

"Anything else special?" I asked.

"I'll leave it to you. Carol and Tom will eat anything as long as it's fattening."

We both laughed, and I told her I'd be over as soon as I'd showered.

* * *

The deli was only a block from their apartment, though a block beyond so I had to pass by their place and come back. I got there around 9.

Carol, it turned out, *had* only arrived shortly before Lisa called. They were playing it cool, too, just in case someone was keeping an eye on their building watching for who came and went. Paranoia ain't fun, but sometimes it's justified.

Tom, I could sense, was getting hyped up for his return to work, though he tried not to show it. We talked and laughed, and all tried to pretend that things were exactly as they should be. And for that little while, it worked.

Tom and Lisa were having dinner with Tom's dad at the Montero that evening at around 7, and Tom was anxious to hear from his dad exactly what was going on with the labor negotiations, and to see for himself how the strike was affecting the operations of the hotel; it remained open despite the picket lines and drastically reduced staff. The papers had, of course, been running front-page stories on both the strike and the talks, and one of the papers began running a little box on the front page showing the projected cost of the strike to the city for each day the union stayed out.

From all indications the negotiations were as rocky as everyone had predicted. While Tom's dad and his team kept a low profile, Joey G. took every opportunity to get his picture in the paper and on TV, complaining to everyone who would listen—including, I'm sure, Joe Giacomino, Senior in his east-coast prison cell—of management's attempts to destroy the working man by refusing to pay a decent wage, etc. All bluster and bully-talk, but it more than made up in volume what it lacked in logic. The fact that the union workers were losing wages while they were out on the unnecessary strike he had called didn't enter Joey's equation.

* * *

I've always wondered why some of the things we do with relative frequency and in the same pattern are considered ruts, whereas others are always anticipated with pleasure. That was what my brunches with Jared had evolved into over time. We'd meet at around the same time, though we'd vary the place, have a couple Bloody Mary's, talk, laugh, have brunch and then go either to his place or mine for the rest of the afternoon spent largely in various forms of horizontal recreation.

Jared had given his two week notice to the beer distributor for whom he'd worked since he arrived in town; he was planning on moving to Carrington, the small town closest to Mountjoy College, where he'd be teaching. He was really looking forward to it, and I told him I'd help him move when the time came. Though it was only about an hour away, we both knew it would probably somewhat limit our get-togethers. It would certainly limit his incredibly active social life, which was always the source for colorful stories of his encounters and conquests, and which he always related with no sense of ego.

I got home around 6, fixed dinner, and settled in for a night of TV. I thought briefly of running out to Ramón's for a drink and a talk with Bob Allen, but then thought better of it.

You're getting old, Hardesty, my mind said.

Bullshit! I replied.

I was just finishing a jumbo bowl of popcorn and thinking about heading to bed when the buzzer rang. When I opened the door I was a little surprised to see Tom coming up the steps. I held the door open as he came in.

"Well, this is a pleasant surprise," I said, and meant it. I motioned him to the couch, then sat down beside him.

"Sorry for not calling first," he said, "but when we got back from dinner, I decided to take a walk, and I ended up here. Who'd a' thought?"

I grinned. "You're welcome any time; you know that." There was a slight pause and when Tom didn't say anything, I stepped in. "So how did it go with your dad?" I asked. "Talks going any better?"

Tom sighed. "Giacomino's a total asshole," he said.

I shrugged. "So tell me something I didn't know," I said.

He gave me a small grin and laid his hand on my leg. "Apparently little Joey is really out of his league, and he knows it. This is his first real negotiation, and he's got not only his old man but the entire union hierarchy watching his every move. Dad says even some of the other guys on Joey's team are obviously not happy with the way he's handling things, especially in calling a strike so early in the game. Of course criticism only drives Joey further out into left field."

"I don't envy your dad," I said. "Or the union members, for that matter."

Tom sighed. "Yeah, and there are four other guys on dad's team, but of course Joey's acting as though he blames dad personally for the strike. Management's offering a really good, solid package, but Joey thinks he's got to prove to his old man that he's as tough as his dad was."

We sat silently for another minute or two, appreciating the more-than-physical sensation of our hands resting on each other's thighs.

"You ready for tomorrow?" I asked.

He nodded. "As ready as I'll ever be," he said. Then he turned to look at me, face to face. "You know I'm going to lose my job over this," he said. I started to say something, but he gave a quick head-shake to cut me off. "Maybe not tomorrow or next week," he said, "but eventually. The only reason I haven't been fired already is because Chief Black is understandably concerned about the reaction of the gay community. He doesn't want another Stonewall on his hands. Any other time, under any other circumstances, I'd be out on my ass already. Chief Black's a good man, and will be good for the department. But even I know the force just isn't ready to integrate gay cops yet. The time will come, but not now. If I could have kept a low profile…."

I knew he was right, and it hurt: For him, for the community, for tolerance.

"I could just quit," he said, almost more to himself than to me. "But I won't. If this is going to be an issue, which it already is, then I'm not going to give anybody the idea that I left because I thought that gays don't have a place on the force—or the right to be there."

"You always were a man ahead of your time," I said, and he grinned.

Glancing at his watch, he said, "And I see it's about time I headed for home. It's going to be an interesting day tomorrow. I hope I don't have any trouble going to sleep."

"Well," I said, "old Doc Hardesty's got a sure-fire cure for relieving tension."

He grinned at me again, and his hand took mine and moved it slowly up his leg. "I'll just bet you do."

And I did.

CHAPTER 8

I spent most of Monday thinking about Tom and wondering how things were going for him. I called Lisa at her work right after lunch to see if she'd heard anything but she hadn't. I could tell she was worried, too, but, like Tom, she always tried to put up a good front. She had hoped to leave work early in order to be home when Tom got there, but her boss had called some sort of office meeting for 3:30, and she couldn't get out of it. I told her I'd stop by the apartment around that time, which is about when Tom should be getting home.

Finishing up the paperwork on another case took my mind off things for a little while, but not too far off. I realized I had to do some more thinking about Jonathan, too. He couldn't stay with Tim and Phil forever, and right now he was practically a prisoner in their apartment. I'd told him not to leave under any circumstances or for any reason, and I think he understood the reason for it. It had only been five days, but I'm sure he'd start to get antsy pretty soon, and I couldn't blame him. I made a mental note to talk to Bob Allen, to see if perhaps he and Mario could put him up for a little while.

I just hoped this entire mess would resolve itself soon, but with so many different elements—the intra-departmental struggle for control, the shooting incident and its ramifications both inside the community and in the department, plus the added problem of the labor negotiations and the strike and Joey G's ties to Deputy Chief Cochran—it didn't, again, seem likely to be over any time soon.

There was something else that had been swimming around the backwaters of my brain for some time, now—one of those infuriatingly elusive thoughts I instinctively knew might be important but couldn't catch. And then it came to me: I'd known the name Giacomino rang a bell, but couldn't place why. And then I remembered Bart Giacomino, whom I'd met in conjunction with another case some time back. Bart was a wheeler-dealer in the gay community who spent money like water and was rumored to be the black sheep of a powerful east coast gang-related family. Could he possibly be related to Joey G? Bart and Glen O'Banyon had been college roommates, so if anyone would know if there was a connection, it would be O'Banyon. Other than satisfying my curiosity, I wasn't sure what practical good having the information might do, but the more I could learn about Joey Giacomino and what might be expected from him, the better I'd feel. Anything was worth a shot.

I called O'Banyon's office and left a message with his secretary, Donna, to have him call me at his convenience.

* * *

I'd gotten to Tom's apartment building a little before 3:30 and when no one answered the buzzer, I figured he hadn't gotten home yet, so went around to the entrance to the parking garage, where I was standing when he drove up at 3:45. He waved, and I followed him through the opened gates into the garage and to his parking spot.

"What, no flowers?" he asked as he got out of the car.

I just grinned and followed him to the elevator.

"Sorry I'm late," he said. "I had a flat tire. The perfect end to the perfect day."

"Problems?" I asked, immediately feeling stupid for having done so.

He shrugged. "Ah, not really, I guess. They assigned me to the property room...*way* in the *back* of the property room, to be exact, going through about four hundred boxes of unfiled reports. That should keep me busy until the turn of the century."

In a way, I was relieved. "No one said anything, then?" I asked as we walked down the hall to his apartment.

"Nope," he said. "No one said anything. All day. Not a word. Literally. A couple of the guys I know pretty well managed to get in a quick nod when they thought no one else was looking, but other than that, I might as well have been invisible. You could have hung a side of beef in the squad room when I first walked in, it was so cold in there. But fuck 'em. I should have expected it."

He opened the door to his apartment and we went in. "Like some coffee?" he asked. "Or I can get you something a little stronger?"

"Coffee's fine," I said. "It's a little early in the day for the hard stuff."

I followed him into the kitchen while he went through the water-and-filter-and-grounds routine and flipped the coffee maker's "On" switch. I sat at the kitchen table while he got out the cups, and we waited while the coffee maker talked to itself in soft burps and bubblings and hissing sounds.

He seemed in fairly good spirits, but I instinctively realized he didn't feel much like talking about his day, so we didn't. I mentioned my thinking of Bart Giacomino, and wondered if the name was familiar to him.

"Sure," he said, somewhat surprised. "Bart's Joey's older brother. I didn't know you knew him. Not much love lost between them, from what I understand. Joe Senior always played his kids off against each other—his way of toughening them up. It didn't work so well for Bart as it did with Joey. I heard that it was Joey who told his old man that Bart was gay. Joe Senior all but kicked Bart out of the family, which of course raised Joey several rungs up the ladder. For most families, blood's thicker than water: For the Giacominos, power's thicker than blood. And now to find out that little Joey's in the same league with his brother... I'd imagine Joey would do just about anything to keep that little secret shut away. If his old man—not to mention his wife—ever found out about it...." He paused and looked at me. "You're sure Jonathan is somewhere safe?"

"As safe as he can be," I said. "I thought of sending him

away, out of the city or out of the state, but if Chief Black might be able to use him to somehow hold Cochran at bay...."

Tom gave a small smile and shook his head. "This is one fucked-up mess, isn't it?"

Truer words, I thought.

The phone rang and I noticed a quick flash of anxiety cross Tom's face. He excused himself and went to the answer. I could read his tension in his body language.

"Hello?" Then, almost imperceptibly but definitely, I could see him relax. "Oh, hi, dad," he said. "How did it go today?...Sure, I'm fine....It was okay; they put me on a desk for awhile, but...uh, yeah...sure...uh, well, I think Lisa's going to play cards with some girlfriends tonight, but...well, sure. What time?...okay, that'll be great. Sure. I'll see you then, then. 'Bye."

He hung up the phone and came back to sit down. "Dad wants to come by tonight; maybe I'll be able to find out what's been happening with the talks."

As if you didn't have enough going on in your own life right now! I thought.

"Great," I said. "Give him my regards."

The phone rang again, and he got back up to answer. "Hel..." he started to say, then immediately hung up.

"Wrong numb...?" I began, then saw the answer in his face.

He didn't say a word, but came back and sat down. The phone rang again.

"Let the machine get it," he said.

"You know, you might want to consider changing your number," I suggested.

He shook his head and got up again to get our coffee. "What good would that do?" he asked. "I have to have my number listed with the department in case of emergency; I could change it every day and someone would still get it."

That told me again that Tom believed the calls were from his fellow officers.

I stayed at Tom's until Lisa got home around 5:30, then headed home.

* * *.

After I left Tom's, I walked back to my place to pick up my car, and headed for Ramón's to kill a couple birds with one stone. I hoped Bob would be there so I could broach the subject of his and Mario's being the second stop in Jonathan's little underground railway journey. And I hadn't been to a happy hour in awhile.

Jimmy was tending bar, and it was a little quiet. I nodded to a couple of the regulars as I took a seat and Jimmy came over to take my order.

"Manhattan night or Old Fashioned night?" he asked, putting a napkin on the bar in front of me.

"Well," I said, "if you can ever come up with an Old Manhattan, I think we can save a lot of speculation. But Old Fashioned for now, I think." We exchanged grins, and as he turned to start making the drink I said: "Bob's not around?"

Without turning back to me, Jimmy gestured with his head. "He's in the office."

"Thanks," I said. I waited until I had my drink, fished a bill out of my billfold to cover it, and gave it to Jimmy before picking up my glass and napkin and walking to the back of the bar. I knocked at the office door, and heard Bob's voice: "Come on in."

Bob was seated at his desk in the small office, but turned in his chair and grinned as he saw me come in. "Hi, Dick. Grab a chair."

I reached behind the door for the folding chair he always kept there and set it up at the corner of his desk.

"You've been pretty scarce lately," he said.

"Last Wednesday, for the group," I said by way of weak defense.

He nodded. "I know, you're a busy guy. How is your friend Tom doing?"

I sighed and put my drink down on the edge of his desk, out of his way. "Rough and getting rougher," I said.

Bob just shook his head. "I wouldn't want to be in his

shoes," he said.

"Yeah," I said. "But Tom's one tough customer: He's not going to give one inch to those homophobes on the force. He knows he's going to lose his job over this as soon as things calm down, but he won't go without a fight."

"Well," Bob said, "the community's behind him one hundred percent; you know that."

"I know," I said. "And so does Tom. We'll just have to see how this plays out." I took a sip of my drink and replaced it on the desk, making sure the napkin was still dry before doing so. "Which brings me around about to asking you for one huge favor."

Bob raised an eyebrow and cocked his head. "Shoot."

I told him about Jonathan, about Giacomino, about Giacomino's ties with Deputy Chief Cochran, and the fact that Cochran's boys were looking for Jonathan.

"He's with Tim and Phil now," I said, "but I can't impose on them forever…" I caught myself and gave Bob a sheepish grin, then added the obvious: "…so here I am to impose on you. Do you suppose…."

Bob didn't bat an eye. "Of course! And this might work out really well, if the kid's willing to earn his keep."

"No doubt about that," I said, telling him about his eagerness to help out at Haven House, and his bartending for Phil and Tim's party, which Bob and Mario had missed because both had to work.

"Well," Bob said, "the house closes tomorrow. Our lease doesn't expire until the end of this month, so we've got plenty of time to start moving things over and getting things started over there. If the kid would be willing to help us out however we need him to, we could sure use him."

"Do you want to check with Mario first?" I asked.

Bob shook his head. "Nah…I can't imagine that he'd have any objections at all. Like I say, we can sure use the help."

"Great!" I said. "God, Bob, what would I do without you?"

"Look in the dictionary under 'Friends,'" he said with a

smile. "It'll be a little spartan over there the first few days, but we can move a bed and some kitchen stuff over tomorrow, if he's willing."

"I'm sure he will be," I said. "And again, thanks…and thank Mario too!"

We talked for a few more minutes then, realizing he had work to do, I excused myself, thanked him again, told him I'd call him during the day tomorrow to iron out the final details.

I talked for awhile with Jimmy, ignored my crotch's trying to call my attention to a guy standing against the wall, finished my drink, and went to the payphone to call Tim and Phil, hoping I wouldn't be catching them in the middle of dinner.

Tim answered, and I asked if I might stop by for just a few minutes.

"Sure," he said. "Have you had dinner yet? You're welcome to join us."

"Well, no I haven't, but I really don't want to im…"

"No problem. Oscar's making a meatloaf that barely fit in the oven. We'll be having meatloaf for a week or two. Come on over."

My stomach voiced its opinion with a small growl. "Okay, if you're sure you don't mind. Can I pick up anything?"

"Nah, we have everything we need."

"Okay," I said. "I'll see you in about ten minutes."

* * *

Jonathan, it turned out, was a damned good cook. The meatloaf was delicious, and he'd made some sort of garlic-glazed new potatoes. He explained that his mom had been sick a lot when he was younger, and that he'd been largely responsible for cooking for the family.

"Better watch it, Jonathan," Phil teased. "Some guy's going to want to carry you off, lock you in the kitchen, and keep you barefoot and pregnant."

Jonathan blushed and shot a quick lowered-head glance in

my direction which, I could tell, was not missed by either Tim or Phil. I felt Phil's foot nudge mine under the table, and I looked up to see him trying unsuccessfully to suppress a smile.

Sigh.

I told them of Bob's offer and, lest Jonathan feel like he was just excess baggage being passed from hand to hand, I stressed that they really needed help with their move.

Both Phil and Tim expressed regret at his leaving, saying that Jonathan was welcome to stay as long as he wanted, but we all knew that it was time they got their own life back—or, rather, given the short time they'd been together, got it started.

I'd noticed, too, during the course of the evening, that without the aid of makeup, Jonathan's wounds were still visible, though now only barely so. And having some sort of stability in his life for the first time since he'd arrived in town was obviously good for him. He didn't look quite so skinny as when I'd first met him, and it seemed somehow that he had gotten even more attractive.

Hardesty!! my mind-voice warned, sternly.

Yeah, yeah, okay, I reluctantly replied.

He had been relatively quiet throughout dinner, but while Phil and Tim cleared off the table, Tim suggested Jonathan show me the new fish they'd gotten with my gift certificate, and Jonathan segued unconsciously into his puppy-dog chatterbox mode, pointing out not only the newest addition to the aquarium—a large, thin silver creature with two large black circles on either side of its body, looking like either portholes on a submarine or the eyes on that ubiquitous yellow "happy face", and which Jonathan had named George—but gave me the names of all the other fish in the tank, which ones bullied the others, which one ate the most, etc. I took a really odd delight in the fact that his enthusiasm was truly genuine. That they all had names and what he swore to be individual characteristics was *important* to him, and he wanted to share it with me.

I explained to him before I left that I probably wouldn't be able to spend much time with him because of everything that was going on, but that he'd like Bob and Mario and that Tim and Phil would keep a close eye on him, too. He said he understood, and that he'd be fine. I hoped he was right.

"I'll miss the fish, though," he said.

* * *

Glen O'Banyon had returned my call to tell me basically what Tom had told me about Bart Giacomino's relationship with his family in general and his little brother Joey in particular. "Bart's not the brightest star in the heavens," O'Banyon said, "and I'm afraid his ego far outdistances his abilities. He could even be called 'shady.' But he has always lacked the 'vicious' gene that Joey inherited from his father. So if you think you can use your knowledge of Bart in any way to try to anticipate what Joey might be up to, just take everything you know about Bart and add 'pathological' and you'll be on the right track."

I tried to call Tom several times in the following days, and stopped by a couple times after work. Lisa was usually there, and I could tell Tom didn't want to talk much in front of her, so we all tried to pretend everything was just fine. The labor negotiations were, according to Tom's dad, pretty much at a standstill, and apparently it might be dawning on Joey that he didn't have much of a clue what was going to happen next. The union's strike fund, which was paying the workers a small portion of their regular wages, was not a bottomless pit. Something had to give, and the only thing Joey knew was that it wasn't going to be him.

It wasn't until Friday morning—Tom's day off—when I stopped over on my way to the office after I knew Lisa had left for work, that I found out what had really been happening at work—or, I suspected, only a small part of it. Getting Tom to talk about it was like pulling teeth, but I could tell it was getting to him and he needed to be able to talk to someone. Lisa would have been more than willing to listen, but he was protective of her and didn't want to worry her more than she already was.

On Tuesday, Tom had left work to find all four tires on his car flattened. He began parking in the underground garage at Warman Park and walking the two blocks to work.

Wednesday, as he went to change out of his uniform, he found an apple on the bench in front of his locker, with a note: "A fruit for the fruit."

Though he had very little contact during the work day with his fellow officers, and a few of them still managed, when they thought they weren't being observed, to say a few words to him, the hostility level from those in Deputy Chief Cochran's camp was rising steadily—unquestionably with Cochran's tacit support and probably even encouragement—and they intimidated the others. No one ever said anything openly to Tom's face, but he was aware he was always being watched, and frequently, after passing a group of fellow cops in the hall, would hear someone say "faggot" or "queer!" He never turned around. And he never responded, never reacted. He refused to give them what they wanted: a physical fight which could lead to his dismissal.

His home phone rang almost continuously.

On Thursday when he got to work, he was called on the carpet by one of Deputy Chief Cochran's upper-echelon cronies: "Why the hell aren't you answering your phone?" he demanded. "Either nobody answers or the damned line's busy. I was looking for an important file in that mess you've made down there and couldn't find it. If you spent less time talking to your...*friends*...and more time thinking about your duties, you'd be better off. The next time I call, I expect to get through!" The fact that he hadn't left a message himself made it pretty clear that it was a set-up, of course, to make sure Tom answered the phone every time it rang and could be subjected to the verbal abuse.

Thursday night, when he opened his locker, glitter powder poured out—someone had painstakingly poured it through the small ventilation slots on the locker door, and slipped in a note: "Fairy Dust." Everything in his locker was covered in it. A bunch of the other officers also changing clothes didn't see the note, but their laughter made it clear they knew about it. Tom just picked up his clothes and left, still wearing his uniform.

As I say, these are only the things I managed to pry out of him. I suspected they were just the tip of the iceberg, and while my admiration for him was already boundless, I was heartsick that I couldn't do anything to help him. He never volunteered any information: He just took the abuse and said nothing. I urged him to go to Lieutenant Richman, but he refused. I was tempted to talk to Richman myself but realized that I couldn't. This was Tom's fight and I had no right to interfere, much as I might want to.

The phone, once he stopped leaving it to the machine to pick up, rang constantly and each time, Tom would simply lift up the receiver, listen for an instant—sometimes I could hear shouting from the phone even as far away as I was from it—and then hang up, his face expressionless.

* * *

Phil had taken Jonathan over to Bob and Mario's new house on Tuesday night, where the four of them set up a bed and unpacked some basic supplies to tide Jonathan over. Bob, to whom I talked after he and Mario had gotten back to their apartment, said they both thought, as I had thought of Mario when Bob first met him, that Jonathan was "a keeper." In addition to his tattered old backpack, Jonathan had brought with him a cardboard box with clothes Tim had given him, insisting he'd "gotten too fat" to wear them (not true, of course), a small portable TV from Phil's old apartment, a good-sized glass bowl, and a large plastic bag filled with water and two small goldfish which Phil and Tim had gotten him as a going away present. Jonathan had duly named the goldfish "Tim" and "Phil."

I've said it before, and I'll say it again: What would the world be like without friends?

* * *

When I arrived at the office after leaving Tom's on Friday morning, I had a message waiting. Two words: "The fountain?"

I was sitting on one of the marble benches circling the fountain in the center of Warman Park at exactly noon. I'd stopped at the diner in my building for a couple sandwiches, a couple orders of cole slaw, and two large cokes to go. I imagined that Richman was giving up his lunch hour and might appreciate something to keep body and soul together.

At ten after, I saw Richman approaching. I got up from the bench, motioned toward one of the picnic tables, and met him there. He seemed happy to see I'd brought some food.

"I was debating on whether to stop and grab something from one of those hot dog carts, but didn't want to take the time," he said, watching me open the bag and remove the contents.

"Ham salad or tuna?" I asked, pushing one of the styrofoam cups of cole slaw across the table to him.

"Surprise me," he said, so I just reached into the bag and grabbed the first sandwich I came to.

"So how is Tom Brady holding up?" he asked, as he removed the plastic lid from his coke and unwrapped his sandwich (the tuna).

"A hell of a lot better than I would under the same circumstances," I said.

Richman sighed. "Yeah, I know," he said. "We're trying to keep as close an eye on things as we can, and if anything overt happens, we'll jump in. But we can't really do much. Cochran's boys are just praying for us to give them something they can use against the Chief Black. Coddling homosexuals or favoritism/nepotism, they don't really care what it is as long as they can use it. And I'm pretty sure Cochran is subtly egging his guys on, watching for our reaction. But the result is—and I'm sure as hell not proud of it—that Officer Brady is pretty much on his own. But he looks like he's strong enough to handle it."

I nodded. "He is," I said. I reached into the bag for the two little plastic spoons for the cole slaw, handing him one, and a napkin. "I just wish he didn't have to."

"Just let him know that we're watching, and if things start getting out of hand... I was going to say he could come to me, but I don't think he would."

I shook my head. "No, he wouldn't. He thinks he can take on the world all by himself, and I feel so fucking frustrated for not being able to help him."

Richman nodded and sighed again, wadding up the sandwich wrapper in one hand and dropping it into the open but empty bag.

"Well," he said, "just let him know that my door is always open for him, if he needs me. Chief Black is between a rock and a hard place on this one. If Officer Brady were almost any other cop...but he's not. He's an outstanding young man who in less than a year on the force has saved the life of a fellow officer and several civilians, he was head of his class at the Academy .... No police force with any self respect or any hope of having the respect of the people it serves can just toss an officer like that aside, which is exactly what Cochran is doing his best to do. And the fact that Brady has an association, however nebulous, with the chief only makes Cochran particularly want to use him against the chief. It's a real mess."

I wondered if he knew about the phone calls, or the harassment at work; but I couldn't mention them, because Tom wouldn't want me to.

* * *

Meanwhile, the labor negotiations dragged on, growing more bitter every day as it became increasingly apparent even to his fellow union negotiators that Joey G. was in over his head. He could bully and yell as well as his old man, but did not have the old man's savvy or negotiating skills. Management had offered a good, solid package, giving some concessions aimed at influencing other members of the labor team to convince Joey G.

to bring the contracts before the union membership for a vote. But Joey wouldn't have it, and the Giacomino name alone kept even those who may have wanted to intervene from doing so. When management gave an inch, Joey took it as a sign that he was winning, and demanded a foot.

Much of this, of course, was played out in the media, and as the management team began to leak the terms and concessions, even the union's rank and file, growing weary of the picket lines, began to wonder what in hell Joey was trying to accomplish.

* * *

Gay Pride weekend was rapidly approaching, and the Pride Parade Committee wrote a formal letter to Chief Black—carefully worded—inviting Officer Tom Brady to be the Parade Grand Marshall "out of gratitude for Officer Brady's actions in protecting members of the gay and lesbian community."

Chief Black wrote an open letter to the Committee, equally carefully worded, thanking them for their offer, but stating that "since any member of this department would have behaved exactly as Officer Brady had under the same circumstances, to single him out for special attention would place too much emphasis on one incident of police bravery to the unintentional detriment of the countless other officers who display equal bravery and courage every day in the course of their service to the city."

By absolutely no coincidence whatsoever, the Journal-Sentinel, the city's smallest-circulation but most strident newspaper, noted for screaming headlines just a step or two above the "Man Eats Own Foot!" style of the supermarket tabloids, ran a front page story of the "rumored rift" within the police department under the thick black-lettered headline: "**A Department in Crisis!**" The fact that this "rift" had been common knowledge since Chief Black was appointed was not mentioned. There was even a short one-paragraph reference to "strong allegations of rampant homosexuality" within the department's ranks. While Cochran's loose agreement with the chief prevented him from speaking out directly, it wasn't too hard to figure out to which "high ranking officials in the department" the story could be attributed. Boldly laying out the obvious friction between the "imported"Chief Black and "the department's proven and respected old guard," the article reported the "deep and growing concern" of many on the force that "certain elements" were trying to ferment civil unrest by undermining the solid Christian family values upon which the force was founded. The fact that this logic would be specious even if it could be called logic mattered not a whit to the paper's editors.

That afternoon, as I was getting ready to head for home, I got a call from an obviously badly shaken Lisa. She had come home to find a note taped to their mailbox. The note said "Fag Cops Die".

CHAPTER 9

I'd of course gone over to their apartment immediately after work, on the pretext of just a casual drop-in visit, but of course Lisa had shown Tom the note and Tom knew the minute I walked in the door that she had told me. While Lisa went into the kitchen to get us some coffee, I sat with Tom in the living room.

"You've got to tell someone at the department," I said. "This is going way too far."

"Like who?" he asked, not quite able to keep the sarcasm from his voice.

"Like Lieutenant Richman!" I said.

Tom gave me a small smile and shook his head. "No," he said. "Richman's one of Chief Black's main supporters. That would play right into Cochran's hands—his boys would just love me running to the chief for help."

"Jeezus, Tom, you've got to do something! Do you still have the note?"

Tom shrugged. "No, I tore it up and pitched it, just like the others."

"*The others?!?*" I asked, incredulous. "There've been *others*?"

"A few," he said casually, then turned his attention to Lisa, who was coming into the living room with three cups of coffee on a small tray. Since I knew Tom didn't want to talk about it in front of Lisa, I dropped it. But the last thing my stomach needed just then was a shot of caffeine.

"I talked to dad just before you got here," Tom said in an obvious attempt to distract me.

"Yeah?" I said, forcing my mind off the notes and what Tom was having to go through. "How are the talks going?"

Tom took a sip of his coffee. "Dad thinks the labor team's

about ready to force Joey to take the contract to the members for a vote. Joey's fighting it every inch of the way, but I think the rest of them know it's a good package and it's not going to get any better. Dad is sure Joey blames him, personally. What a psychotic s.o.b."

"Well, as long as the thing gets settled," I said. "I'll bet your dad is ready to call it a day."

Tom nodded. "Everybody is, I think. Except Joey, of course. He wants to tie a string around the moon and hand it to Joe Senior to show him what a big man his little boy is. It ain't gonna happen."

Carol was expected over for dinner, and they asked if I'd like to join them, but I declined, with thanks. If I'd thought I'd have been able to talk to Tom alone later, I'd have stayed, but… I had talked to Bob earlier in the day and he'd asked if I wanted to go over and see the new house—and though he didn't mention Jonathan's name, I knew he thought it would give me a chance to say hello. I was supposed to meet Bob and Mario at Ramón's at 6; they both had to work later, but were going to take some paint and drop cloths over for a couple of the bedrooms. Jonathan had been busy scraping several layers of wallpaper off and preparing the walls for painting and apparently done a pretty good job of it. They needed to take some window measurements for curtains and shades.

I was a couple minutes late—for the first time in living memory—getting to Ramon's, and every inch of the way I'd thought about Tom and wondered what in hell I could do to help him. To realize the answer was: "Nothing" made me feel like shit, and I refused to accept it.

Bob and Mario were waiting when I got there, and though they asked if I wanted to have a drink first, I realized they both had to work later, and I told them I'd hold off until we got back.

On the ride over to the house, they both said how impressed they were with how hard Jonathan had been working, and how much he'd already managed to do.

Then Bob asked how Tom was holding up, and I told them

everything: just how bad things were at the department, Tom's harassment, the notes, and my concern and admiration for him. Bob and I were each other's sounding boards: We could and did talk about anything that bothered us and, by extension, I included Mario into our little club.

"I hear he's been getting a real hard time from the other cops," Mario said, making me wonder how he might possibly have heard it, since Tom surely hadn't said a word, and this is the first I'd said of it to anyone other than a few friends, whom I trusted not to spread rumors. But then I realized that the situation in and of itself was one that would generate a lot of grist for the rumor mills, especially in light of the department's long and proud tradition of blatant homophobia.

"Yeah," Bob said, "I've been hearing the same. You'd have thought this would have started to fade away a little bit, but it hasn't. Almost like someone out there's trying to keep it on high boil."

I sighed. "Well, not surprising, I suppose," I said. "On our side of the fence are the activists and rabble rousers; on the other side are Cochran's boys who are just hoping for the community to do something stupid so they'll have a reason to dump Tom, root out other gays on the force, and blame everything on Chief Black."

Mario nodded. "The match on one side, the dynamite on the other, and the fuse in the middle," he said. "Let's just hope no one lights it."

"Amen to that," I said.

* * *

When Bob turned a corner and then made a turn into a driveway and pulled up in front of a small coach house, I was duly impressed. The yard was overgrown with weeds and there were several fallen tree limbs lying about; the main house, though obviously long neglected, still retained its dignity, rather like a genteel lady fallen on hard times. It was a great old classic

Victorian, complete with several gables and a large "witch's hat"cupola on the corner facing the two streets.

A large, screened back porch faced the side street and led to the kitchen. Just as we were climbing the steps, Mario carrying the paint and Bob and I with assorted bags and boxes of God knows what, the kitchen door opened and a grinning Jonathan appeared.

Lookin' good, Jonathan! I thought before I was able to catch myself and give me my usual cautionary lecture.

"Hi, Dick!" he said brightly as he hurried across the porch to open the screen door. "Need help with anything?" he asked.

I assumed he was talking to Bob and Mario, but his eyes were on me, as was the smile. Hey, so I like having my ego stroked: Sue me!

"I think we got it all, thanks," Bob said as we all passed through the held-open screen door and into the kitchen.

The kitchen was, as in most old Victorians, rather impractically huge, with 12-foot ceilings, glass-doored cupboards so tall their top shelves couldn't be reached without standing on something, a large pantry, and a narrow maid's stairway leading to the second floor.

The rest of the house, I discovered on the guided tour led by Bob and Mario, with Jonathan not two feet behind me, was equally impressive. An open, wood-columned breakfront separated the formal dining room from the front parlor, with a small study off to one side. Hardwood floors, in need of refinishing but with obvious potential. All the baseboards and moldings had been painted over, but Jonathan had, with Mario's help, begun to remove the several layers of paint on the frame of the doorway to the study, revealing the beautiful natural oak underneath. A small foyer with a leaded-glass entry door, a formal parlor with fireplace and slide-into-the-wall doors off the foyer, a beautiful leaded glass window at the top of the front stairway. Three large wallpapered bedrooms—one of which Jonathan had already stripped and was well along in the second—and a maid's room on the second floor and, of course, only one bath, obviously added after the house had been built, with a claw-foot cast iron tub.

They obviously had their work cut out for them.

"This is our first major project," Mario said of the bathroom. "The plumbers and electricians are supposed to be here later this week. Jonathan will have to take sponge baths and use a chamber pot for a couple days...." He'd said this with a straight face, but when he saw Jonathan's look of horror, he grinned and reached out to punch him on the arm. "Serious about the sponge bath, but think we can avoid the chamber pot," he said, to Jonathan's obviously vast relief. "We've decided to use up most of the pantry area for a half-bath. They'll put that in first."

"That's okay," Jonathan said; "maybe I could go over to Dick's when I have to go to the bathroom."

I let that one slide, and Bob said: "Jonathan, why don't you take Dick up and introduce him to Tim and Phil while we get those window measurements? We shouldn't be long."

"Sure," Jonathan said, breaking into yet another grin. "Come on, Dick: I'll show you where I'm staying." I followed him to the kitchen and up the maid's stairway while Bob and Mario took out tape measures and headed for the parlor.

I'd noticed on the guided tour that Jonathan's bed was set up in the maid's room.

"They said I could stay in one of the other bedrooms," Jonathan said as we reached the top of the stairs, "but I asked them if I could use this one. I like it. It looks out on the back yard and nobody can see in. And the TV reception's better in here. I can't get all the stations with just the rabbit ears, but I get the ones I like best."

He led me into the small room which, I noticed now, had in addition to the bed a wooden rocking chair and two TV trays: On one, near the window, was the TV and on the other, beside the bed, was a large glass bowl with two bright orange goldfish. Beside the bowl there was a tall shaker of fish food. He walked over to the fish and I followed.

"That's Phil," he said, pointing to the one closest to the top of the bowl and seeming quite certain as to which was which, "and that's Tim—he's the funny one: You should see him eat! When I can, I want to get them a little castle to put in there so they'll have someplace to go and sleep. And maybe some of that colored sand."

He stood smiling at the fish for a moment, then turned his smile to me and I felt a flush of awkwardness.

"So how are you doing, Jonathan?" I asked to cover it.

He looked at me and his smile softened slightly; I suddenly got a sense something I'd never really noticed before—maybe it was what Phil had referred to when he said there was a lot going on under Jonathan's chatterbox surface.

"I'm doing fine, Dick," he said. "Thank you. You have really nice friends, and they've all been very good to me. But…" He paused as if looking for the right words.

"But?" I prompted.

He gave a small sigh. "But how much longer do I have to stay inside? I don't mind being here, and I like helping Bob and Mario, but…well…I just wish I could go *out* sometimes. You know, just even to get a castle for Tim and Phil, or…"

"I understand," I said, and I did. I had never really gone into the details of why all this was necessary—I didn't want to possibly frighten him, and all this convoluted business with Tom and Cochran and the Chief and the department and Giacomino probably wouldn't mean much to him anyway, since he hadn't been in town long enough to know all the histories. "It really shouldn't be too much longer," I said. "Maybe only another couple weeks. But there's a lot going on, and you're an important key to it all, and we have to keep you out of sight until we can resolve it. Okay?"

He was watching me with just the hint of a smile. "I'll do whatever you want me to," he said, and once more I felt that flush of awkwardness and…something else.

He's nineteen, Hardesty! my conscience chided.

Gee, another part of me responded irritably, *I had no idea. Why don't you keep reminding me every five minutes or so?*

* * *

Gay Pride was just two weekends away, and on Tuesday, the union membership voted to ratify the labor contract over Joey G.'s sullen objections. He'd wanted to drag it out to the bitter end, but apparently had gotten word from union headquarters—and quite probably via his old man in prison—that enough was enough. The bully had once again been beaten by a Brady.

During our Wednesday night gathering at Ramón's, Tim, Phil, Jared, and I agreed to meet for brunch before the parade and all go together. Bob and Mario both had to work, but said they'd be able to make it at least to the parade, since just about everyone in the community would be there, and business at the bars would be very slow until later. Bob told me, as I could have guessed, that Jonathan really wanted to go, and we all discussed the pros and cons and decided to risk it. Bob and Mario would bring him, then take him back immediately after.

I kept in as close touch with Tom as I could, and was increasingly concerned for him. The phone calls continued; there were more notes and threats, and more open hostility—though still with no open confrontations—at work, and I knew it had to be taking its toll on him. He was relieved for his dad, however, when the talks finally ended, and was going to attend a small management-team celebration on Thursday night. We both hoped it would help take some of the tension off, at least for a few hours.

At 1:30 a.m. on Friday morning, my phone rang. I immediately incorporated it into a dream I was having in a vain attempt to ignore it, but forced myself to reach for the phone before the answering machine kicked in. If this was some drunk wanting to talk to Louise, I was going to be mightily pissed.

"Hardesty," I mumbled.

"Dick, it's Mark Richman. Tom Brady's been killed."

CHAPTER 10

How did I react to the news? I honestly can't tell you. I think there is some sort of protective mechanism in the makeup of human beings that kicks in when one is presented with the incomprehensible. I don't really remember what happened after Richman told me. I recall something about he'd been shot while driving home from the celebration with his dad. He was driving through The Central, which was on his way home, shortly after midnight. From what little was known at the time, apparently he was at the top of the small hill on Beech, where Evans crosses Beech, probably stopped at the light. That's the corner Jared and Tim and I had stood…when?…last year?…the year before?…to watch the Gay Pride Parade. Anyway, two guys standing just inside the doorway of Moxie, saying goodbye to friends, heard what they thought was a gunshot. When they got outside, they saw Tom's car moving down Beech. They thought he was just driving away, but then it drifted across the center lane, bounced over the curb on the other side, crossed the sidewalk and smashed into the front of Reef Dwellers at the bottom of the hill. The guys went back into Moxie and called the police, but when they got there, Tom was dead.

Did Richman tell me all this when he called? Or did I learn it afterwards? I honestly don't know. All I did know was that Richman told me Tom was dead.

How do you react to something like that?

I remember somehow getting dressed and running…literally running…to Tom and Lisa's apartment. Lisa was standing on the curb in the front of the building in a robe and pajamas. She looked at me as I ran up to her.

"I'm waiting for Carol," she said, in a little-girl voice. Her eyes searched my face. "Did you know they killed Tom?" she asked calmly, and when I nodded, her face became a shattered mirror, and she fell into my arms and we both stood on the curb and held each other and cried.

* * *

When Carol arrived a minute or two later, I guess it was—she just pulled up in front of the fire hydrant about ten feet away and ran over to us—we went into the building and up to the apartment. The phone was ringing, and Carol went to answer it. I heard her say "No, it's not. She can't talk right now....What? Oh, yes. Just a minute." She held the receiver out to me: "It's for you," she said. I didn't ask who it was, or wonder who knew I was there, or how they knew. I didn't care, but I made sure Lisa was sitting down before I went over to take the phone from Carol, who immediately went over to her.

"Hello?" I heard myself say.

"Mr. Hardesty, this is Captain Offermann. I tried calling your apartment, but Lieutenant Richman told me if you were not home, this is where you would probably be. I know it's very late, but can you come down to my office immediately, please? We have to talk."

"I...sure. I'll be there in 20 minutes."

The phone just touched the cradle when it rang again, and I picked it up. I recognized the voice immediately. "Hello, Mr. Brady," I said. "This is Dick Hardesty. I...I'm so terribly sorry about Tom."

"Thank you, Dick," he said, his voice calm but obviously stressed. "Is Lisa there?"

"Yes, sir," I said. "Carol is with her."

"Would you ask her if I could come over?" he said.

I covered the mouthpiece with one hand and relayed the elder Brady's request. Lisa nodded 'yes' then resumed her sobbing.

"Of course," I said and then, not knowing what else to say and afraid that if I tried to say anything else I might not be able to hold it together, I just hung up.

* * *

Pretend, I told myself on the way to the City Building Annex. *Just pretend this is a story, and you're reading about a character in it. It's not real. None of it's real.*
But it was, and I knew it.
Still, by the time I arrived at the Annex, I had pulled myself together. I *was* pretty good at playing games, and I could play this one. All the streets at that time of night were marked "No Parking Between 2-6 a.m. for Street Cleaning" so I pulled into the alley beside the Annex where the police cars were lined up, and pulled into an empty space. If they wanted to tow me, let 'em.

The lobby of the Annex was pretty quiet, and when I told the guard sitting at the desk by the elevators where I was going, he just nodded and waved me past.

All the offices on Offermann's floor were dark, except one: Offermann's. There was no one in the small reception area, so I went right to Offermann's door and knocked.

"Come," Offermann's voice said, and I turned the knob and went in.

Offermann was behind his desk. In a chair to his right was Lieutenant Richman, and in a chair to his left a man I recognized from photographs: Kensington Black, Chief of Police.

Captain Offermann made the introduction, and the chief rose from his chair to shake my hand. Neither Offermann and I nor Richman and I exchanged handshakes. There was no need to.

Chief Black motioned me to the remaining chair, and I took it as he sat back down himself.

"Tom Brady was a fine man, and a fine police officer," he said. "Any officer's death is a tragic loss to the department. To me, Officer Brady's death is that and more. I've known Tom for a good number of years and have nothing but admiration for him." He looked at me closely to be sure I was following him. I was. "I want you to understand" he continued, " that the recent rumors of his sexual orientation in no way detract from my admiration." I nodded but remained silent.

"Just before you arrived I spoke with Lisa and John Brady to express my personal condolences and those of the entire department. I understand that you and Tom were…close…and had been so since college. Both Captain Offermann and Lieutenant Richman have told me of your role in hastening the retirement of Chief Rourke, and of their dealings with you in the past."

That's very kind of you, Chief, I thought, *but Tom's still dead.*

I glanced at Lieutenant Richman…Mark…who, as always, was looking directly at me.

"There will, of course, be an immediate and full investigation into Officer Brady's death, conducted by Captain Offermann's division. We are operating on the most logical assumption that the shooting was gang related, in retaliation for Officer Brady's killing of two of their members. But we are deeply concerned by the inevitability of rumors sweeping through the gay community that he could have been killed by someone in this department. This is completely unthinkable but hardly unexpected. I realize part of the fault lies with the department—I'm fully aware of what Tom had been going through for the past few weeks, and I am deeply sorry that he was made the pawn in our current inner-departmental difficulties. They were not of his making, as I am sure you are well aware. I feel in some way responsible because his relationship to me merely complicated the circumstances of the shooting incident."

Yeah? my mind asked as I listened to him through some sort of fog. *If you were 'fully aware' of what he was going through, why the hell didn't you do something to stop it? And do you think for one minute that the fact of wearing a police uniform automatically removes anybody from suspicion?*

Though he had no way of knowing what was going on in my mind, he might have read something in my expression even as he continued talking.

"But if...and I emphasize *if*...some link were to be found between his death and *anyone* in this department, I assure you the responsible party or parties will feel the full weight of the law. There will be no cover-up."

"I appreciate that, Chief," I said. "But I'm a little unclear as to exactly why I'm here."

The chief, Offermann, and Richman exchanged glances as if to see who was going to give the reason. Finally, it was the chief who spoke.

"Whether the rumors of Officer Brady's sexual orientation are true or not, the indisputable fact is that as a result of the shooting incident and the fact that he was in a gay bar with you just prior to it, the gay community apparently considers him one of their own. I am correct in saying this, am I not?" He looked directly at me, and I nodded. He returned the nod.

"This is completely understandable, especially considering the long-standing tensions between this department and the gay community up to the point of Chief Rourke's departure. The emergence of the gay community *as* a community and as an economic and political force to be reckoned with has never been fully accepted by many in the department even today. But if indeed ten percent of the population is homosexual, in a city this size that is a very substantial number of citizens who have every right to demand more respect than they have received from us.

"That Officer Brady's sexual orientation should ever have been a problem at all speaks volumes for how far we still have to go before things can be made right."

He paused again, and looked at me thoughtfully.

"Our point here is that we have a potentially explosive situation we are, quite frankly, ill equipped to handle. If the gay community should choose to overlook the obvious probability of a gang retaliation and concentrates its suspicion—as I strongly fear will be the case given the distrust with which the community views the force—that Officer Brady was killed by a member or members of this department because of his alleged homosexuality, things could get completely out of control." I nodded, knowing that what he said was not only true, but an understatement.

"And the fact of the matter is, like it or not, you are our most direct link to the gay community."

And....' my mind prompted.

"We need time," the chief continued. "Time to conduct our investigation. We need the gay community to bear with us, to stay calm. Gay Pride is one week away. We do not want another Stonewall here, though this has the potential to be much worse than Stonewall. Tens of thousands of angry citizens gathered in one place at one time…well, you can see the danger. You were able to get the community leaders together to keep a lid on the rumors after the shooting. We need you to do it again."

"You know who the leaders are," I said. "You could contact them yourselves. Glen O'Banyon, for example…."

"Mr. O'Banyon," Offermann said, "is well known to be a powerful influence in the gay community, but his position as one of the city's leading attorneys puts him on a tightrope. He must maintain at least the illusion of some degree of distance. For us to go directly to him would be to place him in some professional jeopardy, and we could not ask him to do that."

Richman stepped into the discussion for the first time. "Plus the fact that under the current situation, our own objectivity in the matter would be questioned. We feel someone within the gay community has to pull this together. We'll do everything we can to help, but…"

They were right, of course. I turned to Chief Black. "Would you be willing to talk to the leaders, if I can get them together again?" I asked. "I realize the pressures you are under from within the department."

Chief Black nodded. "Of course I would. Tom Brady's death, and its implications for the entire city is far more important than my concerns over inner-departmental bickering. Get them together, and soon, and I'll be there if they want me. But we've got to act immediately before things get out of control."

I looked from one to the other in turn. They were all looking directly at me.

"I'll do my best," I said. Then, after another long pause, asked: "Is there anything else right now?"

Richman looked at me. "One more thing," he said.

I turned to him, but said nothing.

"Just as we have to ask the gay community to restrain itself, we have to ask the same of you. It's only natural for you to feel obligated to try to find who killed him on your own. But you're much too close to this one. Please, give us a chance to do our job first. Just give us time, okay?"

I found myself nodding. "Okay," I said slowly, knowing they were right, but not knowing if I could do it. "Can I go now?"

In unison, they all nodded without speaking. I got up from my chair, still quite sure all of this wasn't really happening. The others stood, too, and I went around and shook each of their hands, part of my mind idly observing how odd, but how deeply ingrained, these little rituals of civilization really were.

* * *

I think I slept some when I got home, but I'm not sure. It certainly didn't feel like it when I got up at 7:00 and stumbled into the kitchen to make coffee, pausing only to turn the TV on to the morning local news. Tom's ("A decorated police officer's") death was of course the lead story. I didn't want to hear it, but left it on. The phone rang as I pressed the "On" button on the coffee maker.

"Hardesty," I said as I picked up the phone, aware that my head felt like it was full of lead bars.

"Dick, it's Bob. We just heard the news." There was a pause, then: "What can we say? Is there anything we can do?"

"As a matter of fact," I began....

* * *

Bob agreed to call Bar Guild president Mark Graser and some of the other bar owners who had attended the first meeting. We agreed on the urgency of getting everyone together immediately: that evening, if possible. We arbitrarily picked 7 o'clock as a time, and the M.C.C. for a place unless we notified them otherwise. It was presumptive of me to assume the church would be available, but I suspected that, under the circumstances, there wasn't likely to be much of a problem. I told him I'd probably be home all day, and to get back to me when he could.

I didn't even hang up the phone, just pushed the disconnect button and lifted it again, dialing the M.C.C. and, when I got the machine, asked for Tony Mason to call me as soon as he got the message. I then immediately dialed Haven House, in case he might be there. He was.

"Good morning, Dick," he said when I identified myself. "What can I do for you this morning?" Obviously, he had not yet heard the news. I quickly filled him in and then said:

"Can we use the church tonight for a meeting? At 7:00? I know it's short notice, but time is a vital factor here. We'll probably need the whole church—the upstairs, I mean."

"Of course," he said. "Of course. We have a couple activities scheduled for this evening, but I'm sure we can either move them downstairs or reschedule them. I suspect this news is going to hit the whole community pretty hard. I hope it doesn't overreact."

"That's exactly why we're calling the meeting," I said. "And I hope you'll be there to say a few words. We're going to need all the help we can get."

"I'll be glad to do whatever I can, of course," he said. "I'll undoubtedly be hearing from members of the congregation during the day, and I'll do my best to urge them to spread the word to remain calm." There was a slight pause and I was about to say goodbye when he said: "I know you and Officer Brady were good friends, Dick, and I'm so sorry for your loss. Please relay my condolences to his wife."

From the time I'd left Lisa and Carol early in the morning, I'd been so busy that my own feelings had been shoved into a corner. But when Tony said that, I felt a tightening in my throat.

Later, Hardesty, my mind-voice said gently. *Later.* I knew instinctively that the only way I was going to be able to keep my word to the police not to go rushing off on my own was to concentrate fully on the situation at hand.

"Thanks, Tony," I said, clearing my throat. "And thanks for being there for us."

"Always," he said. "'Bye for now."

I hung up the phone and went looking for the phone book, to call Rainbow Flag and the other gay papers when the door buzzer rang.

Jeezus! Enough already! I thought. I had no idea who it could be, but automatically hit the lobby door buzzer and went back to looking for the phone book. Finding it, I started thumbing through to the "R"s when I heard a knock.

I opened it to find Phil…and Jonathan!

"What…?" I started to say, but Phil was hugging me, and then Jonathan.

"I tried to call you," Jonathan said, "but your line was busy, so I called Phil, and he came and got me." I knew Bob and Mario hadn't had the phones installed yet, so that meant Jonathan had to have left the house to call. Under other conditions I'd have been angry with him for putting himself at risk, however remote, but…

Phil shrugged. "I was getting ready to come over here anyway," he said, "but Jonathan was calling from a pay phone just to ask if I'd heard from you, and when he said he was going to walk over because he didn't have enough money for the bus, I figured…."

Friends. Remember?

"Well, I'm glad to see you," I said. "Both of you."

Jonathan smiled, then apparently thought a smile wasn't appropriate, and cut it off like a knife.

"Tim called just before I left," Phil said, "and I told him

where I'd be. He said he'd call as soon as he could—as soon as he knew anything."

"Can I make you some coffee, Dick?" Jonathan asked. "Did you have any breakfast? I can make you something."

I realized I hadn't even had a cup of coffee yet. "I made a pot when I got up," I said, "but never got around to drinking it. You want to go get some for us? Cups are in the cupboard right over the coffee maker."

"Do you want anything to eat?" he asked.

I shook my head. "I'm not hungry," I said, "but thanks."

He started to smile again, thought better of it, and went quickly into the kitchen.

I still had the phone book in my hand, and went back to looking through the "R"s, when Phil stepped over and took it out of my hand.

"Let's sit down for a minute," he said, gently. "You don't have to call anyone right this instant."

Jonathan brought two cups of coffee into the living room and handed one to me, then to Phil. Having done so, he looked a little at a loss as to what to do next.

"Aren't you going to have any?" I asked, and his face brightened—though again he was obviously trying hard not to seem unaware of the somber atmosphere. "Sure," he said. "Thanks." He was gone a minute, then reappeared, standing in the doorway, again not sure of what to do.

"Come sit down," I said, and he came and sat on the couch, but at the opposite end, as though he didn't think I'd want him too close to me.

Though I knew Jonathan wasn't really aware of everything that was happening, or why, I tried not to leave him out as I told Phil everything. The call, the meeting with the chief, Offermann, and Richman, the urgency of getting the community leaders together.

"The main thing we have to get across," I said, "is that the community can't just react until we know the facts, and we have to give the chief and the others time to find out what really happened. We can't just assume it was another cop who killed Tom…even though that's where I'd place my bets right now. He'd been getting death threats…."

The phone rang again.

"Do you want me to answer it?" Jonathan asked, but I shook my head and got up to answer it.

"Hardesty."

"Dick, it's Tim. I've got some really bad news."

What could possibly be worse than Tom's being dead? I wondered. "Yeah?" I said, steeling myself for whatever it was.

"We got the bullet that…that killed him. It's from a .38," Tim said, and I felt the anger rise. While a .38 was a common weapon, it was also the standard-issue duty weapon of the police department.

When I didn't say anything, Tim added. "One bullet. To the left temple. Death was instantaneous. From the position and angle of the wound, he was probably looking straight ahead. There were no powder burns, which means the killer was at least 5 feet away—probably in a car pulled up beside him at the stoplight. He might very well not even known it was coming." There was another long pause, and then: "I'm sorry, Dick. I really am."

"I know, Tim," I said. "Thanks. Did you want to talk to Phil?"

"No, that's okay. I've got to get back to work. I'll talk to him later."

* * *

The day flew by. I was on the phone constantly. I remembered that at the first meeting, we'd asked everyone who attended to sign in with their names and phone numbers. I had the list at the office, and Phil volunteered to go down and get it for me. I gave him the keys, told him where I *thought* the list was; I gave him about ten alternative places to look if it wasn't, too, and he left.

I called Lieutenant Richman to tell him of the time and location of the meeting and he assured me that Chief Black would be there.

If I'd been in much of a state to do any pondering or speculating about things other than the immediate situation with Tom and the fuse that would definitely be lit if word got out that he had been killed with the same kind of gun used by just about every policeman in the city, I might have given a bit more time to wonder exactly why Jonathan was here. But I didn't: I just accepted it and, on some not-too-deeply hidden level, appreciated it. He didn't talk my arm off: He was very quiet, actually. I got the feeling that he simply wanted to be with me, and that was very sweet of him.

When Phil returned with the list, I called everyone on it I'd not already called. Several of them had already spoken to either Bob, or Mark Graser, or Glen O'Banyon. All expressed a great deal of sorrow over Tom's death and apprehension over what it might result in. There was a great deal of anger, too. Even without knowing about the weapon that had killed Tom, many automatically assumed he had been killed by a homophobic fellow officer.

Phil had picked up copies of all the papers which, if not headlining the killing, ran the story on the front page. The two more journalistically responsible papers merely reported the facts—what few were known—mentioning Tom's having been at the head of his academy class, his having saved his fellow officer trapped in the burning squad car, and having come to the rescue of a number of "citizens" being attacked by gang members, and the fact that the police were pursuing the probability that the killing was a gang retaliation. All respectful, all dignified.

But, ah, the Journal-Sentinel: Somehow they had managed to get a close-up photo of Tom's car, looking in the driver's side open door, and showing the hood partially through the wall and smashed display window of Reef Dwellers. The banner headline shouted: "Gay Cop Shot Dead!" While the accompanying article was almost totally devoid of fact, it was of course dripping with innuendo, including making a point of mentioning that the killing had occurred in "the gay area of town" where "gay bars abound." It of course did not mention that so did gay bookstores and gay clothing stores and gay record shops and gay restaurants and...

You're preaching to the choir, Hardesty, my mind said.

* * *

We...Phil, Tim, Jonathan and I...arrived at the M.C.C. at 6:30 and already there were several cars in the church's parking lot. I'd thought of taking Jonathan back to Bob and Mario's, but he wanted to come and I figured 'what the hell, he's as safe here as anywhere.' I could tell he wanted to run next door to Haven House to say hello to some of his former housemates and, after asking if I was sure I didn't mind, he went. I was sure that with Chief Black expected, not even Cochran's boys would dare make a move on Jonathan, even if they knew he was there.

While none of us had intended for the straight media to be there, a van from Channel 6 pulled up in front of the church, and I was sure representatives from at least one of the newspapers were there, too. Everything had happened so fast, we had no way of really knowing who was supposed to be there and who was not. There had been something like 42 people at our first meeting. I expected we'd have quite a few more for this one. But I certainly was not prepared for the crowd that had already gathered by 6:45.

We'd moved around to the front of the church to see who was arriving. Earlier, Lee Taylor of the Gay Business League had agreed to open the meeting, and he and Glen O'Banyon had suggested I introduce Chief Black. I didn't think that was a good idea at all, and suggested that Lee Taylor introduce Lieutenant Richman, whom I was pretty sure would be accompanying the chief: Richman could introduce the chief.

At ten till seven, I checked with Bob and Mark Graser and

Glen O'Banyon and together we went through the crowd looking for those we knew had been specifically invited and urging them to go into the church and find a seat while they still could.

Jonathan made his way to me and I told him to go inside with Tim and Mario to save seats for Bob and Phil and me. As I was saying a few words to Charles Conrad of Rainbow Flag, I was surprised to see Jared coming toward me. As Charles climbed the stairs into the church, I turned to a very sober-faced Jared. We exchanged a handshake and a hug.

"I'm sorry, Dick," he said. He didn't have to say anything more. Looking around at the still-growing crowd, he shook his head: "It looks like we're really in for it, doesn't it?"

I nodded. "I'm afraid so," I said, and suggested he go inside and find a seat with the rest of the gang, then quickly sought out Glen O'Banyon, who was talking with a woman I recognized as the organizer of the Gay Pride parade. I motioned to him and he came over immediately.

"I don't know if we can do this," I said, "but I suggest we post a couple people at the doors. There's a TV crew out there, and I saw a couple still cameras, I think, indicating the papers are here. I think we should keep the cameras out, at least. This is going to be enough of a circus without having people worry that their pictures are going to be splashed across the papers and TV screens."

"You're right," he said. "Let me go find Reverend Mason. It's his church, and he has the authority to keep the cameras out."

By five minutes to seven, the church was completely full, and there were probably 20 to 50 others standing in the doorway and on the stairs. Tony had, indeed, stood in the doorway and refused entry to cameras and the TV crew, which did not make them overly happy. Two other people with cameras were spotted among those in the church, and they were asked to either leave the cameras in the church office or to leave. Both gave their cameras to the Reverend with only minimal objections.

At exactly 7:00, Reverend Mason went to the pulpit, and I

moved to the side door to one side of the altar and went out, circling around the church, to wait for Chief Black's arrival. We had all agreed it would be less disruptive if he could come in through the side, rather than having to walk, like a brideless father, all the way down the aisle to the pulpit.

Fortunately or unfortunately, I was still in too much a state of semi-numbness to be nervous, though I realized that, as Jared had said, this was rapidly turning into something a lot bigger than any of us had anticipated.

At two minutes after seven, two squad cars pulled up in front of the church. The TV crew and one or two still cameramen from the newspapers, who had had nothing much to do in the past several minutes, scrambled toward the squad cars, from which Chief Black, Captain Offermann, and Lieutenant Richman emerged. Chief Black's driver remained in the car. The last thing in the world that I wanted was to see myself on the evening news or in the papers. Richman spotted me, and I turned and walked back around the church to the side door as they followed, saying as little as possible to the insistent reporters.

We gathered just inside the door, on the steps leading to the stage and the altar. Lee Taylor noticed us out of the corner of his eye, and wrapped up his remarks, which from the little I heard and the details given me later, centered on the necessity, if the gay community expected to be accepted into the mainstream, of proving that it could act and react responsibly; that to do otherwise would only prove to our enemies that we were not deserving of inclusion.

"Before we hear from the chief," Lee said, "I have to emphasize that he is here out of concern for the community's reaction over the death of Officer Brady. This is not the time for a town meeting or a press conference. The chief will not be taking questions. Tom Brady has been dead less than 24 hours; so while we all have many questions, there simply has been too little time to find answers. We have got to keep that in mind, and give the chief the time he needs to find those answers."

He then introduced Lieutenant Mark Richman, and Richman, Offermann and Chief Black moved up onto the stage and crossed it to the podium in total silence. I remained on the steps until they had completely crossed the stage, then went through the small door at the foot of the stage which led to the auditorium. Fortunately, Jonathan, Bob, and the rest were seated in the first two rows, on my side of the room. Jonathan saw me and quickly scooted aside making room for me to sit, which I did. Richman stepped to the podium, introduced himself as being in the department's Administrative Division, among whose duties was outreach to the various minorities in the city. He acknowledged the department's long history of discrimination against the gay community, pointed briefly to several steps that had been taken to rectify it, and promised continued and intensified steps in that direction.

He then introduced Captain Karl Offermann as head of the department's homicide division, who limited his remarks to the fact that his presence was intended to show the department's determination to relentlessly pursue Officer Brady's killer or killers until he or they were found and convicted.

"The hope of your police department," he said, "and the hope of the community of which you are all members lies in the ability of our new chief to do the job to which he was appointed. There can be no progress without his leadership, and there can be no progress without your cooperation. With that said, it is my privilege to introduce you to your, my, and our Chief of Police, Kensington Black."

There was some polite applause. Most of the members of the audience appreciated and recognized the significance of the chief's coming to speak to them, but there was too much skepticism, too much anger and sadness and confusion to give him the kind of reception he deserved.

He seemed oblivious to the lack of response.

"I knew Tom Brady long before he was Officer Tom Brady," the chief began, and it was immediately apparent that he was a seasoned and persuasive speaker. "His wife, as most of you know, is my god-daughter. I myself have three daughters, but no sons. But if I had a son, I could not have hoped for a finer one than Tom."

A couple members of the crowd applauded softly, and I could sense that his words had had an impact on the rest.

"As chief of police, I am acutely aware of the tensions which have existed between the police department and the gay community, and I apologize on behalf of the department for its past wrongs against you. I am aware, too, in light of this long-standing distrust of the department, of rumors within the community as to who might be responsible for Officer Brady's death. Rumors unfortunately tend to totally override logic: In this case the more logical probability is that the killing was a gang-related retaliation for the deaths of two of their members and, as a member of the Gang Control Unit, Officer Brady had ample opportunity to make other enemies among the members of numerous gangs.

"Still, I can assure you that we will not dismiss any possibilities out of hand. Our homicide division, led by Captain Offermann, is working around the clock on every aspect of the investigation, and with our Internal Affairs department and Gang Control Unit, to which a number of additional officers have been assigned for this case.

"In short, I am here today to tell you that I do not know who killed Tom Brady, and to ask you to give me the time to find out. I have not been chief of police long enough to expect your trust automatically, but I most sincerely hope you will give me the chance to earn it. And I swear to each and every one of you that the person or persons who caused the death of this outstanding police officer and outstanding young man, no matter who they may be, *will* be found and *will* be punished to the full extent of the law. And when that has been done, I promise I will work diligently to bridge the tremendous gap that has too long existed between the police department and the community you represent. But for right now, our priority—yours and mine—is to not let rumor stand in the way of finding out who killed Tom

Brady. I ask you for the time to do my job. Thank you."

The applause as he stepped back to join Richman and Offermann was much warmer, though far from overwhelming. Chief Black was right: He could not expect the community's trust: He was going to have to earn it. I think he knew that very well. As for his request for time….

Despite Lee's clearly stating that the chief wouldn't be answering any questions, as the three men were leaving the stage, several people in the crowd, including a few I recognized as the community's most militant activists, and one or two I did not recognize but assume were probably reporters, started yelling questions, but the chief's group made no response and went down the side steps and out the door.

Tony Mason stepped quickly to the pulpit and raised his hand to silence the protesters and, as soon as his voice could be heard over the din, asked for a moment of silence in Tom's memory, which effectively silenced the entire room. When the moment was over, the chief was long gone, and the meeting ended with Tony calling once more for the entire community to act responsibly. "And as to the community's long and difficult history with the police department," he concluded, "we should all keep in mind that Tom Brady wore the uniform of that department, and it was to it he had hoped to devote his life."

As the crowd dissolved, Bob, Mario, Tim, Phil, Jared, Jonathan, and I stood by the stage with a group of community leaders, who agreed the chief's appearance had done a lot to show the department's sincerity in dealing with the issue of Tom's death, and in recognizing the power of the gay community. It was definitely a milestone in police-community relations. But none of us knew if it would be enough.

* * *

Jonathan wanted to come home with me. "You shouldn't be alone right now," he said as the others were talking among themselves. "I won't get in your way, I promise. But maybe I can help you somehow, if you need anything. I won't ask you to…ah…."

I understood what he was saying, and I put my hand on his shoulder. "I appreciate that, Jonathan, I really do. But I'll be fine, and Bob and Mario really need you."

He looked disappointed, but I knew full well I was a little too vulnerable right then to be tempted by a cute and willing young guy. It wouldn't be fair to either of us, and especially to him.

* * *

Saturday's papers and morning news all made note of the meeting without making it a big deal, and carried separate short articles on Tom's death, the plans for the funeral to be held Tuesday at noon, and the fact that the police were investigating the gang-retaliation theory of the shooting. Except for the Journal-Sentinel, which had obviously hitched its star to the rumors and sensationalism. "Chief Caves In to Gays!" the cover headline…well, I was going to say 'screamed', but the Journal-Sentinel's headlines never did anything else. And "a reliable source" in the department reported that a large percentage of the force was planning to boycott Tom's funeral.

I'd picked up all the papers on my way back from Lisa's. She wasn't home, and it occurred to me that she must be staying with Carol, just to get away from the phones. I called Carol as soon as I got back home, and Lisa was indeed there. Tom's dad had offered her a suite at the Montero, but she'd naturally preferred to be with Carol. I wanted to call Tom's dad myself, but didn't really know what to say. If he'd not been aware of the rumors of Tom's being gay before Tom died, he certainly had to be now. I determined that I would definitely call him before the funeral, but right now….

Shortly after I arrived home, the phone rang. I thought it might be Jared asking if I'd like to go to brunch, but I remembered him saying at the meeting that he was off to Carrington to see about renting a small house and probably wouldn't be back until Sunday afternoon.

So I was somewhat surprised, when I picked up the phone, to hear Mark Richman's voice.

"I suppose you saw the Journal-Sentinel this morning?" he asked.

"Yeah," I said, "though I resented having to buy that rag. Is there any truth to the part about the boycott?"

I heard him sigh. "I don't know, but I wouldn't be a bit surprised if Cochran wasn't orchestrating something like that. His brother-in-law works for the Journal-Sentinel, I understand. But I spoke to Captain Offermann this morning and he had gotten a call from Chief Black saying that the chief is issuing a departmental memo tomorrow. He is making it clear that the circumstances of Officer Brady's death qualify it to be considered a death in the line of duty, and that any uniformed officer not on patrol duty at the time of the funeral would be expected to attend. He also leaves little doubt that anyone who does not attend will be required to have a damned good excuse as to why they weren't there."

He was quiet a moment, then sighed again. "I probably shouldn't be saying this, but Jesus, to think it would come to this! A policeman's funeral is almost a sacred thing in the department. For anyone to boycott or instigate the boycott of a fellow officer's funeral would be…inconceivable. There is already enough tension in the ranks and there are more than enough truly good cops not to take a boycott quietly. This would be close to declaring civil war within the department, and it would be an insult the gay community could hardly overlook—and who could blame them?"

"I'll spread the word about the memo," I said. "I really do think the majority of the community believes Chief Black is trying to do the right thing, and are on his side. But *somebody* is obviously on a kamikaze mission to take him out at all costs."

"Thanks, Dick. I…we…appreciate it. I'll keep you posted if anything else develops, and you have my home phone number. Don't be afraid to use it."

When we hung up, I went to get the list Mark Graser, Lee Taylor, Glen O'Banyon and I had made up after the meeting, of key leaders to call for constant updating on the situation. None of us, when we called the meeting with Chief Black, had any idea it would mushroom to the size it did. We did not want to make that mistake again.

I was glad I'd volunteered to take the list to my office and make copies for all of us, or I wouldn't have had it available after Richman's call.

I went to the kitchen, made another pot of coffee, and sat down with the list and the telephone....

* * *

Don't ask where the rest of weekend or Monday went: I couldn't tell you. I somehow found myself in the totally unwanted position of liaison between not only Lieutenant Richman and community leaders, but between the leaders themselves. Endless phone calls; endless visits to and visits from people on our contacts list; endless rumors needing attempts at damage control; several visits with Lisa and Carol, and a long phone call with Tom's dad, who would be returning home to Florida on Wednesday with Tom's body, for burial beside his mother and brother. Tom's sister had flown out for the funeral. Under any other circumstance, I would have really looked forward to meeting her. But....

Though the issue of Tom's sexuality was never mentioned during our conversation, it didn't have to be. His dad knew; he'd probably always known. And while I'd fairly much steeled myself against my own emotions, I found I was totally unable to *not* respond to the emotions of others. Talking with Tom's dad practically pulled my heart out. To have lost two sons he worshiped...I could not comprehend how he could hold up as bravely as he did.

Like father, like son; like son, like father, I thought.

Bob and Mario called late Sunday afternoon, I remember,

and asked if I'd like to go out to dinner. When I told them I was practically nailed to the phone, they asked if it would be okay for them to bring dinner over to my place, and I readily agreed. I needed some sort of break, for sure. I suppose I could have gone out, but the steady flow of phone calls, to and from, allowed us all to keep close track of what was going on. The Journal-Sentinel's story on the boycott would probably have been a lot more damaging had I not been able to relay Lieutenant Richman's report of the chief's memo. Still, it was clear that if a boycott should take place, all hell might very well break lose.

Was it just Tom's death that brought everything to the point it was? No, not really…not totally. The current situation was a distillation of the conflict between the police and the community throughout the years. The community needed a hero, and the shooting incident outside Ruthie's had provided it. Tom represented something to the community—a sense of progress, an odd sense of being a part of the mainstream; the Cochran element of the department represented the status quo which had existed for longer than anyone could remember—a status quo which was no longer acceptable to a community which realized it didn't *have* to be pushed around anymore.

The situation was a Grimm's Fairy Tale; an Aesop's Fable; a morality play. And I was in the middle of it all.

* * *

And as I thought that, I was forced to address the one thing I'd tried so hard to repress since the night of Tom's death and my meeting with Richman, Offermann, and Chief Black: What in the hell was I *doing* about all this? I mean, really *doing*? I'm a p.i., for chrissakes! I'm supposed to be out there *solving* cases, not just sitting around with my finger up my nose! And if I can find out who killed people I don't even know, why the hell wasn't I out there looking for whoever killed Tom?

I recognized, of course, when I let myself look at the situation more logically, that this case was very different from any other I'd ever dealt with. For one thing, it wasn't really a "case" at all—it was a murder, yes; it was a mystery, yes, but it was also a part of my life like no "case" could possibly be. I was involved on a totally different level.

And I was in fact lucky that the circumstances were totally different here; there was just too much going on to allow myself to give in to my own feelings. Trying to help keep the lid on a potentially explosive situation had turned into almost a 24-hour-a-day effort. The "usual suspects" pool wasn't really there: Tom was a cop, and chances are that despite what Richman and the others might want to believe, he was killed by another cop. But I had to let Richman and Offermann have first shot: there's no way I could start sniffing around without getting my nose flattened by slamming doors.

Gang members? A possibility, but also a world in which I hadn't a clue as to how to work my way around. There was always a way, of course.

I decided, with a hell of a lot more reluctance than I can possibly convey, that I simply had to concentrate on first things first: preventing an open war between the police and the gay community, giving the police a chance to do their job, and taking the time and effort to put myself in a mental state where I could, if the time came, set out on my own without the emotional baggage I was carrying at the moment. I'd give the police the time Richman asked for, but it wasn't an open-ended agreement.

I'd be a p.i. solving a murder later. Right now….

* * *

Maybe that's why I was so relieved to hear the buzzer ring and, when I opened the door for Bob and Mario, to see Jonathan with them.

We ate the pizza they'd brought, and drank some beer—luckily I had some coke in the fridge for Jonathan—and talked (between phone calls) and tried to pretend it was just a night of pizza and beer. When they left—I have no idea what time—Jonathan did not ask if he could stay, though I could see he wanted to. A little bit too much of me wanted him to, too. But I just couldn't do that to him, and it had nothing whatever to do with his age: I hadn't really had a chance to get to know him, but I could tell he really wanted someone and because I had helped him when he needed it, it was logical that someone would be me. The age thing was becoming less and less important to me, but if I were to in effect lead him on and then find out that it couldn't go anywhere…well, as I say, I just couldn't do that to him.

Probably all this introspection was a good thing, because it took my mind off Tom for awhile.

* * *

Lisa had asked me accompany her and Carol to the funeral, which was to be held at St. Dominic's Cathedral about three blocks from the City Building Annex. The body was to be brought by hearse from Stenson's Funeral Home to the Annex, from which point it would be accompanied to St. Dominic's for the service, with Tom's fellow officers either lining the route or, if the boycott materialized, however many officers did show up would march behind the hearse from the Annex to the church.

Have I mentioned that I do not like funerals? I think I have. Of course, outside of the movie "Harold and Maude," I can't recall anyone who did enjoy them. Still, the only way I could get through them was to simply turn my mind off the minute the service started and turn it back on when I considered it safe to do so.

Tom's father and sister had arranged to pick us up in a limo. We would go directly to the church and await the arrival of the body.

It was going to be a very, very long day.

* * *

The boycott did *not* materialize—at least not in significant numbers—either because of Chief Black's memo or simply because the vast majority of the force were decent men paying last respects to one of their own. As we drove past Warman Park on the way to the church, the streets were lined on both sides by I have no idea how many people: Gays, straights, the curious. I saw at least two large rainbow flags being held by groups on the curb, and spotted a number of smaller, hand-held flags not being waved…just held. I was told later that, as the hearse drove down the street, those with flags simply raised them over their heads in tribute. And as the hearse passed the uniformed officers lining the route, they fell in step behind the hearse and marched with it to St. Dominic's, where they formed into long ranks in the street, facing the cathedral.

Lisa, Tom's father, his sister Maureen, Carol, and I were in the front pew. We sat in leaden silence until the organ announced the arrival of the coffin. We all stood and…I shut my mind off.

It was, from what I understand, a very…well, one can hardly use the word "nice" when talking about a funeral: I can't, anyway. But it was very dignified and I'm sure very comforting to Tom's dad and sister, who were both devout Catholics. I'm sure Tom would have been impressed. Jake Janzer, the officer whose life Tom had saved from the burning squad car, said a few words, which I of course did not allow myself to hear, but which made Lisa cry. Then Chief Black got up and said, I understand, pretty much what he had said at the meeting at the M.C.C.

Tom's dad got up and read a poem Tom had written in college. I remember when he wrote it, and I'd never forgotten it. And while I would not let myself listen to Tom's dad's voice as he read it, I saw it clearly in my mind. It was called "Questions of Valor."

Had we been aboard the **Birkenhead**
could we have held our ground;
giving up our chance to live
so the weaker would not drown?

Were we in the **Titanic**'s *band*
as her stern rose in the air,
could we have kept on playing,
to soothe the doomed souls there?

If we were one of the Sullivans,
five inseparable brothers,
could we choose, as the **Juneau** *sank,*
to perish with the others?

To give one's self for others
is more than bravery:
It illumines words like "selfless,"
And defines humanity.

And then it was over, and when we were back in the limousine, I turned my mind back on. Well, not totally, I guess, because I'm really not too sure on the rest of the day. Needless to say, it passed.

* * *

Tuesday's evening newscasts, I heard, covered the funeral not as a lead story, but in a very responsible manner, as did Wednesday morning's papers. Even the Journal-Sentinel seemed, if one just gave a quick glance at the headline ("Honoring Their Own"), to be showing some journalistic responsibility. But the photo which occupied 2/3 of the front page was not of the ranks of uniformed officers following the hearse or lined in front of the cathedral, or of Chief Black speaking from the pulpit. It was a color photo of one of the groups standing at curbside holding a large gay flag.

I'd managed to oversleep by nearly an hour on Wednesday morning; not that I needed it, of course. But now that the funeral was over, and the boycott had not occurred, and the community had not been slapped in the face, and the police department had not fragmented, I was confident that Offermann and the pro-Black faction could turn their full attention to finding Tom's killer.

I also felt fairly confident that my phone would finally stop ringing except for the normal back-and-forth with friends. I even managed to fool myself into thinking that what I'd been going through the past few days, from the minute I got Richman's call telling me of Tom's death, was just something like a severe bout of emotional flu, and I'd be my old self in no time. Then as I walked into the lobby of my office building, I glanced at the clock and felt as though I'd been kicked in the stomach. It took me a second to figure out why, and then I remembered: It was at precisely that moment that the plane carrying Tom's dad, his sister Maureen, and Tom's body was scheduled to take off. And I realized, maybe for the first time, that Tom was really dead and....

Shhhhhh! my mind said quietly. *It'll be all right.* All right eventually, maybe, I knew; but never the same again.

* * *

The Gay Pride parade was only four days away, and while Tom's death would undoubtedly make it somewhat less joyous and exuberant, and the tension with the police would remain high until his killer was caught, it would be a chance for the community to relax a bit, which it very much needed.

That, of course, was my hope until I stopped Thursday morning at the lobby newsstand on my way to my office and saw the Journal-Sentinel's latest depth charge: "Police Gun Killed Gay Cop!"

My immediate reaction was to wonder how in hell they had

found out about that: I was sure the police would not have released such potentially damaging information. I wasn't about to spend a cent of my money on buying the rag to find out if it was total speculation or if it was attributed to the ubiquitously anonymous "reliable source" in the department.

When I got to the office, I had a message to call Mark Richman, which I immediately did.

"You saw the Sentinel?" he asked.

"Yeah." I didn't tell him Tim had told me that it had been a .38 which had killed Tom. "Is it true—though I know the words 'true' and Journal-Sentinel are almost never used in the same sentence."

"Between us, it was a .38 slug, yes. But we don't know that it came from a department service revolver. We're zeroing in on the gang connection—retaliation for Brady's having killed two gang members, any run-ins he may have had while on the Gang Control Unit. But we are very concerned about how this might appear to the gay community. We'd hoped the funeral, following after Chief Black's being at the M.C.C. meeting, would bring the community to our side. Will you keep your ear very close to the rail on this one? If it might trigger a strong reaction from the community, we'd like to be prepared for it."

I wasn't quite sure what he meant by being "prepared for it," and I didn't think I'd like it if I was sure.

"I'll definitely keep you posted," I said. "How is the investigation going?"

"We're on it," he said, a little noncommittally.

"Anything solid?"

"Not yet," he said. "We've been tracing Officer Brady's movements since he left his father at the Montero. We know what time he left and though it's impossible to be completely accurate, taking into consideration the light traffic flow at that time of night, we've timed as closely as we could how long it would have taken him. He had a full tank of gas, so we think he may have made a quick stop either for gas or to get something to eat, and if he did, maybe somebody saw something. We're checking every gas station and convenience store along the route. We do have a witness who saw a late-model car going pretty fast down Evans near Beech at about the same time, but no make, specific model, or other features other than it was *not* a squad car."

Not a marked one, anyway, my mind observed, but I didn't say anything.

And I for one didn't exactly relate gang members and late model cars.

* * *

At 2:36 a.m. Thursday morning, my phone rang.

Oh, Jeezus, not again! I thought, instantly awake.

"Dick, it's Jared," the voice said. "You might want to come down to The Central."

"What's going on?" I asked, considering all the possibilities, none of them good.

"The new police substation's on fire. It looks bad."

"I'll be right there," I said, and hung up, hurriedly getting out of bed and looking for my pants.

And what the hell was I supposed to do when I got there? God only knows: I didn't. All I knew was that lately my whole life had become a series of knee-jerk responses.

The substation was at the corner of Ash and Beech, and as I turned down Ash I could see the flames from several blocks away. A police car, strobes flashing, blocked the street a block before Beech, and I turned the corner and parked as soon as I could. Despite the late hour, there was a large crowd on Beech, mostly standing against the buildings as close to the fire as the police would let them get. Several fire trucks were pouring huge streams of water onto the two-story substation which was completely engulfed in flame, and another truck several doors down was trying to put out a sizeable blaze on the roof of a clothing store, apparently started by sparks showering down from the substation fire.

I spotted Jared and made my way through the crowd to him. He saw me, nodded, and returned his attention to the fire. Suddenly one of the fire engines gave three sharp blasts of its horn and began to back up quickly, running over one of its own hoses and pulling others as the firemen standing closest to the building moved back into the street. With a muffled roar, first the roof caved in and then the entire front of the building collapsed onto the sidewalk.

I made it a point to look carefully around the crowd to see if there was anyone there I knew or recognized—I was especially looking for guys I knew to be militant activists. I was mildly relieved not to see any.

"What happened?" I asked Jared as the firemen moved again toward the fire, continuing their efforts, though it was clear there was now nothing to save. The fire on the clothing store roof appeared to be under control and the billowing smoke was changing from black to white.

"I was at Pals earlier," he said, "and picked up a trick around 11. We went over to his place—he lives just down the block on Carter. I was headed back to my car around 2:20 when I saw smoke coming out of the substation. I knew Coffee & was open, so I ran over there to have them call the fire department, but a couple guys already had, and the trucks and squad cars started coming a minute or so later."

"I just hope it wasn't arson," I said, knowing full well the odds were 99.9 to 0.1 that it was.

Jared pointed to the parking garage construction site directly across Ash from the station. The wind had shifted slightly, clearing enough of the smoke away to show what someone had spray-painted in 6-ft high letters on the high wooden fence surrounding the site: "No 'Fags' on the Force, No Cops in The Central!"

Shit!

CHAPTER 11

I'd noticed, while watching both the fire and the crowd, the arrival of more and more uniformed police. When I decided it was time to head home and was walking back to my car, I saw that where one squad car had been blocking Ash a block up from Beech, there were now two more, facing in opposite directions on the side street. As I passed the first car, an officer stopped me.

"Where are you going?" he asked, not threateningly, but with a definite no-nonsense tone.

Normally, I'd have started bristling right then and there, but I took the question in light of the overall situation, and understood.

"Home," I said.

He was joined by another officer from one of the cars on the side street.

"You live around here?" the second officer asked.

"No," I said. "I'm going to my car."

The second officer took his flashlight and shined it in my face, though there was plenty of light from the corner streetlight.

"Can I see some I.D.?" the first officer asked.

Again, I allowed my rational side to overcome a quick surge of annoyance, and fished out my wallet, opening it and handing my driver's licence to the officer, who turned the flashlight's attention to it.

"What are you doing in this area at this time of night?" the first officer asked.

Hey, this is my city and I can be any damned place I want to be, my mind voice said. I told it to shut up.

"A friend called me and told me of the fire," I said.

Now <u>there's</u> a good reason, I thought.

"You like going to fires in the middle of the night?" the

second officer said, handing my license back to me after jotting my name and license number down on a notepad he'd taken from his shirt pocket.

"This isn't just any fire, obviously," I said.

"No, it isn't," he said.

I saw a couple women approaching, walking up from Beech.

"You can go," the first officer said, and raised his hand to stop the approaching couple.

* * *

I got to my car, observing two or three more squad cars arriving, and started to drive off. I'd gotten two blocks when another squad car began to follow me.

Shit! I thought as he turned on his flashers, and I pulled over.

The second interrogation was much like the first and I realized the guy was just doing his job. I told him the first set of officers had already taken my name and driver's license number, knowing it wouldn't do any good, which it didn't, and finally—after going back to the squad and calling my information in to headquarters—he returned my license and told me I could go.

I passed at least two more squad cars heading for The Central before I managed to make it home. Fortunately, I was far enough from The Central at that point that they couldn't be sure where I was coming from.

When I finally did get home, around 4:45 a.m., I debated on whether I should even try to go back to bed. I was pretty certain I'd be getting a phone call in a couple hours from Mark Richman. But I'd been running pretty much on caffeine and adrenalin for the past several days, and was really beat. So I compromised and just sprawled out on the bed without taking my clothes off and that's the last thing I remember until the phone rang again, at 7:02.

I was aware I felt like a salmon swimming upstream against

the rapids while I struggled to reach a state of consciousness that would allow me to reach for the phone, and I made it just before the machine kicked in.

"I understand you were at the fire last night," Richman said without even a 'hello.'

"Yeah," I answered groggily, not even wondering how he might know that..

"Well, the shit's really hit the fan now. Cochran's demanded a meeting with the chief, and it's scheduled 8 a.m. How soon can you be down here?"

"I'm on my way," I said.

Water-splash face wash, quick pass at my hair with the brush. No tooth brushing. No shower. No shave. No change of clothes.

I didn't care.

That I couldn't find a parking place and had to park in the Warman Park underground garage and walk the two blocks to the City Building Annex would normally have pissed me off royally. But I had to spend every ounce of energy I had just getting my head together. There was a coffee vendor's cart halfway between Warman Park and the Annex, and I stopped long enough to order a large black. It was hotter than hell, but I'd chug-a-lugged it by the time I reached the Annex and pitched the cup in a curbside trash receptacle. I looked up at the huge clock in the lobby as I entered. It was 7:49.

Richman was at his desk when I knocked on his office door.

"Well," he said, "you look like hell." He pointed me to a chair, and I sat down.

"Thanks," I said.

"Sorry to drag you out of bed," he said. "…I guess you didn't get much sleep."

"Good guess. How did you know I was at the fire?" I asked. I didn't think he could possibly know from my being stopped by the officers: There were too many people and too much confusion for anyone to be that organized.

"Jake Janzer was there," Richman said. "He recognized you

from Officer Brady's funeral."

We sat in silence for long enough for me to want to just close my eyes and nod off, but I forced myself to sit up straight in my chair and ask: "So what, exactly, am I doing here?"

He leaned back in his own chair, elbows on the chair's arms, fingers spread, tips touching. "The chief wants to see you. I don't know if he'll want Cochran present or not."

"Where's Captain Offermann?" I asked.

Richman gave the slightest hint of a smile. "He's more involved right now with finding who killed Officer Brady; the loss of a half-million dollar police substation isn't in his jurisdiction."

"Black thinks *I* had something to do with it?" I asked, immediately wondering where I'd come up with that one.

The small smile became a quick small grin. "Uh, I don't think so," he said, and his face became serious. "But you know damned well this fire couldn't possibly have happened at a worse time. And that graffiti doesn't even allow us to gain a few days time by pretending it might not have been arson. The Gay Pride parade is three days away. Three days! Just as almost everybody in the gay community automatically assumes a cop killed Tom Brady, that graffiti makes it pretty damned obvious to *us* that somebody gay set that fire. Gays aren't the only ones who can jump to conclusions or deal in generalities: They still insist on painting the entire police department as being out of control homophobes. Well, there are a lot of people in the department who assume that everybody in the gay community is capable of civil unrest and violence against city property. We can all do with a little less conclusion jumping and a lot more logic.

"And the upshot is that Cochran wins! He'll do whatever it takes, short of calling in the national guard—and if he had the authority to do so himself, I wouldn't put it past him—to see to it that tens of thousands of potentially violent gays are not allowed to congregate, let alone hold a parade, on Sunday. And if we try to pull the parade permit, we'd have to seal off The

Central to prevent gays and lesbians from gathering there…!"

Well, maybe a little overstating, there, I thought, but he'd made his point, and I could certainly share his frustration over the entire situation.

At about 8:15, Richman's phone rang.

"Lieutenant Richman," he said, picking up the receiver. There was a pause, then "Yes, sir. Yes, we'll be right up." He hung up, got up from his chair, and said "Let's go."

The chief's office, on the floor above Offermann's, was duly impressive. A considerably larger reception area than Offermann's had doors to each side of the receptionist's desk. To the left, I could see through the open door into a large conference room. The door to the right was closed, and Richman knocked—more a token, two-knuckle rap, and Black's voice said: "Come in."

Richman opened the door and made a small "after you" gesture, then followed me in, closing the door behind him.

It was a rather comfortable room. A large desk flanked by the American flag on one side and the state and city's flags on the other. Two smaller desks, one in each far-wall corner of the room, and perhaps eight comfortable-looking but definitely business chairs arranged in conversational semi-circles.

Chief Black sat behind his desk and made no move to get up, not that I'd expected him to. He made a palms-up "be seated" motion toward the two chairs a few feet from the front of his desk, and Richman and I sat.

"Thank you for coming, Mr. Hardesty," he said, and I merely nodded. He sat just looking at me for a moment, then said: "I am gravely disappointed by the burning of The Central substation."

Jeezus, he is blaming me! I thought for an instant until reality smacked me on the side of the head and said: *Get a grip!*

"The question," he said without waiting for any response from me, "is what we are going to do about it. Deputy Chief Cochran, with whom I've just spent a few instructive minutes, is right in one thing: There can be no gay pride festival this weekend. Not in The Central. Our problem is in how to stop a massive confrontation between the gay community and the police. Whomever it was who set fire to the substation did the gay community an incalculable disservice and opened the door to official retaliation. Plus the fact that it takes time and manpower away from the investigation into Officer Brady's death. All of which plays directly into the hands of…those in the department who will go to great lengths to maintain the old ways. Deputy Chief Cochran is demanding that the parade permit be rescinded immediately, and a curfew ordered in The Central—which would almost positively guarantee an insurrection."

I suddenly wondered if Cochran and his followers could possibly be so desperate to get rid of the chief that they might themselves be involved in the fire? Highly unlikely, but…well, if Hitler could come to power by setting fire to the Reichstag and blaming the communists, what's one little police substation to someone who wanted the chief out? Cochran was the only one to really gain anything out of it. And if the thought occurred to me, it almost certainly had occurred to the chief.

While I was riveted on his every word, I questioned once again what the hell I was doing here. Apparently that question was written all over my face, because he leaned forward in his chair and put his arms on the desk.

"You are here as our sounding board and because, while you do not consider yourself a community leader, you are a community member with, we believe, a better grasp of both sides of this situation than most. If we can reach some sort of consensus here, I will ask to speak with a very few of those you gathered for us before: The president of the Gay Business League, the president of the Bar Guild, the chairperson of the Gay Pride parade and the head of the Festival Committee, and perhaps the editors of the gay papers, though those are weeklies and I don't know if there is enough time for them to be of much help unless we could convince them to put out a special edition."

He leaned even closer and said: "But first I'd like to hear any suggestions you might have to help us avoid what could very well lead to a total disaster for both the gay community and the city at large."

I didn't have to think long on that one. "There is one thing you could do immediately that would help relieve a lot of the tension, on the part of the community at any rate," I said.

"And that is?" he asked.

Now it was my turn to lean forward. "When I left The Central this morning," I said, "I was stopped twice by the police asking what I was doing there. I understand why, but I'm sure a lot of those who were also stopped don't. The entire Central was practically crawling with police: Squad cars everywhere. I even saw a couple mounted units: Where in hell they came from at that time of the morning I have no idea, but they were there and it somehow gave me the impression of the Germans marching into Poland." I gave a quick look at both of them and shrugged. "A little melodramatic and unfair, perhaps, but that's what it reminded me of. If there'd been a bigger crowd of gays and lesbians there…." I gave a small mental shudder. "Anyway, tempers are understandably high on both sides. I'd strongly recommend the first thing you might do is to reduce the visible police presence to an absolute minimum. The city needs to provide a presence of authority in The Central, let it be the fire department. They have to be there to handle the arson investigation anyway. The community has no beef with the fire department; they won't be perceived as a threat. Keep a couple of the big rigs on the street and maybe put a few more people on the investigation than are really needed. It would show the presence of city government without overwhelming us with it. Perhaps even keep squad cars as much out of the area as you could—maybe more plainclothesmen and unmarked patrols?"

Chief Black looked at Richman, then back at me. "We could do that, yes. But that does not address the problem of the parade and festival," the chief said. "The fire gives a good reason for not allowing the parade to go past the fire scene—it's still a crime scene, as well. But the parade route is straight down Beech, from

Olive to Crescent; Ash is almost exactly in the middle of the route, and there's no way the parade could be rerouted around it: None of the other streets in The Central are wide enough, and most of them are residential anyway. Shifting the parade to another part of the city at this late date would be next to impossible, even if we were willing to risk the serious problems the sheer number of participants would represent. I agree with Deputy Chief Cochran on this one. Mobs have very short fuses, and tension is simply too high on both sides right now."

Richman, who had been quiet since we'd walked in, sat idly chewing the corner of his lower lip in thought, then said: "Do you think they would go with a postponement? Move it back a week? It would give both sides some breathing room and it would be a form of mutual concession: The community conceding the practicalities of our arson investigation and the tension level in exchange for our not guaranteeing a confrontation by cancelling the festival and parade outright. I'm sure we can do whatever permit reissuing/ rescheduling might be needed."

"It's certainly worth trying," I said. (I'd started to say "What have we got to lose?" but the answer to that one was all too obvious.)

"Can you get Lieutenant Richman a list of the people I mentioned and their phone numbers?" the chief asked. "It might be better if we initiated the calls this time. We want to keep it down to a manageable number, but can you think of anyone else we should include?"

I thought it over a moment: Lee Taylor of the Gay Business League, Mark Graser from the Bar Guild, Charles Conrad of Rainbow Flag, Cathy Holms and Marty Green from the Pride Parade and Festival—those were probably the most key people. I didn't think Glen O'Banyon or I needed to be involved, though I was nosy enough to want to be there.

"I think the ones you mentioned should do it," I said. "Everything can filter down from there. I have the list at home, and I'll call Lieutenant Richman as soon as I get there. But I hope you'll also be doing something with the straight media. We're all in enough trouble without their making the situation even worse than it is. I know the Journal-Sentinel will milk it for everything they can get out of it."

Chief Black nodded. "I have calls in to the editors of all the papers, and the management of the TV and radio stations. We started getting interview requests about ten minutes after the first alarm on the substation fire came in. I don't want to call a press conference right now; I'll try the one-on-one approach first. I think most of them realize what is at stake and will be responsible. As for the Journal-Sentinel, I've instructed the head of our legal department to advise them that if so much as a single incident of violence or civil disobedience can be traced to their irresponsible handling of this story, we will have them in court and keep them there until they go bankrupt. I don't think they'll want to call our bluff on that one."

Sensing that we'd said just about everything there was to be said at the moment, I got up from my chair. "If we're through here, I'll head home and get those numbers."

Both the chief and Richman got up and extended their hands. We shook, and I turned and walked out of the office.

* * *

Got home, called Richman with the numbers—I gave him the Tattler's and Bottom's Up's editors' numbers on the basis that they probably should be included, though neither one could probably afford to put out a special edition, and their current editions were either just out or at the printers. Still, the editors had a lot of contacts within the community. Richman invited me to attend: They hoped to get everyone in to the chief's office at 2 p.m., but much as I wanted to go, I declined. I knew if I didn't get some sleep I'd be a zombie. I could find out how it went afterward.

"Oh," Richman said before he hung up, "I do have one bit of news. Officer Brady did stop for gas at a QuickieStop. The attendant didn't notice anything strange, though, and didn't see anyone else around."

Another dead end. I said goodbye and thought longingly of sleep.

I did call Glen O'Banyon's office to let him know what was going on and left a message with Donna, his secretary, to have him call me at home. Then I went into the bedroom, fell face-first across the bed, and went out like a light.

I dreamt of Tom, standing in front of the burning Central substation as it started to collapse, and I wanted desperately to run to him, to pull him away, to save him, but I couldn't move.

* * *

O'Banyon called at 2:15, interrupting another dream—one in which I was holding a copy of the Journal-Sentinel with the photo looking through the open door of Tom's car. There was something on the front seat....

I filled O'Banyon in on everything that had happened. He'd seen the morning news reports on the fire and tried to call me, but I was on my way to the Annex by that time. He said he'd be in court the rest of the afternoon, but asked me to call—or that he'd try to reach me—later to find out how the meeting had gone. We both had our fingers crossed.

I noted as we talked that the little red light on my answering machine was blinking—probably calls that came in while I was with the chief and Richman—but I just didn't feel up to checking them right then.

When we hung up, I got up, made a pot of coffee—oh, boy! caffeine!—went back to the bedroom to strip off my clothes, and spent the next twenty minutes in the shower. When I'd finished and dressed and had a cup of coffee, I checked the machine. Bob, Phil, Jared, Lee Taylor. I tried returning them all, except for Lee, who I hoped was at the meeting with the chief. No one was home except for Jared, who was packing for his move to Carrington. I told him about everything that had happened since we'd parted ways at the fire. He said he had been stopped, too, just as he was getting into his car, by one of the horse-mounted officers, who was apparently watching for people getting into cars parked along Beech. Jared said the cop tried to pretend he didn't recognize him, but Jared swears he'd tricked with the guy one night at Thorson's Woods.

Ah, Tom, ye weren't alone, lad! I thought.

* * *

Though I'd only had about four hours of sleep, I didn't even try to go back to bed. I was hoping Richman or maybe Mark Graser would call to let me know what happened at the meeting. I knew everyone there was aware of the stakes and the danger of any open confrontation between the police and the community.

I found myself thinking about the dreams I'd had. The first one, of Tom standing in front of the burning substation, was pretty text-book symbolism. The one of the Journal-Sentinel was a little less clear. Something on the seat? I didn't remember that from the actual photo, but I'd kept it, for some perverse reason, and it was at the office. I'd check, just out of curiosity.

I toyed with the idea of going down to the office anyway, just to check messages and get the mail, but I didn't want to miss a call from anybody at the meeting.

At 3:12, the phone rang.

"Dick Hardesty," I said as soon as I picked it up.

"Dick, Mark Richman."

Ready or not... I thought.

"Did they go for the postponement?" I asked, not wanting to beat around the bush.

"Yes," he said, and I heaved a long mental sigh. "It got pretty hot and heavy there for a while, but the chief managed to convince them that it was the only way to avoid a disaster and let both sides save face. I'm not sure what an extra week will buy us, but it's better than nothing. And of course they wanted to know what was happening in Officer Brady's death. The chief called Captain Offermann in to talk briefly to the group."

It struck me that Chief Black was a pretty damned shrewd politician as well as a good chief. He knew full well that he was going to be asked about Tom's death, but calling Offermann in in response to their questions rather than having him there from the start gave the impression that he was going out of his way to be cooperative. Subtle but impressive.

"And what did Offermann have to say?" I asked. I felt a little guilty to realize that the fire had moved to the forefront of my thoughts in the past…what…twelve hours?

Sorry, Tom, I thought.

Don't sweat it, buddy, Tom's voice said somewhere in my head.

"He didn't really have too much to say," Richman continued. "Homicide has been doing everything it can, but these things take time. He stressed that the gang-retaliation theory was far more logical than that a cop might have been responsible, but confirmed that the gun had been a .38—one of the few things the Journal-Sentinel's ever gotten right. He told them that the markings on the bullet were being compared against those of every .38 registered to the force. Chief Robertson, shortly before he died, required each officer to test-fire his gun specifically to be able to determine, in any shooting involving the police, which bullets came from a police weapon, and to which officer it belonged. Thus far there have been no matches. He told them we were also checking the markings against those in our crime files to see if the gun had been involved in previous shootings."

I hadn't realized just how tense I'd been about the meeting, but I could feel the knot at the back of my neck fading away. "And what about Deputy Chief Cochran?" I asked.

"Chief Black invited him to the meeting as a matter of courtesy, and to prevent him from saying later that he'd been cut out of the loop. He just sat there, mostly, but it was obvious that he was not happy, you can be sure. But the fact of the matter is…I'm sorry, Dick; this sounds pretty cold, I know…that with Officer Brady no longer being Cochran's trump card against the chief, he doesn't have too much to bargain with at the moment except the potential for disaster the substation fire presents, and I'm sure Chief Black wanted to put him in the actual presence of leaders from the community to show him we're all just human beings dealing with a mutual problem. Not that anyone has any illusions that Cochran will ease up on his efforts to discredit the chief, but for the moment…."

He was quiet a moment, then said: "The chief passed along your suggestion about limiting the obvious police presence in The Central, and that went over pretty well. It's still a dicey situation, and nobody's home free yet, but it's a start."

"I really appreciate your filling me in," I said.

"Well, we owe you," he said. "I think that the one good thing to come out of all this is that the chief, at very least, recognizes the need for a permanent, direct liaison with the gay community." Another pause, then: "Well, I've got to head back up to the chief's office. He's decided it is time to call a press conference to discuss the fire and, now, the agreement with the community. It'll help get the word out."

"Okay," I said. "And again, thanks."

* * *

I'd just started to think about lying down for awhile when not ten minutes later, the phone rang. It was Richman again. "Meet me at the corner of Collins and Warman in 20 minutes. I've got some really bad news."

Oh, great! Some 'really bad news.' That'll be a switch!

"I'm on my way," I said.

Collins and Warman formed two sides of Warman Park. I parked in the underground garage and was standing on the park side of the corner when a blue 4-door pulled up and Richman, in uniform but without his hat, leaned over to open the passenger's side door. I got in.

"I didn't make it to the press conference," he said, pulling out into traffic. "Just as I was leaving my office, the report came in that we found a match for the bullet." He paused, whether for effect or because he didn't like what he had to say, I couldn't tell. Finally he said: "It isn't from a police issue service revolver."

"Well, I'd imagine that would be *good* news for you," I said, puzzled.

He gave me a glance out of the corner of his eye, without turning his head. "It's from a weapon used in a liquor store holdup and shooting about six months ago."

"And...?" I said, still confused.

"A weapon we took from the suspect and had in our possession. It was stolen from the evidence vault in the police property room."

"Jeezus!" I said. "How in the hell could that happen?"

"Gee, Dick," he said, his voice echoing his frustration, "we sort of wondered that ourselves." There was a slight pause, then: "I'm sorry; I didn't mean to take it out on you. But the doors this opens up.... It was there the week before Officer Brady was killed: It was officially entered in the property log at that time; when exactly it was taken from evidence storage, we can't say. The undeniable fact is that it had to have been taken by someone on the force, and that means... The most important thing right now is that whatever happens, we can *not* let word of this leak out until we know exactly what happened!"

The implications of Richman's news was slow to filter through everything else that had been clogging my mind for the past week.

"I appreciate your telling me," I said, realizing that he had not had to and probably should not have for sake of the investigation, "...but *why* are you telling me?"

We had, I realized, made several right turns and were now back on Collins, paralleling the park heading toward Warman.

"We need you to keep your ears *wide* open, he said. "If you hear anything about this—any rumors at all, call me immediately."

"I will. I promise," I said as he pulled up to the corner where he'd picked me up.

"Good," he said. "Now I've got to get back to work."

He reached his hand across and we shook hands. I opened the door and got out, then stood there a moment, my mind racing, and watched him drive away.

* * *

Despite Richman's bombshell about the murder weapon, by the next morning I was a little more alert and got to the office by 8:30. I noticed, as I left the ground floor diner with my large styrofoam cup of black coffee and stopped to pick up a paper at the lobby newsstand, that while the headlines of both major papers were on a disastrous bridge collapse in Oregon, they both carried front page stories on the fire, the investigation and/or the meeting with Chief Black. The Journal-Sentinel, of course, ran a nearly-full-page shot of the ruins of the burned-out substation with the headline "Gays Throw Down the Gauntlet!" I was rather surprised to realize the Journal-Sentinel even knew what a gauntlet was.

Once in my office, after a quick check of my messages, I sat down at my desk to drink my coffee and read the paper—hey, routines are good to have. My eye was immediately drawn to an article at the top right hand corner of page 2:

A.H.W.A. Local Head Resigns

> Joseph Giacomino, head of Local 344 of the Amalgamated Hotel Workers of America has resigned his position to accept a new assignment at the union's headquarters in New York City. Giacomino, who led the union's recent labor contract negotiations, will become liaison to John Corello, A.H.W.A. president….

Aha! So little Joey G. was being yanked back home. I was sure the "new assignment" was just a face-saving move for the union. Undoubtedly Joey's handling of the negotiations had not met the approval of the union's higher ups—or of Joe Sr. from his prison watchtower. I could only imagine how Joey must be feeling about that.

But far more importantly, I realized that once Joey was out of the city and out of the state, bringing him back for any sort of charges Jonathan might be able to bring against him was extremely remote. I knew Lieutenant Richman already had more to do than he could handle, but I owed it to Jonathan, and who knows how many other kids like him, to make sure that Joey G. didn't get off on this one. Now that Tom was…gone…there wasn't any need to use Jonathan as a counter-trump to keep Cochran from running with the "gay cop" issue. If the chief decided to use the Jonathan-Giacomino-Cochran chain to investigate just what skeletons might be in Cochran's closet, fine. That was up to him. But Jonathan deserved justice, and I was going to be damned sure he got it.

And while I was sitting there thinking these things over, I remembered my dream about the Journal-Sentinel photo of Tom's car and there being something on the seat. I really didn't remember seeing anything when I first looked at the photo, but then my mind wasn't exactly operating on all cylinders at the time. I rummaged through my desk and found the paper in a bottom drawer, again not quite sure why I'd kept it in the first place—I realized even at the time that whenever I would look at it, it would hurt. It did.

The photo was newspaper-grainy with the individual pixels readily visible with just a little bit of effort to see them. And sure enough! There *was* something on the front seat, barely visible near the passenger's side door. I couldn't make out what it was—some sort of small box or package, or maybe a paperback book? I remembered that Richman had said something about the police thinking Tom might have stopped somewhere on his way home for gas or for something to eat. That last part stuck me as odd, especially since Tom had just come from a party where I'm sure there'd have been more than enough food even for Tom's legendary appetite. Still….

I folded the paper and put it back in the drawer, then dialed the City Building Annex.

"Lieutenant Richman," the voice said.

"Lieutenant, it's Dick. Sorry to bother you: I know you're busy. How are things going?"

"You have no idea," he said. "You're lucky to have caught me; I've been in and out of the office since 7:30 this morning." He paused, then said: "What can I do for you? You haven't heard any…rumors, I hope?"

"No, thank God," I said. "But I was wondering if you'd seen the article in today's paper about Joey G.'s being called back to union headquarters in New York?"

"I haven't had much time to read the papers lately," he said.

"Understandable," I said, "but I don't want that bastard to get out of town before Jonathan has a chance to file charges against him for the beating."

There was another slight pause, then: "Good point. Why don't you bring the kid in…uh…let me check…" yet another pause… "I don't have a single minute free today. Why don't you bring him in tomorrow morning, around 8?"

"Tomorrow's Saturday," I said.

"So I've heard," he replied. "But things are still too tense for anybody around here to be taking a weekend off. If we don't find Officer Brady's killer and/or who set the substation fire before next weekend comes around, we'll be right back to square one with the Pride Festival problem."

"I'm sorry, Lieutenant. I realize your priorities…"

"Well," he interrupted, "we can't afford to let this Giacomino situation go away, either. You just be here tomorrow morning. I'll make the time. And speaking of time, we can save some if you have…Jonathan…write out in longhand and in detail exactly what happened to him that night, from the time Giacomino picked him up to the point where he drove away. We'll need it for the report."

"He'll have it for you," I said. "And thanks again. We'll see you in the morning." I was almost ready to say goodbye when I remembered the paper. "Oh, and I have a question you might be able to answer. That photo the Journal-Sentinel ran the morning Tom was…" I hesitated, the word caught in my throat "…Tom died: It looks like there was something on the front seat…a little package or box or something? The photo was too grainy to tell."

"Yeah? What about it?"

"Do you know what it was?"

He was quiet a second. "Ah…not off-hand. A box of mini-donuts or a bag of chips or something like that, I think…remember, I told you he stopped at a QuickieStop on his way home. But I'm sure whatever it was shows up on our own photos. Why…?"

"I'm not sure," I interrupted, feeling suddenly a little guilty for bothering him over something so minor. "But could I see those photos sometime?"

"Sure," he said. "Well, look, I've got to go. I'll see you and…Jonathan…in my office tomorrow morning at 8."

"Thanks again," I said, and heard the 'click' of his hanging up.

* * *

I realized that I'd not seen Jonathan in what I was rather surprised to think of as a very long time. I tried calling Bob and Mario—I assumed they'd be up by this time—to see if they could tell Jonathan I'd pick him up at 7 the next morning, but no one was home. It occurred to me that they were probably over at the house, working, and I knew they hadn't had their phone installed yet.

I decided to take a drive over and tell Jonathan myself. Besides, I wanted to see the progress they'd been making, and what was going on with the new bathroom, and…*'fess up, Hardesty!*…okay, and Jonathan.

What's with you and this kid, Hardesty? my mind voice asked. *This isn't like you at all.*

* * *

I had to park on the side street, just beyond the driveway, which was filled by a plumber's truck, Mario's car, and an exterminator's van. I'd gotten halfway to the house when I remembered that I'd left the legal pad and pen I brought for Jonathan—I didn't know that there'd be anything for him to write on in the house—and went back for it. I could hear the sounds of hammering and a circular saw as I walked up to the porch and knocked. When nobody responded, I assumed they just couldn't hear me over the work going on, so I just went in. I saw a couple guys working in what had been the huge pantry and now was on the way to becoming a half bath. They didn't look up as I walked through and, after a quick check of the main floor, I headed up the maid's stairs to the second floor. I found Mario and Jonathan in what would be the master bedroom but was now a bleak tundra of drop cloths, stepladders and assorted paint cans, brushes, rollers, and roller pans.

Jonathan was edging the lower half of the window frame, the tip of his tongue sticking out the corner of his mouth in total concentration as he tried to avoid getting paint on the wall.

Mario saw me first. "Ah, just in time!" he said with a grin. "Grab a brush."

Jonathan looked up and, seeing me, broke into a full-sunrise smile. "Dick!" he said. "Hi!"

"Hi yourself," I said, returning the smile. "Looks like you've been busy."

"Yeah!" he replied enthusiastically. "It's sure going to look nice, isn't it?"

Mario'd set down his paint brush and came over to shake hands, first carefully checking to see that he didn't have any wet paint to transfer. He glanced at the legal pad in my hand but didn't say anything. Taking his cue from Mario, Jonathan did the same. He'd apparently at some point tried to scratch his nose while holding on to the paint brush—he had a little swatch of paint over his left eyebrow. Why did I find that sexy?

Oh, fer chrissake! my mind-voice snorted.

Jonathan hadn't stopped smiling since he first saw me, a fact not lost on Mario, who glanced quickly from Jonathan to me and gave a quick raised-eyebrow grin.

"Why don't you finish that edging, Jonathan, then show Dick what we've been doing since he was here last."

Well, it hadn't been *that* long, but....

"Bob not here?" I asked as Mario and Jonathan returned to their work.

"Yeah," Mario said, pouring more paint into his roller pan. "He's in the basement with the exterminator."

"Oh, oh," I said. "No problems, I hope."

Mario shrugged without looking away from his rolling. "Well, when we bought the place, the pre-sale inspection showed that there was some minor termite damage, but we were in a hurry to close, so we made an arrangement with the former owners that they'd pay for any problems. We brought another inspector in to see just what needs to be done. We'll probably have to fumigate, though."

Jonathan finished the window frame, put his brush down on top of the open can, and came quickly over to me. "Come on, Dick, I'll show you the new bathroom!"

He led the way back down the maid's stairs to the kitchen where a gaping hole in the wall led to the new half-bath. One of the workers, who had been apparently framing in the new wall, gave Jonathan a big grin and a wink. Jonathan blushed and gave me a quick glance out of the corner of his eye.

"Bob said I could help decorate it when it's ready," he said, ignoring the worker. "He brought a book of wallpaper samples and some tile samples for the floor. It'll be really nice."

The worker kept looking at Jonathan with a small smile and an expression that reminded me of the wolf eyeing Red Riding Hood. Jonathan quickly turned and led me into the dining room where either he or Mario had stripped most of the woodwork.

"It looks like you have a new friend," I teased, giving a head-jerk in the direction of the new half bath.

Jonathan looked uncomfortable, making me wish I hadn't said anything. "Yeah," he said. "He wants to have sex with me. He told me so. But…" His look of discomfort did not go away.

"But?" I asked.

He looked at me and gave a semi-frown, then a quick sigh.

"Nothing," he said, and moved toward the main staircase. I followed. About halfway up the stairs, he turned to me.

"Is it because I was a hustler?"

Now *that* one caught me by surprise. "Is *what* because you were a hustler?" I asked, confused.

"Is that why you don't want…?" He shook his head. "Never mind; it's not important."

"Yes it *is* important," I said, "whatever it is. I don't think…"

At that point, I heard Bob's voice, talking with someone as they entered the dining room.

Seeing me on the stair, he said: "Well, hello, stranger; I'll be right with you." He then turned back to a large man with a beer belly that stretched the buttons on his uniform shirt and flowed over the top of his belt, completely hiding the buckle. They continued walking to the front door as the man took a large measuring tape from one side of his belt. Bob opened the door for him, then closed it behind him and turned toward me. When I glanced toward Jonathan, I saw he had gone on up the stairs and disappeared.

Now what have you done? I asked myself.

Like you had <u>no</u> idea! my mind answered. *God, you can be such a jerk!*

"Busy place," I said, moving back down the stairs to shake hands with Bob.

"The joys of home ownership," he sighed. "And now it looks like we'll definitely have to fumigate."

"When?" I asked.

"By sheer luck, he had a job cancellation for tomorrow, if you can believe that!" Bob said. "So it's either tomorrow or wait nearly a month. It'll take three days. I hate to bring all the work to a halt right in the middle of everything, but it's better to get it done now than when we're moved in—which we hope will be in three weeks."

He started up the stairs and I followed. When we reached the top, he said: "Which creates something of a minor problem."

"Jonathan," I said.

"Yeah," he said. "He can't stay here, obviously, and he'd be welcome to stay with us, but as you know we've only got a one-bedroom, and…"

I raised my hand to stop him. "I understand," I said. "Completely."

"Maybe Phil and Tim can put him up for a few more days," Bob said.

"Oh, I'm sure they'd be willing to," I said, "but they really need their time right now. I've imposed on them…and you…too long as it is."

Bob reached out and touched my arm, then started toward the master bedroom. "Hell, it's no imposition at all for us!" he said. "Jonathan's more than earned his keep. We'd be glad to have him stay here as long as he needs to. But it's the next three days we have to think about."

"I'll have him stay with me," I heard myself saying, surprising the hell out of the part of me that *hadn't* said it. With everything that was going on being in a constant state of flux: Tom, the department, Cochran, Giacomino, the fire, the community, and God-knows-what-all else, I didn't think Cochran's boys would be spending too much time looking for one hustler who they must now believe, after some time with nothing seen or heard from him, that he'd gone back to Wisconsin. With Tom…dead…*yeah, dead*…I couldn't imagine that I was of any value or interest to Cochran.

But I knew the main reason I was hesitant was because of my uncertainty about myself and exactly what I thought might be going on with Jonathan. On the one hand, being relatively alone with him for three days would give me a chance to get to know him a little better and get a better handle on where I thought this might or might not be leading. But on the other hand, I really didn't want to hurt him, and I knew that I'd have to fight myself like hell to keep from what they still euphemistically call "taking advantage"of him. And it would be taking advantage in spite of the fact—or more exactly *because* of the fact—that he obviously wanted to be more than just friends.

Oh, fer Chrissakes, Hardesty, my mind snapped. *Aren't you overdoing this 'I'm so noble' crap? The kid's 19, not twelve. He knows what he wants. Stop behaving like something out of Victorian novel! What you're <u>really</u> afraid of is getting involved with someone again! You're not worried about your hurting him—you're worried about him hurting you!*

Oh, shit!

When we got to the bedroom, Jonathan had started painting the other window frame. Bob announced that the house would have to be sealed for the next three days, work would have to stop on the bathroom, and Jonathan would be staying with me. Jonathan, who had not smiled since Bob and I entered the room, merely looked at me, expressionless. "I can sleep in the coach house," he said. Bob and Mario exchanged glances, then looked at me with slightly raised eyebrows.

"They'll be tenting the coach house, too," Bob said.

"And I want you to come and stay with me," I said.

"Really?" he asked, still suspicious, but reminding me somehow of the reactions of a puppy to whom a hand is held out just after having been scolded.

"Really," I said, and hoped to hell I meant it.

I then told them all of Giacomino's "reassignment" and what that would mean if Jonathan didn't file charges before he left town, and that Richman wanted Jonathan to come down in the morning to sign the paperwork. I gave him the notepad and pen and told him to write out everything exactly as it happened. He took them to put in his room and came quickly back, his spirits seeming to have once again picked up.

"I'll pick you up at 7," I told him.

"I can I bring Phil and Tim, can't I?" he asked. "I can't leave them here; they'd die."

"Well," I said, "we won't have time to take them home before we have to be downtown, and…"

"That's okay," Mario said. "We can take them home with us tonight and watch out for them until it's clear to bring them back."

"Thanks, Mario!" Jonathan said. "I'll show you how much to feed them and I'll change their water tonight so it'll be fresh."

A voice called from downstairs: "Mr. Allen?"

"Ah," Bob said. "The exterminator. He was measuring for the tent. I'd better get down and see if he needs anything."

"I'd better get going, too, and let you guys get back to work," I said. "I'll see you at 7, okay, Jonathan?"

"Sure," he said with a big smile.

I followed Bob back downstairs and, with a wave to the workers in the half bath, I left.

* * *

It was Friday night, and I had only been out cruising once since Tom died. *There! I was getting used to saying thinking it.* But that encounter had been about as exciting as an oil change, and while sheer habit is a powerful force, I realized I really still wasn't in the mood for trolling for tricks. So I just stayed home, went to bed fairly early, and watched some porn videos. I was more than a little surprised, while taking care of business, to find myself thinking of Jonathan.

* * *

Jonathan was waiting on the front porch as I pulled up at ten minutes to seven. He had the legal pad in one hand and his old backpack in the other which, I assumed, contained clothes to last the three days he'd be at my place. He was wearing some of the clothes Tim had given him, and looked really nice.

Har-des-tyyyyyyy! my mind cautioned softly.

Okay, okay.

It being a Saturday morning, we made it downtown by quarter after and found a parking place about a block away from the City Building Annex. There was a coffee shop on the corner, and I asked Jonathan if he'd eaten. When he said "no", we went in and ordered a quick breakfast. He was back to being the old talkative Jonathan I remembered from our first meeting at Hughies, but there seemed to be a subtle change, somehow. He told me all about working on the house, and how he really liked Mario and Bob, and how his goldfish Phil and Tim—especially Tim—seemed to be getting bigger and how real-person Phil had stopped by one afternoon and brought some cheeseburgers and chocolate shakes, and how they'd talked about all sorts of things and really had a good time, and…well, maybe it was just that he was talking about things and people we had in common. I don't know.

We walked into the Annex at exactly three minutes until 8. From the amount of traffic we saw going in and out of the alley next to the building and the number of people in the lobby, I never would have guessed it was a weekend. There seemed to be an inordinate number of civilians around—mostly men; and then I realized they were obviously cops in plainclothes assigned to keep an eye—a very *close* eye, I'd judge from the number of them—on The Central.

We got to Richman's office at exactly 8 o'clock, and he must have seen us through the opaque glass on his door because he said "Come" before I'd even had a chance to knock. We entered, did our handshake ritual, and he motioned us to sit down with Jonathan in the chair closest to the desk. Richman returned to his seat and opened a manila file folder on his desk, taking out an assortment of official-looking report forms. Picking up a pen from a desk set in front of him, he began asking Jonathan the requisite questions, writing rapidly as Jonathan responded. I could tell Jonathan was embarrassed to talk about his hustling—an interesting change from the day we'd first met, I noticed—and that even a sketchy outline of what had happened that night disturbed him.

When they'd finished, Richman asked him to sign in several places, and then asked if he had brought his written statement of what had happened. Jonathan handed him the notepad, and Richman flipped quickly through the two or three pages he'd written. Noting that Jonathan hadn't signed it, he asked him to do so, then signed his own name and the date under it.

"And you're prepared to testify against him in court?" Richman asked. Jonathan nodded. "Good," Richman said. "We'll take it from here."

He was silent a moment, then looked slowly from Jonathan to me, lips pursed. "I have to be honest with you, Jonathan," he said finally. "Giacomino is a very powerful man and a very wealthy one. There is an outside chance that he will not go to jail for what he did to you."

Jonathan nodded and said "I know. But I want *him* to know he can't go around beating people up and get away with it."

Richman sighed. "You're right, of course, and we'll do whatever we can to see that he pays for his actions. I'm sure just the nature of the charge will encourage his wife to make his life a living hell. Couldn't happen to a more deserving guy."

Figuring we were just about done for the moment, I was about ready to get up from my chair when Richman opened a drawer in his desk and brought out another manila folder.

"These are the photos taken at the scene of Officer Brady's death," he said, moving the folder across the desk toward me. "I took out those that…ah…those that weren't necessary."

Thank God for that! I thought. I don't think I could have looked at any pictures that showed…well…Tom.

There were probably a dozen showing the car from all angles, most from the outside, starting from the back of the car and working around the passenger's side. There were a couple taken from inside Reef Dwellers, showing the damage the car had done when it crashed through the wall and display window. But the ones I was most interested in seeing were the ones taken through the open driver's side door. When I reached one showing the full front seat, I froze, my eyes riveted to a small box on the seat near the passenger's door. I could almost feel the blood draining from my face, and I felt lightheaded.

"Dick! Are you all right?" I heard Jonathan ask, his voice anxious.

I forced myself to lean forward to hand the photo to Richman.

"That's who killed Tom," I said.

Richman took the photo, looked at it carefully, then looked at me, his confusion written clearly on his face.

"What is it?" Jonathan asked.

"It's a box of Cracker Jack," Richman said.

CHAPTER 12

Jonathan was staring at me, obviously totally confused, as apparently so was Richman, though his face had regained its normal composure. I knew he was giving me time to pull myself and my thoughts together.

There had to have been a full minute of total silence while I tried to figure out how to make anyone but me understand what was going on. Finally I decided just to plunge right in and hope the water wasn't too far over my head.

I explained—mostly to Richman, of course, since poor Jonathan had no idea of all the twists and turns this story had taken—about the long and bitter history between the Giacominos and the Bradys; of how the Bradys suspected Joe senior had caused the death of Tom's older brother; of the fight Tom had had with Joey G. over the box of Cracker Jack when they were kids, and of Tom's dad's observation that the Giacominos never forgot or forgave. I'd thought at the time that he was exaggerating, but I believed it now with all my heart.

Joey G. had just been humiliated, as an adult, by Tom's dad at the labor negotiations. What better way, in Joey's reptilian way of thinking, to get back at both Tom's dad and at Tom for that long-ago defeat? The Cracker Jack box was unopened—I'd bet anything that Joey had known about the victory celebration Tom's dad threw the night after the contract was signed and had waited outside the Montero. Whether he was waiting for Tom or Tom's dad probably didn't matter: Either Brady would do, but Tom was frosting on the cake.

"Is there another convenience store close to where Tom got his gas?" I asked.

Richman thought a moment, then said: "Yeah there's one a block closer to town. Maybe Brady realized as he passed it that he needed gas, and stopped at the next one. Why?"

"I think Giacomino saw Tom come out and followed him at a safe distance so Tom wouldn't notice he was being followed. When he saw Tom pull in for gas, he probably pulled into the one closest to him, went in, and bought the Cracker Jack. He knew full well what he was doing."

"Yeah," Richman said, "but isn't it possible Tom Brady bought the Cracker Jack for himself?"

"He loved it as a kid," I explained, "but he ate so much of it he couldn't stand it as an adult. Of course Giacomino had no way of knowing that."

Richman nodded. "I'll have a squad check that out," he said. "If Giacomino did stop and buy the Cracker Jack it wouldn't be enough to convict him, certainly, but it would be a good bit of circumstantial evidence. And there might be fingerprints...."

"I might tend to doubt that," I said, "given Joey's background. He'd probably be smart enough not to leave prints."

Richman nodded. "So go on with your scenario."

"So," I finished up, "Joey G. waited for Tom to drive off, followed him to the stoplight at Evans and Beech, and pulled up beside him. Tom's window was rolled down, I saw in the photo. He probably had it down because it was warm. If he'd seen Giacomino in the car next to him, I don't think he would have rolled it down for a chat. And since Tom was apparently looking straight ahead when he.... Giacomino just shot him and tossed the Cracker Jack in through the window as his sick calling card: His little private joke, his revenge. He thought nobody else would know, but *he*'d know."

I suddenly felt very much like a balloon when all the air has gone out of it: Almost limp. I sat back in my chair, and was aware of Jonathan just staring at me, slack-jawed. Richman, too, was silent. We all sat there without speaking for what seemed like an eternity.

Finally, I heard Richman give a deep sigh. "I'll buy it," he said. "But buying it and proving it are two very different things. Assuming that he would have made sure his prints weren't on the box, other than maybe being able to put him at the convenience store…. We'll do our best to see what else we can find, but my guess is that we won't be able to get enough to convict him. He's a snake, but as you pointed out, he's not stupid. Once we find out who got the gun for him, we might be able to make some tie-in there."

He looked again from me to Jonathan. "And this throws a different light on this whole assault charge. I never realized just what a psycho Giacomino really was until now. Jonathan, for you to press charges against him could put you in very real danger. Normally, I would put you in protective custody, but since it's apparent that someone within the department is working with or for him, I couldn't risk your safety."

"Then let's get him for the murder," I said.

"How?" he asked. "We can arrest him for the assault and maybe tie him up for a few days at most, but I don't think that will give us enough time. Once he's free to leave the city, he'll be gone, and even if we get enough to convict him later, his lawyers will be able to fight extradition for years. And short of getting out the rubber hose, we can't make him confess to Tom Brady's murder."

"I can," Jonathan said, which snapped both Richman's and my eyes open.

"That's nice of you to offer, Jonathan," Richman said after a moment, "but I'm afraid that's totally out of the question."

"Why?" Jonathan demanded. I was so taken aback by the whole idea, and by Jonathan's boldness, that I didn't say anything.

Richman gave him a soft smile. "Well, mainly, that's why we have a police department …to protect citizens from having to confront dangerous criminals directly. You'd be putting yourself at great risk, and we couldn't allow that."

I'm sure he didn't mean it to be condescending, but that's the way it came out, and Jonathan's awareness of it was reflected in the tight smile he returned.

"But you're right," Jonathan continued calmly—again

surprising the hell out of me—"the police probably can't get a confession out of him. I can. I'm the only one who can tie all this stuff together, and he knows it."

Who the hell is this guy? my mind asked, admiringly, *and what happened to that scatterbrained kid I met at Hughie's?* And at the same time, several rows of stadium lights began to go on in my head.

"He thinks I went back home," Jonathan continued. "If I called him up and told him I wanted money for what he did to me or I'd go to the police...."

Richman shook his head. "Sorry," he said. "Too dangerous. *Way* too dangerous. Now that we know what he's capable of..."

"What he did to me was really bad," Jonathan stated simply. "But what he did to Dick's friend is a lot worse. And he wasn't just Dick's friend, he was a policeman. You shouldn't let him get away with that!"

"He's right, you know," I said to Richman, then turned to Jonathan. "But Lieutenant Richman is right, too, Jonathan: it could be really dangerous."

Jonathan shrugged. "So's hustling," he said.

I looked at Richman, who looked back and forth between Jonathan and me, and then sighed. "I suppose we could run it by Captain Offermann," he said, "but I'm pretty sure he won't go for it."

"We can try," I said, and Richman reached for the phone.

* * *

Offermann couldn't see us right away, so Richman cancelled his morning meeting and we spent the next twenty minutes talking, figuring possible strategy. The more we talked, the more I could sense Richman coming over to our side. When Offermann returned Richman's call and told us to come to his office, we had fairly well firmed up a scenario that provided the best possible protection for Jonathan.

Richman was right: Offermann's initial reaction was, in

effect, "No way in hell," but Richman convinced him to hear us out.

It boiled down to the fact that either we take a shot and hope Jonathan might get something out of Giacomino, or sit back and watch Joey G. leave town with a dead cop's murder just hanging in mid air.

Offermann heard us out, then said: "There's no other way?"

"Not in the time frame available to us," Richman said. "We're still sitting on a time bomb with the gay community. If word of the murder weapon's having come from our own property room gets out, there's no telling what will happen. I'm afraid that with or without Jonathan's pressing charges, Giacomino will be leaving the state very shortly. If we can nail him for Officer Brady's murder before he has a chance to skip out, it will diffuse a lot of tension."

Offermann was silent for what seemed like an eternity, then nodded and looked to Jonathan. "And are you absolutely sure you are willing to do this, Mr. Quinlan?" Jonathan nodded and Offermann was silent again before saying: "While we will do everything we can to protect you, we cannot guarantee your safety 100 percent. And we will have to ask you to sign a waiver releasing the city and the department from any liability should something unforseen happen. I want to be sure you understand."

Jonathan nodded again. "I understand," he said.

"Very well," Offermann said with a sigh. "Let's break for about 45 minutes while I set things up. We'll meet back here at…" he glanced at his watch, "…eleven o'clock."

Richman, Jonathan, and I got up and left the office as Offermann picked up the phone.

* * *

The three of us walked the two blocks to Sandler's Café. Etheridge's, where I'd frequently met Glen O'Banyon for lunch, was directly across the street from the City Building, but was closed weekends. Jonathan and Mark had coffee and pie: I was still too emotionally numb from thinking of Tom and how he had died to even consider eating anything. Jonathan was uncharacteristically quiet—whether from thinking of what he'd volunteered to get himself into or out of concern for me I couldn't tell. Mark, who apparently had relatives living somewhere close to Jonathan's home town, engaged Jonathan in some Wisconsin stories, but I'm afraid I missed most of it.

When we returned to the Annex, we met Captain Offermann who led us upstairs to the large conference room next to the chief's office. At one end of the long conference table, a uniformed officer was hooking a small tape recorder to an odd-looking telephone. Another phone, a regular one, was about halfway down the table. When he'd finished doing whatever it was he was doing, the officer nodded to Offermann and left the room. Offermann motioned Mark...Lieutenant Richman, that is, since we were on official territory...and me to a seat and indicated Jonathan should sit by the regular phone.

"Do you know what you're going to say?" Offermann asked.

Jonathan nodded. "We went over it earlier in Lieutenant Richman's office," he said.

I'm sure he was nervous, but it didn't show—maybe a hangover from his hustler days, where it doesn't pay to be shy. I was probably nervous enough for both of us, but hoped mine didn't show, either. Jonathan sat where Offermann had told him as Offermann stood at the end of the table in front of the phone with the recorder.

Though the police had Giacomino's phone number in their files, of course, luckily, if a little surprisingly, he was also listed in the phone book. If he hadn't been it would be very difficult for Jonathan to explain how he'd gotten it. There were four Joseph Giacomino's listed, but only one J.G. Giacomino. Richman had written it down, and handed it to Jonathan, who picked up the phone to dial. There was a moment of silence, then he nodded to Offermann, who picked up the other receiver and pressed a button on the recorder.

Showtime!

"Is Joey there?" Jonathan asked. There was a pause, then: "Tell him it's Jonathan...he'll know." He put his hand over the receiver and swivelled it up away from his mouth to whisper: "He's in the yard with the kids."

I felt a quick wave of deep empathy for the kids, imagining what it must be like to have a father like Joey Giacomino.

He quickly swivelled the phone back to his mouth, took his hand off the receiver and said: "This is Jonathan...don't you hang up on me; you do so know who I am. Your van? Pritchert Park?...I want my watch back...yes, you do....What do you think I want? I want my watch back, and my money back, and I want you to pay me for what you did. And my rates have gone *way* up!...Yes, you will...because I know something nobody else besides you and me knows: You killed Tom Brady!" There was a long pause, then: "Because I like cops and he was my boyfriend...Yeah, he was married, just like you, and he liked to fuck guys, just like you. He was really mad when I saw your picture in the paper and told him it was you who beat me up. How else do you think I'd know how he beat *you* up when you were kids because he wouldn't let you steal his Cracker Jack? He said you cried like a baby." Another long pause. "I thought so....Oh, no!...I'm not that stupid...I'm not going to be alone with you *anywhere*....You meet me by the Collins Street entrance to the garage under Warman Park at 7 o'clock tonight...I don't care where you're supposed to be; you meet me, and you bring me $25,000 dollars in cash and...I know it's Saturday and I don't care where you get it. Just bring it....Oh, that's okay, I'll recognize *you*, that's for sure. 'Bye." And he hung up.

Everyone remained silent for a moment, and then Offermann said: "Nice job. Now let's see if it works."

* * *

Offermann played back the tape. I was surprised how much Joey G. sounded like his older brother Bart. Joey's part of the conversation was in something of a stage whisper—obviously because he didn't want his wife to hear. But his arrogance came across loud and clear. Giving Joey the information about the fight over the Cracker Jack should have assuaged any fear he might have about it's being a police trap—it's the kind of tiny life-detail only a few people could possibly have known about.

I was momentarily concerned that Giacomino might send someone rather than showing up himself, but then I realized that he would be very unlikely to risk anyone else, even the hired goons and bodyguards he had at his disposal, finding out about his taste for young men. And I wouldn't have been surprised if he couldn't even remember what Jonathan looked like.

Jonathan and I left the Annex shortly after one p.m., having made arrangements for a police technician to come over to my apartment at 6 to have Jonathan fitted for the wire he was to wear—the fewer people who saw Jonathan around police headquarters, the better. Richman had chosen the spot for the meeting for several reasons: There was a concert at the Warman Park band shell that night, so there would be a lot of people around as extra protection for Jonathan. And meeting close to the street would be in easy range of the listening van. I'd had some slight experience with how electronic eavesdropping other than telephone wiretapping worked from an earlier case, though it hadn't involved personal wiring. The police department had just acquired a new electronics van with state of the art equipment and, unlike the van it was replacing, this one carried the markings of the local power company so its presence anywhere would not be suspect.

Although I still wasn't very hungry, I was sure Jonathan must have been, so we stopped for lunch at my favorite deli where I tried to introduce Jonathan to the joys of bagels and lox ("Raw fish?! Do I have to?"). I had the bagel and lox, Jonathan had a Reuben. Apparently there weren't any deli's in or around Cranston, Wisconsin, so even a Reuben sandwich was new to him, though he liked it ("Sauerkraut on a sandwich! Wow!").

We got to my apartment around 2:15 and spent the afternoon mostly talking. Jonathan was understandably somewhat subdued, but I used the opportunity to find out a little more about him. He came from a large family, of which he was the youngest child: In addition to his brother Samuel, who was four years older and to whom he felt the closest, he had three sisters, ten, twelve, and fourteen years older than him, with whom he had little in common. Money was tight and, as he'd told me when we first met, he'd been working since he was twelve: Paper route, grocery store stock boy, busboy at a restaurant and, when he got out of high school, at the local nursery, which is where he got his love of plants. His dad was a truck driver with, I gathered, something of a drinking problem. He was gone most of the time, and Jonathan's mother had died of lung cancer the year before, which had devastated him.

As far as being gay, Samuel had brought him out at the age of 12 and maintained a sexual relationship with him until he got married. Jonathan obviously worshiped Samuel, and I got the impression that he felt somehow betrayed when Samuel got married and stopped having sex with him. He adored his dad, too, but the older man had little time to spend with his kids. Jonathan's face lit up when he described having gone with his dad on some of his shorter cross-country hauls.

He'd graduated from high school but didn't have the money to go on to college. He worked at the nursery until, after his mother died and he was basically at home alone, he decided to step out into the world. Everything seemed to fascinate him; so much so that he apparently never had taken the time to concentrate on any one thing before something else got his attention. I got the distinct impression that Jonathan was something of a diamond in the rough: A lot of untapped potential if he could just focus.

Ah, my mind voice whispered, *Dick Hardesty, savior of lost souls and molder of futures.* Well, I did have to admit that I really did like to try to influence other people's lives—that's probably one of the reasons I became a p.i. But if I could help

Jonathan become aware of his potential for...whatever...I'd be more than willing to do it.

Yeah, and you don't have to paper train him, another voice said.

What a fucking cynic!

Jonathan asked me as many questions as I asked him, though as always I was mildly uncomfortable talking about myself. He seemed particularly interested in hearing about my five year relationship with Chris, what it was like to have a lover, and why we had broken up. He seemed fascinated with the idea of being with someone: Until he had left home, Samuel had pretty much been his life, and his only sexual contact. I was curious as to how he ever even thought of hustling, and he said that the guy who had given him a ride on the last leg of his trip here had made a pass at him and, when Jonathan readily agreed, had given him $20 and dropped him off near Hughie's, apparently assuming Jonathan was already a hustler.

He—very carefully, I sensed—avoided any talk of the two of us together, but I'm pretty good at reading between lines, and have enough of an ego to be flattered knowing he was interested.

At about 5: 30, Jonathan began to look at the clock on the mantle, and I could sense him tensing up.

"Now look, Jonathan," I said. "You don't really have to go through with this. We can just have the police arrest him on the complaint you made out this morning. This thing with Tom isn't your affair."

Jonathan shook his head. "No, I want to do it," he said. "I want to help you like you helped me."

"Well, I really appreciate it," I said. And I did.

I found myself glancing at the clock, too. "Are you hungry?" I asked. "We can grab something before we leave if you'd like, or..."

"I'm not hungry right now," he said. "Are you?"

I shook my head. "Not really," I said. "We can get something after...afterwards, then."

Jonathan smiled. "Great! But no raw fish."

At five minutes to 6, the buzzer rang. On my way to answer it, I took a quick trip to the window and looked out to see a familiar CityPower van at the curb.

I opened the door to both Richman and what as I remember now was a really hot looking guy in a CityPower uniform, carrying a tool box—the fact that his being hot didn't strike me at the time says a lot about my frame of mind. Richman introduced him as Detective Carey.

They had Jonathan remove his shirt and Carey opened his tool box and went to work. He had Jonathan put his shirt back on, then frowned. "Do you have a slightly heavier shirt?" he asked. "I can see through the fabric on this one."

Jonathan went to his backpack, which he'd put down near the doorway to the hall, and rummaged around in it, picking out a sleeveless sweatshirt, which he held up for the officer's approval. After receiving a nod, he removed his shirt and put the sweatshirt on.

Carey looked it over carefully, walked over to Jonathan and patted him lightly around the chest, then gave another nod. "Yeah, this'll do," he said.

The officer's two-way radio, which was attached to his belt, buzzed, and he unhooked it and brought it to his ear in one smooth motion. He listened for a moment, then pressed a button and returned it to his belt. "They want us to come outside so they can test it for distance: They're having some bad static problems from here."

We all—I probably didn't have to go, but of course did anyway—left the apartment and walked down the hall to the stairs.

"Now remember, Jonathan," Richman said, "to always keep the van in your line of sight. People walking past won't present much of a problem, but anything solid and stationary will block the signal."

Jonathan nodded.

When we got outside, Detective Carey told Jonathan and me to walk slowly down the sidewalk toward the corner and to keep talking. Richman got in the van and the officer stood outside, watching us.

There's nothing harder than to find something to talk about when you're supposed to keep talking, but we managed somehow, though I haven't a clue now what we talked about. When we reached the corner, we turned around and Carey waved us back, signaling for us to stop from time to time and giving us a rolling-index-finger "keep talking" gesture.

When we got back to the van, Richman and another man dressed in plain clothes, whom we hadn't seen before, got out.

"This is Officer Clark," Richman said by way of introduction, and Jonathan and I shook hands with him. "Officer Clark will stay as close to Jonathan as he can. Giacomino is a pretty street-smart character and he can probably spot a cop at 20 paces. So he'll mainly just be sure Jonathan gets into position without problem." He looked at Jonathan. "You and Officer Clark will take the bus downtown," he said. "We'll leave now and get set up, so we'll be there when you arrive."

Jonathan looked at me. "Where will Dick be?" he asked Richman.

The question apparently caught Richman by surprise. "Well, he..." he looked at me and obviously read my face "...he'll be in the van with us," he said.

"Good," Jonathan said.

"And remember what we talked about this morning...what you're supposed to say. We need to provoke him into admitting he killed Officer Brady. But be very careful. Don't agree to go *anywhere* with him, not even behind a tree; not for the money, not for anything. There will be a lot of people around, heading for the concert, so I don't think he'd try anything physical. Understood?"

Jonathan nodded again.

"Okay," Richman said. "We'd better get going. We'll see you downtown."

Officer Clark and Jonathan headed for the bus stop as Richman, Detective Carey, and I got into the van to join the driver and another man in a CityPower uniform, and headed toward Warman Park.

* * *

We got there at about 6:40. There was already quite a bit of traffic, both auto and pedestrian—the park concerts always drew a big crowd, and many people brought picnic baskets and made a night of it. The van pulled up into a yellow zone on the park side of the street, about twenty feet from the down ramp leading to the underground garage. The other uniformed man, who was never introduced formally, but who I'd heard called "Johnson," put on a hard-hat, got out of the van, walked to the rear, and opened the back doors to a partitioned utility area to take out several yellow traffic cones which he placed in the street in front of and behind the van, then returned for a couple Day-Glo white and black striped sawhorses with the word "Caution" and set them around a manhole a short distance in front of the van. The main body of the van was windowless except for a couple small, slotted smoked-glass windows through which those on the inside could get some idea of what was going on outside. There was a second partition between the driver's area and the main section, which extended about three-quarters of the way to the roof to keep passers by from seeing fully into the interior. The main body of the van, other than the space taken by the side door, was lined with an impressive and totally confusing array of built-in electronic gear, the purpose of which I could not even imagine. There was a small desk with a swivel chair opposite the door, and a regular bench seat against the back partition.

At about ten 'til seven, Carey also put on a hard-hat and got out to help Johnson remove the manhole cover, then went around to the back of the van, opened the door to the utility area, and pretended to be busy doing whatever CityPower guys do. With Johnson in the front of the van, and Carey behind, they could keep a good eye on the area.

The man who'd remained in the van with Richman and me sat at the small desk and began pushing buttons and flipping switches and being no-nonsense efficient. I heard a small crackle and Johnson's voice on his two-way: "They just got off the bus."

By looking over the front partition, I could see the bus pulling away from the curb on the other side of the street, and Jonathan walking to the corner. Several other people had gotten off, and one of them I saw was Officer Clark.

The man at the desk fiddled with some knobs and levers as I watched Jonathan approach. Two teenagers walked past him, talking and laughing, and the sound of their laughter came into the van. Richman and the man looked at each other and exchanged nods.

I didn't want to get in the way or make my concern for Jonathan too obvious, but Richman sensed it. "You can look out there," he said, motioning to the small slot closest to the rear.

"Thanks," I said, and moved to it.

I'd lost sight of Clark, but Jonathan walked to one back corner of the down-ramp and stood leaning against the railing, watching the entering cars passing below him. While he was a little too far away for me to see his face clearly, he looked very calm—well, a hell of a lot more calm than I probably would have been under the circumstances.

Seven o'clock came. And went.

Five after seven. Nothing.

And with every second I, for whom patience has never been much of a virtue, got more and more edgy.

Jonathan had turned around, and was leaning backwards against the railing, looking up at a large elm tree about fifteen feet from him.

"Heads up!" I heard Carey say. Looking around, I saw a guy I assumed to be Giacomino—I'd never seen him in person, just his photo—walking along the side of the ramp toward Jonathan, who had his back to him. He was dressed casually, wearing a light windbreaker, and looked exactly like everybody else moving toward the band shell.

"I thought it was you," Giacomino's voice said, though it wasn't completely clear. The man at the controls adjusted a knob and moved a lever to clear the static.

I saw Jonathan turn around to face him. "Did you bring my watch?" Jonathan's voice asked.

There was what sounded like a contemptuous snort. "I don't have your fucking watch," Giacomino said. "Forget your fucking watch. What's your game here?"

"No game," Jonathan said. "Did you bring the money?"

There was a pause. "And exactly why, again, should I be giving you a fucking dime?"

"Come on,...*Joey*...you know why. You beat me up. That's worth a lot. You killed my boyfriend: That's worth a lot more."

"Why in hell would a cop pick up a cheap hustler like you? I don't buy that for a second."

"Hey," Jonathan said, "a union boss picked up a cheap hustler like me. Why wouldn't a cop?"

"You're scum," Giacomino spat.

"Scum who knows enough about you to put you in jail for the rest of your life. Now where's my money?"

Another pause. I was watching through the slit, straining to try to see the expressions on their faces. To others passing by, they appeared to be just two guys, talking.

"So how did you get hooked up with that faggot Brady, anyway?" Giacomino asked.

"Same way I met you," Jonathan said. "He was going to bust me, but I convinced him not to, and...well...we saw each other a lot after that. Then, when Tom's dad came here for the labor talks, Tom started telling me about you. He laughed a lot. I didn't know who you were: Not even when you beat me up. But when I saw your picture in the paper and told Tom... and he told me what a pathetic excuse for a man you were. Told me about having beaten you up when you were kids...."

"Shut your fucking mouth!" Giacomino hissed, the fury showing itself not so much in volume as intensity. "Do you realize who you're talking to, you pathetic piece of shit? Do you realize what I could do to you if I wanted? I could squash you like a fucking bug!"

"I'll bet you didn't even kill Tom yourself!" Jonathan said. "You wouldn't have the guts to pull the trigger!"

"I pay my own debts," Giacomino spat. "I didn't need anybody else to pull the fucking trigger. Your fairy boyfriend never even saw it coming, and neither will you."

Richman picked up a two-way radio. "Go!" he said.

I watched as Giacomino reached quickly into his jacket and pulled something out.

Jonathan!

I saw Giacomino's arm make a quick forward motion and heard a sharp, exhaled *"huhh!"* And the sound went dead.

Richman already had the van's side door open, and was halfway out as I turned to follow him.

I remember running up the side of the ramp, of seeing Officer Clark struggling with Giacomino as Johnson and Carey raced up to join them. And I remember seeing Jonathan slumped on the ground, his back against the railing. Richman had his two way in his hand and I heard him say "Get an ambulance!"

* * *

It was a beautiful Sunday afternoon: Warm, crisp blue sky. Music, flags, floats, and thousands upon thousands of us stretched out as far as the eye could see. Tim, Phil, Jared, Bob, Mario, me…and Jonathan, who had insisted on being there even though he was still in some pain from his stitches. The doctors had said that if Giacomino's knife had struck three inches in any direction other than where it did, it would not have been blunted by the transmitter Jonathan was wearing and would almost surely have killed him.

We stood at the corner of Beech and Evans, near the Moxie, within 200 feet of the spot where Tom had died. We chose that place to watch the parade deliberately…for Tom, who I knew was standing there with us.

The gun Giacomino used to kill him was never found, but the fact that Deputy Chief Cochran announced his "retirement" the day after Giacomino's arrest struck me as a little more than coincidental.

At the bottom of the hill, at the corner of Ash and Beech, bulldozers had almost finished clearing the site of the burned-out police substation. The arsonist(s) still hadn't been caught, and maybe never would be. But work was progressing on the parking garage across the street and the fence surrounding it had been repainted. Construction on the replacement substation was scheduled to begin shortly.

Joey G. was still in jail, of course. He'd have the best lawyers his old man's money could buy for his trial for Tom's murder, but there was no way he could avoid spending a lot of time in prison for his attempted murder of Jonathan.

* * *

And Jonathan? Well, he's been staying with me since he got out of the hospital. The first couple days any kind of moving around was pretty painful for him, so I set him up in the guest bedroom and played Florence Nightingale. The day of the Parade was his first full day out of bed. And while Jonathan slept in the guest bedroom, I found myself getting less and less sleep every night as my crotch grew increasingly pissed with me for not doing what I increasingly wanted to do. In a way it was very much like that game of Tease Tom liked to play, only I was playing it by myself. I even forced myself to shut my bedroom door when I went to bed—I didn't think I could take seeing a naked Jonathan padding past my door on the way to the bathroom in the middle of the night.

It was pretty late when we got back from the Pride Festival, and I could see Jonathan was tired, so I suggested we go right to bed. I got into bed and tried to sleep. No luck. I decided to try the one thing that usually relaxed me when I was too uptight. I closed my eyes and, as usual, began thinking of Jonathan.

Suddenly I heard a slight sound and opened my eyes. Jonathan was standing in the opened doorway, wearing one of the most beautiful birthday suits I think I'd ever seen, and a smile that turned me to jelly.

"Can I help with that?" he asked.

What about your steadfast rule against getting involved with anyone under 21? My mind voice chided primly.

Well, Jonathan was turning 20.

Close enough. I threw back the covers and welcomed him to bed.

THE END

Copyright 2002
Dorien Grey

OTHER DORIEN GREY MYSTERIES

AVAILABLE DIRECTLY FROM

GLB Publishers
P.O. Box 78212
San Francisco, CA 94107

THE 9TH MAN	There's a serial killer in the Gay Community and the police don't seem to care.	US $ 14.95
THE BUTCHER'S SON	A gay bar arsonist, a bigoted gubernatorial candidate, and mysterious twins draw Dick into a fast-paced adventure.	US $ 14.95
THE BAR WATCHER	Gay men are being killed right and left but they are all "nasties." What does that mean?	US $ 14.95
THE HIRED MAN	It was a modeling agency and escort service, but then some of the men were killed...	US $ 15.95

To order directly, send purchase price plus $2.50 per book. Mailing address:

_____
_____
_____

YOUR PRIMARY SOURCE
for print books and e-books
Gay, Lesbian, Bisexual
on the Internet at

http://www.glbpubs.com

e-Book Fiction by such leading authors as:

Bill Lee	Chris Kent
Mike Newman	William Tarvin
Byrd Roberts	Veronica Cas
G-M Higney	Jim Brogan
Robert Peters	Thomas R. McKague
Kurt Kendall	Richard Dann
Marsh Cassady	Byrd Roberts
Jay Hatheway	James Hagerty

and of course, **Dorien Grey**

The Good Cop is also available as a print book directly from the publisher:
GLB Publishers
P.O. Box 78212
San Francisco, CA 94107

$15.95 by check or money order (no charge for shipping)

or as a download file from the Web Site
in your choice of formats:

http://www.glbpubs.com $8.00

Credit Cards and checks honored